For my hero . . . Leslie Valentine Myers

"BEFORE WE GET STARTED, I SHOULD MAKE SOMETHING ABSOLUTELY CLEAR."

"Okay," Cal said, while driving his convertible and waiting for the other shoe to drop. Not that he had any sexual intentions toward Holly Hicks, but now that she'd kindled a few pleasant flames, he didn't want cold water thrown on his newly awakened fantasies. "Go ahead. Shoot."

"I don't believe in heroes."

"What?" He'd heard her well enough. He just couldn't quite believe his own ears.

"I said I don't believe in heroes."

Cal laughed out loud for the first time in months. The sensation was like champagne. Like his bloodstream fizzing and popping a cork. "Neither do I," he shouted back above the wind.

"Pardon?"

"That makes two of us."

Holly cupped a hand to her ear, still not comprehending.

"I said we're going to get along just fine," he yelled, settling more comfortably behind the wheel, taking nearly criminal pleasure in speed and hot moonlight and the company of an honest, windblown woman.

❦

Also by Mary McBride

Still Mr. & Mrs.

MY
HERO ♥

MARY McBRIDE

WARNER BOOKS

An AOL Time Warner Company

WARNER BOOKS EDITION

Cover design by Diane Luger
Cover illustration by Mike Racz

Warner Books, Inc.
1271 Avenue of the Americas
New York, NY 10020

Visit our Web site at www.twbookmark.com

An AOL Time Warner Company

Printed in the United States of America

First Paperback Printing: June 2003

10 9 8 7 6 5 4 3 2 1

MY
HERO ♥

Chapter One

"I don't believe in heroes."

"Holly, for crissake." Mel Klein wanted to tear out his hair. What was left of it anyway after thirty-five years in television news production. "Do you want to be a producer or not?"

He was bellowing. Okay. He couldn't help it. No more than he could keep his blood pressure from skyrocketing. He'd just spent the entire morning with the idiots in charge of programming for the VIP Channel, pleading Holly Hicks' case, practically begging Arnold Strong and Maida Newland to give his assistant a chance to produce a single segment for Hero Week.

One lousy hour out of the seven hundred they were projecting for the coming year. Forty-eight minutes of actual footage if you figured in commercials.

He'd sung Holly's praises, handed out copies of her creatively padded resume, passed her picture around, and popped in one of her tapes. With over three decades in the broadcast news business, Mel knew talent when he saw it, he told them. Holly Hicks had a real flair for putting together a story. She could write an opening sentence that nailed the average viewer to his BarcaLounger. Her sense of timing was impeccable. Her sense of balance was right on. She had a rare eye and an intuitive appreciation for the blended power of pictures and words.

All morning he'd virtually tap danced on the big teak conference table on the nineteenth floor. He had a headache now, not to mention carpet lint on his knees and elbows from practically prostrating himself between Arnold on his frigging treadmill and Maida in her black leather, NASA-endorsed, ergonomic executive chair.

Then, just as he was about to toss his next raise and his firstborn grandson into the bargain, the idiots said yes.

They said yes!

He'd nearly given himself a coronary rushing back to his office to tell her the news. And now Holly—the Holly who'd been on his ass ever since the day she walked into the building three years ago in one of her itty-bitty, primly tailored, "This is how a producer looks" suits—the Holly who wheedled and needled and wouldn't let go of her smoldering desire to produce anything—*I'll do anything, Mel. Anything!*—the Holly who left homemade, but not half-bad demo tapes on his desk every Monday morning—*that* Holly was blithely telling him she didn't believe in heroes.

He bellowed again. "Do you want to be a goddamn producer or not?"

"Of course I want to be a producer. It's all I've ever wanted to be." Her chin came up like a little Derringer aimed at the frazzled knot in his tie. "I just thought I should be up front about my prejudices, that's all."

"Fine. Great." He waved his hands like a maniac. "Hey, I don't believe in Santa Claus, but that didn't keep me from producing 'Christmas Around the World,' did it?"

"No."

"I don't believe in capital punishment either, but I still did a helluva job on 'Drake's Last Meal,' right?"

"Right."

"Well, then . . ." Mel Klein planted his hands on the top of her desk and leaned forward, lowering his voice, allowing himself to grin for maybe the third or fourth time in his grouchy life. "You got it, kid."

Her pretty little face lit up. Two hundred watts at least.

"I got it!"

Then—*Cut!*—the light went out.

"Mel, I think I'm going to be sick."

♥

In the ladies' room, Holly Hicks splashed cold water on her face, then slowly lifted her gaze to the mirror above the sink, hoping to find Joan Crawford staring back at her. Big-shouldered. Yeah. Hard as a diamond. Tough as nails.

Or Bette Davis—even better—with her bold, unblinking eyes.

Madonna would be good.

Instead Holly saw herself.

She shook her head and watched her strawberry blond bangs rearrange themselves in a series of sodden spikes on her forehead. She was hardly big-shouldered. In fact, at five foot three inches, she wasn't even tall enough for her shoulders to be reflected in the glass. As for her eyes, rather than bold and unblinking, they were a pale green, smudged with mascara at the moment, and the left one was definitely twitching.

God. She'd waited her whole life for a chance like this. If not her whole life, then at least since she was twelve. While the other little girls in Sandy Springs, Texas, drooled over

Donny Osmond, Holly had been a *60 Minutes* groupie in love alternately with Harry Reasoner and Mike Wallace. But she didn't want to kiss them. She wanted to *produce* them. It was why she'd come to New York in the first place.

Not once had she taken her eyes off the prize.

Not while growing up in a house where watching the news was considered a foolish waste of time, where reading was deemed eccentric at best, subversive more often than not. *What's that you're reading, girl? A Separate Peace? Some kind of Commie Pinko story, I'll betcha. Lemme see that.*

Not while attending a high school where her nickname was El Cerebro, or The Brain, in a school where beauty and brawn were prized over intelligence, where the football coach was the only PhD on the faculty, and where her classmates put far more effort into getting laid than getting an education.

Not while filling out reams of scholarship forms each year at the University of Missouri's School of Journalism or practically indenturing herself every semester to the campus bookstore.

Not while working her way east for so many years at so many stations she could have thrown darts at the alphabet and come up with the call letters of at least one of her employers. Not through downsizing, takeovers, cutbacks, drawbacks, freezes, firings, new regimes, old boys' clubs, pink slips, and innumerable *sorry*s and *so long*s.

Hers had been the great American migration in reverse. Go east, young woman, go east. With her journalism degree hot in her hands, Holly had crossed the wide Missouri and the mighty Mississippi to a station in Peoria, Illinois, where the phrase "entry level" meant being solely responsible for a temperamental, two-pot Bunn-o-matic. Across the moonlit

Wabash, in Terre Haute, she graduated to a three-pot coffee machine. Ohio took a while to traverse, and a lot of coffee, from Cincinnati to Columbus to Canton. In Wheeling, West Virginia, she'd actually been Acting News Director for two days before they brought somebody in from outside. She spent a winter in Buffalo that lasted a millennium. One wet spring in Syracuse. Then she'd bided her time in Albany before crossing the Hudson and hitting the Big Apple at the ripe old age of twenty-eight.

Here at the VIP Channel, Holly had finally found a mentor in Mel Klein, a man who not only appreciated her abilities, but who also supported her goals. A man of uncommon generosity in this notoriously cutthroat business.

You got it, kid.

"I got it," she repeated now as her adrenaline surged again and her heart began to race with a weird combination of high-flying excitement and lowdown fear.

"Breathe, dammit." She sucked in a huge breath and held it while she kept her eyes closed. She counted to ten, slowly letting the air out through pursed lips, telling herself there was no one at the station, no one in New York, and probably no one on the planet more ready for this assignment than she was.

Then she opened her eyes, and there she was.

Holly Hicks. Producer.

Hot damn.

♥

"You sure you're okay?" Mel asked her. "You want to take the afternoon off and we'll go over this tomorrow?"

"Not on your life. Are those the production notes for Hero Week?"

"Yep." He slid the folder across the top of his desk, somehow managing to avoid a calendar, a tower of pink while-you-were-out notes, an electric razor, three empty coffee cups, and a bottle of Maalox. Bless his heart. Mel's little office was an oasis of friendly clutter in the otherwise sterile chrome and glass headquarters of the VIP Channel.

Holly held the dark blue binder a moment before she opened it, then she read the first page with its list of the five heroes Programming had chosen for the special week. Other than Neil Armstrong, she didn't recognize a single name.

"Who are these people?" she asked. "Who's Al Haynes?"

The springs of Mel's chair creaked as he leaned back. "He was the pilot of United Flight 232. Remember? The plane that pinwheeled down the runway in Sioux City, Iowa, in 1989?"

"Oh, sure. Good choice," she said. Great footage!

"Thelma Schuyler Brooks is the woman who started the music school on the Wolf River Reservation in Arizona, and now has at least one student in every major orchestra in the country."

"Okay." Holly was thinking she'd have to work closely with her sound man on that one, not to mention brush up on her Beethoven.

"Howard Mrazek is the NYPD hostage negotiator who saved all those people a couple years ago during the standoff at the Chemical Bank."

"Mm," Holly murmured as her eyes drifted further down the page. "Who in the world is Calvin Griffin?"

"The Secret Service agent who took the bullet for the President last year. He's your hero."

"Excuse me?"

"He's your hero, Holly. He's your guy. That's the segment Arnold and Maida want you to produce."

"I'd rather do Haynes," she said. She was already imagining how she could use repetition of that fiery runway footage to come up with a really dramatic piece. Hadn't they been in the air a long time, flying touch and go, trying to bring that sucker down? Had Haynes flown in Viet Nam? Was the crash footage in public domain? What was her budget? Her mind was going ninety miles an hour, so she was barely aware of Mel's reply. She knew he'd said something, though, because the little office was still reverberating from his growl.

"You're doing Calvin Griffin," Mel said. "You don't have a choice, kid. That's what Arnold and Maida want. Griffin's how I sold them on the idea in the first place."

She glanced down at the name on the page. "What do you mean?"

"I mean because you're both from Texas. Because you know the territory. You speak the language."

Holly wanted to laugh, but it would have come out high and maniacal, like a person being carted off to an asylum. She didn't know the territory. She hadn't been back to Texas in over a decade. Thank God. As for speaking the language, she'd had six months of very expensive lessons with a voice coach in Cincinnati in an attempt to bury her accent. She hadn't said *y'all* in years.

"I do not speak the language, Mel." She rolled her eyes. "When was the last time we went out to lunch and you heard me tell the waiter *bring me a slab of baby back ribs and a big ol' beer*?"

Her mentor narrowed his eyes. "When was the last time you didn't have to remind yourself not to ask for mayo on pastrami?"

He was right, of course, and Holly could feel her lips flatten in a thin, stubborn line. Why couldn't she have been born to a lovely couple in Connecticut, instead of Bobby Ray and Crystal Hicks of Sandy Springs, Texas?

"Hey. Come on, kid. The accent's cute. Refreshing." Mel's chuckle was just obscene. "Plus it got you the job. Not to mention an all-expense-paid trip back home."

"Where I get to interview some good ol' boy who got shot just doing his job," she added glumly.

"Take it or leave it, kid."

♥

Well, of course, she was going to take it.

Hollis Mae Hicks might have been a rube, as Mel had so deftly pointed out, but her mother hadn't raised a fool. Which wasn't to say that Crystal Hicks hadn't tried to raise one or done her damnedest to quash her daughter's unquashable broadcast dreams. Even as Holly was filling out the application for the Journalism School at the University of Missouri, her mother was waving a brochure from the Bi-County School of Cosmetology under her nose.

"Mama, please."

"Do you know how much Marsha Stiles makes in a good week at her shop? A bundle, that's how much. She sets her own hours, too. If she wants to take off for Padre Island in the middle of the week, by God, she does it. Beats me why anybody as smart as you would turn up her nose at a career like that. Just fill out the application. They're picky, Marsha says. You might not even get in."

Holly got in, of course. To the Bi-County School of Cosmetology as well as the University of Missouri's School of Journalism. When she chose the latter, her mother had washed her hands of "so-called" higher education.

Being no fool, Holly left work half an hour early in order

to stop at the Gap on her way home. Maybe she didn't speak the language anymore or know the territory, but she still had a pretty firm handle on the couture of South Texas, where dressing for success meant wearing clean jeans and a T-shirt with no obscenities printed on it.

She couldn't produce a story if she couldn't get that story in the first place, and she doubted anybody in Calvin Griffin's hometown of Honeycomb, Texas, would be very forthcoming to a woman in a banker's gray chalk-stripe suit.

So, after wriggling into a pair of sandblasted, five-pocket, overpriced denims, she plucked two more just like them off a pile, gathered up an assortment of T-shirts, and then handed her credit card to the clerk.

"I'm going to Texas tomorrow," she said with a slight roll of her eyes, feeling compelled to justify not only her taste in apparel, but the sheer magnitude of it, as well.

"Yee-hah," was all the salesgirl said as she proceeded to scan and bag the clothes.

Holly signed the receipt, vaguely wondering if it was Thoreau who cautioned wariness of any endeavor that required new clothes. Obviously Henry David had never been sent to Honeycomb, Texas, on assignment. But, hey, with a name like that, he would have fit right in with all the Billy Joes and the Jim Bobs. Come to think of it, there had been a Henry David in her class in Sandy Springs. Henry David Thibault, otherwise known as T-bone. Good God. She hadn't thought of him in years.

Since it was only a few blocks from the Gap to her one-bedroom sublet on East 59th, Holly decided to walk. It was late spring with the temperature a perfect seventy-five degrees. There was a swath of blue sky above her and even the pavement beneath her feet seemed cleaner than usual this afternoon. Still, dirty or clean, gray skies or blue, she loved

Manhattan. She'd been here for three years and it still amazed her that within a ten- or twelve-block radius of her cramped little apartment was . . . well . . . everything, including the United Nations and Simon & Garfunkel's Feelin' Groovy bridge.

To celebrate—the promotion, not the upcoming trip—she stopped at a liquor store along the way for a split of champagne. "I just got promoted to executive producer," she told the clerk, whose reply was either a muttered *lucky you* or *fuck you*. It was hard telling which from the man's deadpan expression. After that, she splurged on take-out from Ming's, then kicked herself the last half block for neglecting to ask Mel if a raise went along with the promotion.

At last, entering the lobby of her building, she smiled cheerfully at the terminally crabby doorman and called out, "I'll be out of town for a week or so, Hector. Could you keep an eye on my mailbox?"

Holly took his grunt for a yes, and then, even though she could have ascended on her own, newly acquired executive producer wings, she took the elevator up to her tiny twelfth-floor apartment.

♥

She courted sleep that night the same way she had every night since she was twelve years old, by packaging a story in her head. She did it all—the producing, the writing, the reporting—with the exception of the camera work, which, since about 1992, had been handled by an imaginary cameraman named Rufus who, for some unknown reason, had gone through three imaginary wives in the past eleven years.

Sometimes Holly would do a re-take of a story she'd seen on the news that day, and she'd craft an opening sentence that blew the actual televised one out of the water, then she'd get better sound bites, each of them guaranteed to play forever in broadcast archives. Other times she'd invent murders or scandals or disasters, but the creative effort of doing that usually got her so jazzed that she couldn't fall asleep at all.

Sometimes the voiceover in her head was in Charles Kuralt's plummy tones. Sometimes it was in Jane Pauley's crisp, Midwestern, no-nonsense voice. Most of the time, though, it was Holly's own voice, minus any residue of drawl.

Tonight she had Rufus panning Honeycomb High School, a single story, distinctly ugly, Texas-Danish modern building of fake stone and glass erected in the '50s to replace the old, red brick two-story school that had stood on the site since 1896.

As Rufus panned in on the portable marquee in front of the building—*Honeycomb High School, Home of the Hornets*—Holly voiced over.

Despite appearances, tradition runs deep at Honeycomb High, where the great-great grandchildren of . . .

Cut.

She flopped over on her side, swore softly, and jammed the pillow under her ear. There probably was no Honeycomb High. Not anymore. It had probably gone the way of Sandy Springs High, consolidating with Gardenville and Cholla and Roper and Spurge, to become the Bi-County Consolidated High.

Okay.

Rufus panned Main Street, closing in on the limestone court house in the town square. Holly voiced over, maybe with the merest hint of a drawl for effect, assuming she had any hint of a drawl at all.

Heroes are hard to come by here in Honeycomb. In 1874

they hanged Horace McGinty for stealing two horses, one for himself and one for his neighbor's wife. Sixty years later, in 1934, the notorious Bonnie and Clyde stopped just south of here . . .

Cut.

Wait. A person could make a pretty cogent argument that Bonnie and Clyde were heroes in their own perverse fashion, which made heroes even harder to come by, assuming they existed at all.

Holly sighed as she punched her pillow and kicked the covers off her feet.

Rufus, yawning, panned over a vast, flat landscape, roughened by mesquite and prickly pear and the occasional live oak. A pickup truck spewed dust in its wake. An armadillo bumbled along the side of the road. And nary a hero in sight.

Chapter Two

Cal Griffin hated it when Ramon hired a new bartender, and this kid with his hay-colored hair, pierced ears, and erupting skin didn't even look old enough to work at a lemonade stand, much less at a rundown tavern in Honeycomb, Texas. Cal took another swig from his beer bottle, idly watching the baby barkeep wipe the counter again and again, nearly rubbing the cigarette burns right out of the Formica. Well, hell. It was pretty obvious the kid was working up the courage to start a conversation. Might as well get it over with, Cal thought.

"What's your name, kid?" he asked him.

"Ricky. Well . . . Rick." He shrugged and passed the rag across the bartop again, not quite able to make eye contact. "Say, I was just wondering, aren't you that Secret Service guy who was such hot shit a while back?"

Cal almost laughed. "Yeah, but I'm lukewarm shit now." He drained his bottle and set it down with a dull thump. "You want to reach back there and get me another one of these?"

"Sure." Young Rick used the rag to twist off the cap before he put the cold, wet bottle in front of Cal. The kid swallowed, making his Adam's apple bounce off the collar of his shirt. "So, what was it like?" he asked.

Cal cocked his head. "What was what like?"

"You know. The White House. The President. All that."

"It was okay."

He lifted the bottle and let the chilled lager slide down the back of his throat. There. He had conversed, goddammit. He hoisted himself off the bar stool and carried his beer to a table on the far side of the glowing jukebox, pulling out a chair and settling in for a long, liquid day. Alone.

Nobody had to tell him that he wasn't very good company these days, or that his knack for small talk, if he'd ever had one, had gotten into the wind, along with his agility, his physical endurance, and his ability to run a six-minute mile. Mile, hell! Six months into his rehabilitation, he could just barely make it twice around the Honeycomb High School track, and that was at a pace which allowed Bee, the school's ancient, gray-muzzled mascot, to happily lope alongside.

And since he was such lousy company, he particularly liked sitting here at Ramon's in the morning, after yet another lousy workout, before any of the regulars arrived, when there was just the bartender to ignore. What better place to hunch down in a corner and feel sorry for himself? If he were an injured dog, nobody would think twice if he ran into a crawlspace. Now there was a perfect name for a tavern, if ever he'd heard one. The Crawlspace.

Then, just as he was really settling into his comfortable funk, the front door opened, sending a hard shaft of sunlight across the bar's dark interior. Cal immediately recognized his brother-in-law's rangy silhouette in the doorway. It was probably too late, he decided, to make any kind of decent, much less graceful escape out the back door. Busted. Damn.

"I figured I'd find you in here." The heels of Dooley

Reese's boots clacked on the linoleum floor as he approached the table. His droopy, sand-colored mustache appeared to be sagging more than usual as he reached out a long arm, twisted a chair around, and slung it between his knees. "Starting a little early, aren't you, Cal?"

"Actually, Dooley, I'm late." He raised his hand in the air, snapped his fingers to get young Rick's attention, and then held up two fingers.

"Yessir. Coming right up," the kid called. "You want a glass with your beer, Mr. Reese?"

"No. Nothing for me, Rick. Thanks." Dooley edged his chair closer, draping his bony wrists over the slatted back. He cleared his throat. "I came to apologize for your sister, Cal. Ruthie didn't mean what she said this morning."

"What part didn't she mean, Dooley?" he asked in a voice that was affable and insidious all at once. "The part about me being a drunk, or the part about being glad our mama was dead so she didn't have to see this?"

The droopy mustache twitched uncomfortably. "I told you she didn't mean it. Any of it. She's just upset."

"We're all upset," Cal said coldly.

Ruthie. God bless her. She was only four years older than Cal, but sometimes it seemed like forty. After their mother died, Ruthie had taken on that role with a nearly religious fervor.

After the assassination attempt, she'd dropped her own life to oversee his care during his extended stay in the hospital, and then she'd brought him home to the family ranch to recuperate. Ruth Griffin Reese was loyal and generous and tough as nails, but these days she seemed to be in the throes of some kind of mid-life crisis, constantly talking about her turn and her dreams and pointing to Cal as a clear example of just how short and unpredictable life could be.

Lately, she'd been making noises about selling the ranch, her half at least, in order to fund her dream of opening a restaurant.

Poor Dooley walked around half the time like he'd just been hit by a two-by-four or kicked in the head by one of the champion bulls he raised for rodeo stock. For his part, Cal just stayed out of Ruthie's way as much as possible. Mostly here at Ramon's. The Crawlspace.

Across the table, Dooley sighed. "Look. Ruthie said you got a couple phone calls this morning. Come on back to the house. See who called. We'll have some lunch. Ruthie's trying out some damned new recipe she saw on TV yesterday."

He didn't want to answer any phone calls. He didn't want some experimental lunch that he'd be forced to critique, and then get in trouble no matter what he said. All he wanted to do was stay right here at Ramon's and watch the day shake out. In a few hours Skeet Crawford would wander in after his lunch business petered out at the Longhorn Café. Tim Begley would arrive once he delivered the mail. There would be others, all unemployed or disabled one way or another, like himself. Patsy Holling usually showed up about four-thirty, teetering in on her spike heels, trailing a different fragrance—lilies or lilacs or rosewater—for every day of the week.

"How about it, Cal?" Dooley asked quietly.

Cal pondered the label on the beer bottle while he dragged his thumbnail through its wet center, effectively slicing it in two. Not so different from what had happened to his life nine months ago when he took the bullet meant for President Randolph Jennings. One minute he'd been at the top of his game—strong, agile, in control. The next minute all of that was gone.

Those seconds flashed before his eyes again. He preceded

Jennings through the hotel door, out into the bright September sunlight. He could still feel the change in temperature and humidity as they passed from air-conditioning to the heat of the D.C. afternoon. He could feel the distance between himself and the President, a palpable measure, close enough to protect the man yet removed enough so the man didn't trip over his feet. Right where he needed to be. On point. In control. Ready. For anything. Everything.

He heard the first bullet. It went thunk as it bit a chunk out of the pavement just ahead of him, and his body reacted instantly, independent of his mind, twisting sideways, inserting himself just as he'd been trained between . . .

"Cal?" Dooley asked again. "How about it?"

"What?" He blinked the dark bar into focus.

"Come on home, Cal."

He sighed. Hell, why not? Where else was there to go?

♥

It didn't take long to quit the town limits of Honeycomb, whose population had slipped to about seven hundred souls in the two decades that Cal had been away. Out on the state road, he stomped on the accelerator of his rebuilt '64 Thunderbird convertible—his convalescent gift to himself despite the vertigo that had kept him from driving it for a lousy three months—and blew past Dooley's pickup at eighty-five miles per hour with plenty of juice to spare.

Okay. So it was a high-school stunt, a stupid testosterone trick. Still, it managed to lift Cal's spirit a notch for a couple of seconds. The hot wind scrubbed his face while the summer sun beat down on the top of his head. From horizon to horizon, there wasn't a cloud in the sky, and since it was nearing noon, there were no ragged shadows to smudge the landscape or dull the greens of the mesquite trees and the prickly pears along both sides of the road. It was as pure a summer day as they made in this part of South Texas.

The ranch appeared in the distance, what was left of the land that had been in his family for nearly a hundred and fifty years. With each successive generation selling off a parcel here and a couple hundred acres there, Rancho Allegro was down to twelve hundred acres now. At the going rate of about eight hundred bucks an acre, Ruthie's half would net her a nice half million to pour into a restaurant venture, but Cal was hoping she'd reconsider. As little as he'd been back here these past twenty years, the place was still home, and at the moment he didn't have any other.

The house itself was no great shakes. Just a single-story yellow stucco with several cinderblock and aluminum siding additions. The outbuildings, all pre-fab, were a sandy color that matched the dry ground on which they were lashed.

He eased his foot off the gas, close enough now to see Dooley's lineback mare shoving her muzzle over the fence and swishing her tail. His sister, Ruth, was outside, her skirt whipping around her legs as she tended her tomato plants. At this distance, with her long, dark hair, her tiny waist and narrow shoulders, it would have been easy to mistake her for their mother.

Cal pulled into the gravel drive, half expecting to see his sister beat an angry and hasty retreat into the house to avoid another confrontation. When she stood her ground, he mouthed a silent curse. She had already ripped him a new one this morning. Wasn't that enough?

By the time he was out of the car, Ruthie had crossed the yard with a basket of tomatoes slung over her arm.

"I'm glad Dooley found you," she said.

Cal breathed a faint sigh of relief, recognizing an apology, even a grudging one, when he heard it. "I wasn't all that hard to find, sis," he answered in his own conciliatory code. One of these days, he thought, he and Ruthie might actually say "I love you" out loud, surprising the hell out of each other.

She lifted a hand to shield her eyes from the sun, and then said, "Diana called."

The headache Cal had been nursing all morning blossomed inside his skull. He swore softly.

"She wants you to call her lawyer," Ruth said. "Something about the divorce. She said—"

"Yeah. Yeah. Okay."

"And you got another call." Ruthie was on a definite roll, if not a direct mission. "From the White House, Cal. A woman named Janet Adler. She—"

"Janet Adcock?"

"Yeah, maybe that was it. She said it was important that you get back to her as quickly as possible. I nearly called you at Ramon's, but then Dooley offered to drive into town and get you."

As if on cue, Dooley, who had obviously maintained the proper speed limit, swung into the drive. He aimed a dark "you damned fool" glare at Cal before he smiled at Ruth. "Hi, honey," he said, angling his long bones out of the dusty pickup.

"Hi, yourself. I'm going in to slice these tomatoes. Lunch will be ready in about twenty minutes. Cal, that'll give you time to return at least one of those calls, so you do it, you hear?"

He nodded even as he wondered why the hell Diana wanted him to call her lawyer. This divorce was supposed to be a no-brainer, wasn't it? And what did Janet Adcock want?

♥

The conversation with Diana's lawyer quickly deteriorated to a childish chorus of *Did, too's* and *Did not's*. Frederick Burton, of Bishop, Burton, and DePew, was looking for some paperwork he claimed to have mailed to Cal three weeks ago for his signature.

"I never got it," Cal told him.

"It was sent in care of Mrs. Ruth Reese on Rural Route 3, Honeycomb, Texas."

"I don't care. I never got it."

The more Cal insisted he hadn't received the papers, the more the lawyer argued that he had. Of course, the difference between them was that Burton was probably consulting an actual file while Cal was depending on his not-so-reliable gray matter. He really wasn't all that certain the paperwork hadn't arrived, only to be crammed in a drawer or shoved in the glove compartment of the Thunderbird. But one of the things he'd learned in the nine months following the assassination attempt was that a little belligerence went a long way in covering up short-term memory problems.

"Why don't I just fax them to you?" Frederick Burton suggested, then didn't find it so hilarious when Cal informed him that the nearest fax machine was probably two counties over. "I'll get them in today's mail, then," he said. "You really need to sign them, Mr. Griffin, for the divorce to proceed."

Cal could feel the headache flare in his right temple, somewhere in the vicinity of the metal plate. He closed his eyes a moment, then asked, "How's Diana?" There was no longer any trace of defensive anger in his tone.

"Excuse me?"

"How's my wife?"

The silence at the other end of the line was eloquent. Well, hell. Diana was a beautiful woman, and one who enjoyed, even craved, sexual encounters of the dramatic kind. Why wouldn't she be sleeping with her divorce attorney?

Finally Burton replied, "She's fine. She sends her regards, as always."

"I'll bet."

Cal broke the connection and stared straight ahead. They had met in First Class on the red eye from L.A. to New York. Diana Koslov was a honey blonde with a honey voice whose job description with a D.C. PR firm was fairly loose. He was never sure exactly what she did except get off airplanes into limousines, take phone calls from people whose names she thought he ought to recognize, and strike terror in the hearts of maître d's in every major city in the contiguous forty-eight.

During that flight, somewhere over the heartland, they had renewed their dues in the Mile High Club. Diana liked it rough, and Cal, tough guy, had been only too happy to accede to her demands. The six or eight weeks after that were a blur of hotel rooms, twisted sheets and gardenia-scented sex. How they wound up getting married, he wasn't quite sure. He'd probably repressed it, although he had a vague recollection of the Fourth of July celebration on the Mall and Diana's beautiful face framed by the most spectacular fireworks he'd ever seen. More than likely it had something to do with his inability to spend his nights as a sexual athlete and his days protecting the President of the United States. Part of it was just that he was thirty-seven years old with not much to show for his life except a couple medals and an address book that was the envy of every agent on the White House detail.

The marriage didn't go to hell right away. It took at least six weeks. Then, on a warm September Sunday afternoon, Thomas Earl Starks made his bid for the history books by trying to kill the President, and the sole fatality had been Cal's marriage. Well, his marriage and maybe his career. The jury was still out on that.

"Cal, lunch'll be ready in five minutes," Ruth called.

"Great."

He didn't even realize he was still holding the phone until it rang in his hand. It was Janet Adcock. After the formalities, she softened her starched Deputy Director of Communications voice and asked, "How are you doing, Cal?"

"Tolerable." It was his standard reply. Nobody really wanted to hear that his head was still aching, his balance was often touch and go, his leg hurt like hell and his knee had locked up on him again this morning. Plus he didn't want word to get back to his superiors at the Secret Service that his recuperation wasn't right on track as he'd led them to believe.

"I'm glad you're doing well," she said. "The President sends his best."

"Thanks."

"We need to ask a favor of you, Cal."

Oh, brother. The *we* implied there'd been at least one meeting and his name had been mentioned. Janet had probably drawn the short straw and got to make the call.

"No," he said.

"What do you mean, no? You don't even know what it is."

"I don't need to know. Whatever it is, Janet, I can't help you."

"Just listen for a minute, will you?"

She didn't give him much choice as she immediately launched into some long-winded monologue about a TV doc-

umentary, the upcoming one-year anniversary of the assassination attempt, and Randolph Jennings' eternal gratitude for
Cal's cooperation.

"The documentary is tentatively scheduled to air in mid-
September," Janet said, "and could be a real boon to the re-
election campaign. It'll be part of the VIP Channel's
biography series. You've probably seen it. The shows are
very well done."

"Nope. Haven't seen them. We don't get TV out here in
Honeycomb," he drawled at the same time he was looking
out the window at Dooley's huge satellite dish that brought
in something like eleven thousand channels, only two of
which were ever watched for cooking shows and rodeos.

He could tell from Janet's faint, sympathetic, Sarah
Lawrence murmur that she believed him. "Well, trust me,"
she said. "They're quite good. They'll be calling this segment 'Hero Week,' Cal."

He snorted.

"Let me tell you a little more . . ."

"Not interested, Janet."

"Cal, if you'd just—"

"Sorry."

What followed next was a stubborn silence, a staring con-
test across two thousand miles. Cal could just picture Granite Janet sinking her eye teeth into her lush bottom lip,
pulling at a hank of light brown hair, twisting it around her
index finger before she planted the abused lock behind the
ear unencumbered by the phone, all the while glaring out
through her always open office door, ready to bite off the
head or gonads, depending on his crime, of the next guy who
dared to enter.

For a minute—oh, damn!—he missed his job and the
West Wing so much he almost wished Starks' bullet had

wiped his memories clean instead of just short circuiting some of them.

"Cal, maybe I'm not making myself clear. The VIP Channel is going to do this profile of you whether you cooperate with them or not. Their producer is on her way to Texas this evening, I'm told. President Jennings would be extremely grateful if—"

"All right, Janet. God dammit." Hero Week. Shit.

"Oh, good." She didn't dwell on her victory. Janet had way too much class for that, and was too smart to give him an opportunity to renege. "Let me give you the producer's name. I have it here somewhere. Cal, I'm going to put you on hold a second. Don't you dare hang up on me."

Hero Week. He wanted to snap the receiver in half, maybe bash it against the metal plate in his skull and see which dented first. After nine months, interest in the assassination attempt had slackened. It was yesterday's news. Old stuff. Nobody had called him in weeks, thank God. Even the Secret Service wasn't trying to trot him out as their poster boy anymore.

He wasn't a hero. He'd just been doing his job, and if he had to do it again—which admittedly he did just about every night in his brutal dreams—he'd zig rather than zag when he threw that body block into the President to push him back through the door they had just exited. That way the bullet that grazed his head before it smashed into his thigh might have just hit the leg. Of course, without his head to slow it down a bit, the slug might have shattered his femur. You never knew. The hero business was pretty unpredictable.

"Cal?"

"I'm still here, Janet."

"The producer's name is Holly Hicks. She'll be flying into Houston tonight, and we thought . . ."

There was that *we* again.

". . . it would be a nice touch and show a real spirit of cooperation if you were the one who met her at the airport."

"In Houston?"

"Yes. She's flying from Newark to . . ." He could hear papers shuffling. "Yes. Intercontinental Airport in Houston. She's on Continental. ETA is nine P.M."

Cal shook his aching head and considered telling Janet that Houston was over two hundred miles from Honeycomb. But then he thought about his Thunderbird and the top down under clear blue skies and his foot jamming the accelerator while the T-bird ate up and spat out big stretches of road going northeast on 59.

"Okay. Nine P.M. I'll be there," he said.

"Great. I'll let them know in New York."

"What was her name again? The producer?" Cal reached for a pen and a scrap of paper, suppressing the frustration he felt at having to write down even the most minor items before they eluded his memory.

"Holly Hicks," Janet said.

He was grateful when she repeated the flight information for him in addition to the name.

"I'll fax her your picture from our press file so she can find you at the airport."

"That'll work," he said. "You've still got my press file?"

"Damned right I do. You don't think I want to do all that work all over again when you come back, do you?"

"Janet, I'm not . . ." Hell. Cal forced a laugh. "Yeah. Couldn't have been easy, tracking down all those credentials and awards."

"You've got that right." Her voice went soft. "I heard about the divorce, Cal. I'm sorry."

He never knew how to reply. Did he laugh it off and say

"It would have happened anyway"? Or choke up, as was often the case, and try not to say "I'm ashamed because I don't know why I married her in the first place"? What?

"Yeah, well . . ." he finally replied, hoping it translated as *hey. No big deal.*

"So, when can we expect to see your indestructible bod and your stony expression back here in the White House?"

"Soon," he lied.

After hanging up, Cal dragged his fingers through his hair, encountering the subtle indentation of his repair job, wondering why Janet bothered faxing this Holly person a photo by which to identify him when a metal detector would have accomplished the same damned thing, maybe even better. He probably didn't even look like any of his old pictures. He probably looked as different, as terrible as he felt.

Suddenly he regretted every word he had just spoken on the phone. Except for his agreement to make the drive to Houston. That he was looking forward to.

Chapter Three

The plane was crowded, which came as a complete surprise to Holly who couldn't for the life of her imagine why so many people were headed—and apparently quite willingly— to Texas. She was seated toward the rear of the plane, between a large man and his equally large wife, both of whom carried on a conversation during most of the flight. Holly had offered to exchange seats with either one of them, but, no, Norman sorta cottoned to the aisle seat while Denise was happy being by the window. That's how they always flew. They thanked her kindly and then went right on talking to each other as if the seat between them were empty.

Holly kept her elbows to herself and almost wished she were deaf while she stared at the screen of Mel's laptop on the pull-down table in front of her. At her feet, tucked safely in her handbag, was the fax from the White House that had come in just moments before she'd left the office for the airport. When she got back home, she was going to have it framed. Not the picture of Calvin Griffin, even though he was nice looking enough, but the cover sheet bearing the seal of the President of the United States. It was a pretty good bet no graduate of the Bi-County School of Cosmetol-

ogy had ever received a fax like that, and she wished her
mother were still alive to see it.

Her parents had died when she was in college, the victims
of a joy-riding fourteen-year-old in a stolen Camaro. The
state troopers had been pursuing him down I-37 just as
Bobby Ray and Crystal Hicks, their radio blaring "Stand By
Your Man," happened to get in the way. Holly hadn't been
back since the funeral, although she did correspond with her
cousin, Cassie Hicks Devane, who had a daughter, Madison,
with a vague interest in broadcasting and a powerful desire to
be Miss Texas.

Now, in Seat 25B, wishing she were flying to Peoria or
Nome or Siberia—anyplace but Texas—Holly was trying to
come up with a decent hook for the hero story.

She'd spent the morning boning up on the assassination
attempt in Baltimore last September. Predictably, all the wire
services and major news magazines had devoted the bulk of
their coverage to the shooter, Thomas Earl Starks. He was a
disgruntled postal worker—weren't they always?—with ties
to several foaming-at-the-mouth right-wing militia groups,
although the general consensus was that the man had acted
alone when he fired his M-16 rifle from an upper level of a
parking garage. Starks' confiscated diaries indicated an
intense hatred of Randolph Jennings as well as the belief that
the President was the unwitting pawn of several foreign gov-
ernments, primarily Denmark and Iceland, which might have
been funny if the man hadn't actually acted on his bizarre
notions.

It was no surprise, either, that the twenty-nine-year-old
Starks was a loner whose family, which consisted of a
mother and two sisters in Valparaiso, Indiana, hadn't even
heard from him in years. Apparently Thomas Earl Starks fit

the assassin profile from the top of his schizophrenic head to the tips of his toes.

As far as Calvin Griffin went, the coverage was mostly about his actions in those frightening seconds that sent scores of people—press, White House staffers, bystanders— scrambling for cover while he threw a hard body block into Starks' target, quite literally taking one of the bullets meant for President Jennings. Heroic as it sounded, the fact remained that it was Special Agent Griffin's job to do just that.

Personal details about the agent, however, were few and far between. He was thirty-seven years old, a Texan, recently married at the time of the shooting, with no children. Actually, his wife got more attention from the press than he did last September, especially in the tabloids where she was pictured coming and going from the intensive care unit, usually in a limo, always dressed to the hilt with her hair perfectly done and enough gold bracelets and rings to set herself up in the jewelry business. Holly had a vague memory of seeing her on *Larry King Live*.

As for Griffin himself, he had been a Secret Service agent for about a dozen years following what appeared to be an undistinguished career at Texas A & M and a stint in the Marine Corps.

His photograph, in black and white, didn't help much. With his clipped hair and cool gaze and stern mouth, Calvin Griffin looked like a recruiting poster for the Treasury Department. Alert. Athletic. Bright enough. A suggestion of arrogance, perhaps, in the tilt of his head. A stubborn angle to his jaw. Maybe the slightest hint of humor in the crow's feet at the corners of his eyes. Interesting? Not very. A hero? Hardly.

Holly didn't really have a handle on him yet. As a producer, that handle was what she desperately needed to put together a solid piece for Hero Week. She needed a hook to hang her story on, a way to organize and present all the facts and opinions she was about to learn. So far, she figured she had two choices for her hook. The story of Calvin Griffin, Hero, was either "We always knew he would be" or "We never thought he'd amount to a hill of beans." A few preliminary interviews ought to point her in one direction or the other.

All things considered, she really wished she'd been asked to produce a segment on Thomas Earl Starks, who was now in a federal penitentiary in Indiana. The shooter struck her as far more interesting than the victim. Starks had spent years working his way up to his heinous crime while the Secret Service agent had merely reacted in a split second to the gunfire. Not much there to work with as far as a story went. For all Holly knew right now, Calvin Griffin didn't even have a middle name.

Her seatmate, Norman, leaned to his right, further encroaching on her space. "You see any lights down there yet, Denise?"

"Not yet, honey bunch."

He sighed. "Well, we oughta be landing soon."

Holly glanced at her watch, then closed Mel's laptop. In another few minutes, she'd be back in Texas.

Yippee ki oh.

♥

Cal checked his watch. The plane was half an hour late, which had allowed him ample time to question his sanity in the airport bar.

The White House wanted a hero? Fine. Great. He'd showered and shaved and even splashed on a little Calvin Klein prior to putting on a suit and tie and his shoulder holster for the first time since the assassination attempt. This Holly person was going to be looking for a Secret Service agent, so he figured he might as well look the part even if he felt like a damned imposter.

Hero Week.

Shit.

Over his sister's vehement objections, practically over her dead body, Cal had gotten to the airport without a hitch, and he even remembered what color the level was where he'd parked in the garage. Yellow. He stole a quick glance at the palm of his hand where he'd written it, just to be sure. Only the "Y" was visible, the rest having been washed away by the moisture from several bottles of beer.

He left a twenty on the table in appreciation of the waitress' reliable service and blessed reluctance to chat, then he made his way toward the gate where the plane from Newark was due to arrive.

With his badge and photo ID and a working expression only slightly softer than Mount Rushmore, he cut through airport security like a blade through butter, and for a moment—a few curt nods, a pleasant tension in his jaw, and several confident, purposeful strides—it felt as if he were back on the job. Back in control. There was the warmth of his firearm snug against his ribs. The military shine of his wing tips. The subtle pressure of a perfectly knotted tie that signified he was on the job. Cal knew he missed it, but only now did he realize just how much. Desperately. Achingly.

As quickly as the realization occurred, he shunted it to the farthest reaches of his consciousness. He wouldn't let himself think about how much he missed the job. He didn't dare.

Starks' bullet hadn't only affected his physical health and short-term memory, but it had also played havoc with his emotions. They'd been dangerously close to the surface these past nine months, and even though he seemed to be getting better in that department, he wasn't always sure what might spark a rage or sneak up on him to make his throat close and his voice break and his eyes burn with tears. The unexpected rages were at least macho. But the tears. Jesus. They ought to be putting him on Freak Week instead of Hero Week.

His head was relatively clear and his emotions in check by the time he got to the gate, where people were already coming through the door from the jetway. Men, mostly, in suits, juggling briefcases and carry-on bags and cell phones. Cal leaned a shoulder against a concrete post while he surveyed the crowd from behind his dark glasses.

A small, pretty brunette paused in the jetway door, gazed hopefully around the waiting crowd, then lifted a hand to wave at a man with a toddler slung under his arm.

The next likely candidate for a producer was a tall redhead in a big-shouldered pinstripe suit who looked like she'd had a few too many Bloody Marys between Newark and Houston. She walked his way, but then Big Red lugged her one-suiter right past him without a second glance.

Okay. Maybe this Holly wasn't on the plane. Maybe there'd been a change of plans. Maybe they'd canceled Hero Week. Maybe . . .

He saw her, frowning down at the photo in her grasp, eyeballing the crowd before she consulted the picture once again. She wasn't any bigger than a minute. A strawberry blonde in curvy jeans and a luscious strawberry-colored tee. The fact that she looked good enough to eat didn't entirely escape him.

Her gaze slid right past Cal, not once but twice. He

must've looked worse than he imagined, or else this Holly wasn't all that bright. Then all of a sudden he realized he was wearing his shades, a hard habit to break after so many years of scrutinizing crowds. He dragged the glasses down his nose, and when her gaze traveled back, it stayed.

A smile—half recognition, half relief—worked its way across her mouth. She took in a visible breath and started toward him in a succession of movements that signaled firm flesh over delicate bones and devilish hips. Fine, feminine attributes that Cal hadn't been even remotely aware of during the past nine months. He shifted off the concrete post, more than a little aware of them now, as well as the effect they had on him.

Her hair was chin length, curly, just this side of wild, and the color of a pale lager laced with pink glints from the glow of a jukebox, a jar of honey on a sunset window sill. She really did look good enough to eat, this Holly, and much to his dismay, Cal realized he was famished.

"I'm Holly Hicks," she said in a voice that was part sugar, part Cayenne pepper, and a pinch of Texas. "The producer from the VIP Channel. Are you . . . ?"

"Cal Griffin."

The hand she offered him was small and sleek, with short nails and no rings to cut into his palm.

"I really appreciate your meeting me," she said, her tone brisk and businesslike. Her green gaze broke away from his to search the general vicinity. "Oh, good. There's a rest room. If you don't mind . . ."

"No. No problem."

"Could you hold this for me a moment?" She shrugged a black strap from her shoulder and handed him the laptop case. "And this?" She set her carry-on bag at his feet. "Thanks. I appreciate it. I'll be right back."

"I'll be right here," he said.

She was so tiny that Cal lost sight of her once she edged into the flow of passengers making their way toward the main terminal. He located an empty chair and sat, laptop on lap, carry-on bag beside him, hero turned baggage handler.

♥

In a stall in the ladies' room, Holly stomped on the flush handle so hard she nearly broke it off. Of all the chicken-hearted things she'd ever done in her life, rushing away from Calvin Griffin the way she just had probably topped the list.

After the near miracle of actually finding the man who matched the photograph in the crowd at the gate, she'd drawn in a calming breath, walked up to greet him, and then promptly panicked.

She pummeled the soap dispenser at the sink now, trying to figure out what had just happened to her, deciding it had nothing whatsoever to do with Calvin Griffin, and everything to do with her native state. Airports all looked pretty much the same, but one glance at the people milling around the gate had proven without a doubt that this airport was in Texas where the Stetson still ruled, where shirts tended to snap instead of button, where "Howdy" was the greeting of choice.

For one unsettling moment, it seemed as if she'd never left at all. She was almost afraid to speak to Calvin Griffin for fear the first word out of her mouth would be Howdy. She was reluctant to look into the mirror over the sink right now for fear of seeing herself at seventeen. God. She was half afraid to turn around for fear that Rod Serling would be standing back by the handicapped stall.

Producer Holly Hicks boarded a plane in Newark believ-

*ing she would safely arrive in Houston in a matter of two
and a half hours. What she didn't know, however, was that
the destination on her ticket was clearly marked* The Twi-
light Zone.

Do do do do, do do do do.

After punching the knob on the hand dryer, Holly stood
there telling herself she was being stupid and really, really
overreacting. She was back in Texas, sure, but she wasn't
going to *stay*, for heaven's sake. This wasn't a permanent
assignment. She'd get her story, set up potential interviews,
scout out a few locations for film—it would take a week if
she was lucky, two weeks tops—and then she'd be on her
way back to New York.

Texas, after all, wasn't a giant pool of quicksand that was
going to suck her back in. It wasn't flypaper, for God's sake.
It was just a state. A big piece of geography. Okay, maybe it
was also a state of mind. But more than anything, it was the
past. Her future was in New York.

When the dryer cut off, she headed out of the rest room,
realizing she wouldn't need a picture to find Calvin Griffin
this time. The black and white photo didn't do him justice. It
didn't capture the incredible blue of his eyes. She'd noticed
that the moment he had taken off his shades. Those eyes, set
deep within a nest of sexy crinkles, were an astonishing hue,
somewhere between periwinkle and cornflower. They were
truly beautiful.

The rest of him wasn't so bad either. For somebody still
recuperating from a serious injury, the Secret Service agent
looked extremely fit. Even his gray suit couldn't conceal the
fact that he was muscular and required no extra padding in
the shoulders. Rather than pale and sickly, his face was bur-
nished from the sun. His hair was sun-tipped, too, a lovely

light brown, just a shade or two removed from blond, and a tad longer than in the photograph.

Her professional eye told her that Calvin Griffin's athletic good looks would be a boon to her piece. They could shoot him up close, really tight, to get the full effect of those marvelous eyes and the deep creases that parenthesized his finely shaped mouth, assuming of course that her "hero" would agree to go on camera.

Holly caught sight of him then, sitting just about where she'd left him with her laptop and carry-on bag, looking patient as any saint. Scratch that. Patient as a man whose job it was to stand around for hour after hour guarding the President of the United States. As when he'd been shot in place of the President, Calvin Griffin was pretty much just doing his job.

♥

Cal had forgotten that in femalespeak "I'll be right back" was usually good for fifteen or twenty minutes. It was worth the wait, though, when he saw her walking toward him once again. Holly Hicks apologized for keeping him waiting, took back her carry-on bag, but seemed to forget about her computer. That was all right, though. After he grabbed her suitcase from the carousel, the laptop slung over his shoulder helped to balance him.

The airport was crowded enough to make chitchat impossible, which was a good thing since Cal was concentrating on where he had parked the Thunderbird. Yellow level, wasn't it? He glanced at the palm of his hand, only to see a little smudge of ink that could have been any letter at all. A line of Y. Part of a G for green. The tail of the final D in red. A half-loop of the E in blue. Damn. He'd start on the Yellow level, and work his way down if he had to, all the while railing at the idiots responsible for color-coding to cover up his own ineptness. Hell, he would have used the same macho ploy even before a .22 caliber slug had scrambled his head.

What difference did it make? Sooner or later, this Holly was going to realize his mental elevator stopped one floor short of the penthouse. Sooner was probably better, humiliating though it was. And the sooner he got it through his damaged skull that bright, beautiful lady producers were way out of his league now, the better off he'd be.

The doors leading to the Yellow level of the parking garage swooshed open, and there, parked not too far away, in all its chrome and turquoise glory was his T-bird. Cal rolled his eyes gratefully toward heaven.

"Here we go," he said, grasping her elbow and leading her across the line of exiting traffic toward the car. Her arm was so tense it felt as if he were gripping a mannequin.

He had put the top up after he'd parked, but it was a hot night with a full moon and he was suddenly, inexplicably feeling like a seventeen-year old. "Mind if I put the top down?" he asked, sliding behind the wheel.

"The what?"

"The top. Down."

"Oh, sure. Go ahead."

He hit the button and listened to the smooth glide of the ragtop receding and tucking into its well behind the back seat. Backing out of the parking place was inelegant, to say the least, because of his inability to turn his head quickly, but he remembered where he had stashed his ticket to exit the garage, so Cal was feeling, if not quite manly and in control, then at least somewhat competent when he hit the highway for Honeycomb.

"Nice night," he said, settling in at sixty-five and enjoying the way the moon reflected off the polished hood of the car.

"Pardon me?"

"Nice night," he shouted over the wind and the ambient road noise.

She nodded, a tight smile on her face as she used both hands to brush her hair out of her eyes.

"Too much wind?" he shouted.

"No. It's fine."

"Okay." He kept his eyes on the road for the next few miles of interchanges and ever-present construction barrels while his passenger seemed content enough to take in the moonlight and the ever-widening sky as they approached the open road.

"How far is it to Honeycomb?" she shouted.

"Not far," he said. "About two hundred miles."

She laughed. "Now I know I'm really in Texas. It's the only place in the world where two hundred miles isn't far."

"How long ago did you leave?"

"New York?"

"No. Texas."

It took her a moment to answer. "A long time ago."

Then, when she didn't say anything more, Cal glanced to his right to find his passenger gnawing on her lower lip, frowning. All of a sudden she shifted sideways in the seat, cocking one leg up and looping an arm over the seatback. The expression on her face was eager now, if not urgent.

"I need to be really up front with you about something, Mr. Griffin."

"Cal."

"What?"

"Call me Cal."

"Okay. Cal. I think before we get started, I should make something absolutely clear."

"Okay," he said, waiting with a sort of bleak patience for the other shoe to drop. The last time he'd heard a similar preamble from a woman sitting in the passenger seat, it turned out to be a frank disclosure of herpes, putting a right good crimp in his plans for the evening. Not that he had any sexual intentions toward this Holly Hicks, but now that she'd kindled a few pleasant flames, he really didn't want cold water thrown on his newly awakened fantasies.

"Go ahead," he said, yelling over the wind, sounding a lot more irritated than curious. "Shoot."

"I don't believe in heroes."

"What?" He'd heard her well enough. He just couldn't quite believe his own ears.

"I said I don't believe in heroes."

Cal laughed out loud for the first time in nine months. The sensation was like champagne. Like his bloodstream fizzing and popping a cork. "Neither do I," he shouted back.

"Pardon?"

"That makes two of us."

She cupped her hand to her ear, still not comprehending.

"I said we're going to get along just fine," he yelled, settling more comfortably behind the wheel, taking nearly criminal pleasure in speed and hot moonlight and the company of an honest, windblown woman.

♥

The next time he glanced her way, Holly Hicks was sound asleep. Asleep! So much for his dazzling company.

Dammit. He should have asked her where she planned to stay in Honeycomb so he knew where to drop her off. How could he have overlooked such an obvious and important question? Why couldn't he anticipate anymore, but only react?

Still, it wasn't as if there were all that many accommodations from which to choose. To Cal's knowledge there was only the old Mesquite Inn on Route Six, which was essentially a diner with three tourist cabins out back, and then there was Ellie Young's bed and breakfast downtown. The only visitors who ever came to Honeycomb were there to attend weddings or funerals or else they were rodeo people doing business with Dooley. It was more a town for leaving than for coming to.

The little producer barely stirred when he stopped for gas in Hungerford, and was still asleep when he drove past Ellie Young's big house at almost two o'clock in the morning. If Ellie was expecting her, she hadn't left the light on.

It was time for a command decision, and the last time Cal had made one of those he'd gotten half his head blown off.

Hell. He didn't have much choice except to take Sleeping Beauty back to Ruth and Dooley's for what was left of the night. Even when he made a hard right into the gravel drive and then cut the engine, she didn't rouse. Her head was tipped back against the seat, allowing moonlight to cast the shadows of her eyelashes onto her cheeks where she hadn't bothered to cover up a sprinkling of freckles. Those, along with the chaos of curls on her head, made her look more girl than full-grown woman.

He couldn't help his gaze moving along the strawberry-colored contours of her T-shirt, no more than he could suppress his body's reaction to those fine, first-class breasts. The past nine celibate months suddenly felt like nine years, and Cal sighed with a mournful mixture of lust and nostalgia and more than a little self-pity, grateful that the sound didn't wake the object of his unexpected and inappropriate desire.

There was a time he could have carried the tiny producer, her suitcase, her carry-on and her laptop all at the same time from the car to the house, but since he didn't want to fall flat on his face with Holly Hicks in his arms, he carried her in first through the back door of the dark house.

It figured she'd wake up just as he lowered her onto the unmade sofabed in his room.

"I must've dozed off," she murmured, as if it had only been for ten minutes instead of nearly four hours. When Cal turned the light on, she blinked. "How long was I asleep?"

"About two hundred miles."

She swore under her breath. "I'm so sorry, Mr. Griffin. This is really embarrassing. I took a muscle relaxant when I got on the plane, but I—"

"It worked," Cal said, feeling stupidly relieved somehow that it wasn't his company that had made her comatose. "I didn't know if you'd arranged to stay any place, so I brought you here."

She looked around. "Where's here?"

"My place. Well, actually it's my sister and brother-in-law's place." Cal looked around, too, at the sorry space he inhabited. The sofabed spilled out from one wall. Another wall was stacked with boxes, two deep and three high, which held most of his worldly belongings. Diana had paid somebody to pack it all up and ship it off. There was a blue reclining chair tucked into a corner, and on the table beside it were some paperbacks and three, no, four empty bottles of beer. He picked them up and dropped them in the wastebasket.

"I'll go out and get the rest of your stuff from the car," he said.

"Wait." She jumped up from the bed. "I don't want to put

you out. I didn't make any reservations, but maybe there's a motel I can go to tonight?"

"There's a nice bed and breakfast in town, but it's pretty late. I'll take you there in the morning." From the doorway he said, "If you want to help, just pull those sheets off. I'll be right back with some clean ones."

♥

Holly muttered to herself as she yanked the sheets from the mattress. The Valium she'd swallowed at the Newark airport was supposed to calm her down, just chill her out, for heaven's sake, not put her out like a light. Calvin Griffin probably thought she was some wigged-out media jet-setter who always traveled as high as the plane.

Way to go, Holly. She balled up the sheets and punched her fist into the bundle. Good way to begin a job, too. You've been with your subject for almost four hours and you slept through all but fifteen minutes. Of course, the good news was that it was three hours and forty-five minutes less of the Lone Star State that she'd be forced to endure.

Calvin Griffin dropped her suitcase just inside the door, then put her laptop on the dresser. "Be right back with sheets," he said, then disappeared again.

When he returned, Holly said, "Look, I really don't want to put you out, Mr. Griffin. Isn't there a couch I can just curl up on for a few hours?"

"Nope. And it's Cal, okay?"

"Okay. Here. Let me have those." She pointed to the pale blue linens in his hand.

"I bet you didn't expect to be making up a bed tonight, huh?" He shook out a sheet. Holly took a corner and helped align it on the sofabed's thin mattress.

"I didn't know what to expect, to tell you the truth. This job only materialized yesterday. And it's . . ." She pressed her lips together. She'd been about to confess that it was her first producing job, which wouldn't exactly instill inordinate confidence in her subject. "It's been a little hectic," she said, reaching for an edge of the top sheet and tucking it in on her side of the bed while he changed cases on the pillow.

"There," he said, tossing the pillow against the sofa back that served as a headboard. "The bathroom's just across the hall." He gave a nod to the boxes along the wall. "Sorry about the mess."

"I don't mind."

"Well, good night then. I won't be far away, so just holler if you need anything."

"Thank you, Mr . . . Cal. I really appreciate this."

"No problem. Good night, Holly."

After the door closed, Holly took off her shoes and wriggled out of her jeans. When she opened the closet door to stash them away, she was greeted by the sight of half a dozen suits, in varying shades of gray, all neatly aligned on their hangers. Conservative, blend-into-the-woodwork, Secret Service suits, not so different from the one Calvin Griffin was wearing tonight. There was a tux, too, in a dry cleaner's plastic bag. It made sense that he'd have his own tux in light of all the formal functions the President had to attend.

Suddenly the horrible news footage of the assassination attempt ran through her head again, and she wondered sadly if Calvin Griffin had been wearing one of these suits when Starks had fired his gun, then even more sadly she concluded that that particular gray suit had probably been soaked with blood and tossed in a trash can at the hospital. Or would the authorities have bagged it and kept it as evidence? She probably ought to find that out, but she was too tired to even make a note to herself right now.

She turned out the light, then slipped between the fresh sheets, flopping around until she found the place where the pull-out sofa's metal bar didn't cut across her spine. Closing her eyes, she let out a long sigh.

Texas. God. If she worked fast—really, really fast— maybe she could go home in a week.

Rufus panned the crowd waiting at the gate, then homed in on a powerfully built man, his shoulder slanted against a post, his blue eyes beckoning while Holly voiced over.

Heroes are where you find them. In a sea of Stetsons, in a desert of denim and dusty boots, one man stands out . . .

Chapter Four

The next morning Holly awoke with her usual sense of anticipation. Maybe today would be the day when Mel would finally pass a producing assignment her way. Maybe today somebody at CBS or ABC would finally call about one of the dozens of demo tapes she'd sent them. Maybe today her dream would finally come true. Then she realized where she was, remembered that Mel already *had* come through for her and that she was indeed a producer. Her anticipation fizzled in the face of reality. The good news was that her dream really had come true. The bad news was that it had come true in Honeycomb, Texas.

She had no idea what time it was, but the sun was well up and there were sounds of life in the house.

Oh, Lord. Whose house was it? What had Calvin Griffin said last night? Was it his sister and brother-in-law's place, or his brother and sister-in-law's? She'd find out soon enough, she supposed.

She put yesterday's jeans and tee back on, slipped into the bathroom across the hall, and then located the kitchen from the clattering sound of pots and pans.

There was a woman standing at the sink, humming softly

to herself. After Holly said good morning, the woman turned and it was immediately obvious that she was Calvin Griffin's sister. Her hair was long and dark, but the blue eyes were nearly identical. Those eyes were also wary and not the least bit warm. Her lips formed a downward curve.

"I'm Ruth Reese," she said. "Cal's sister. He says you're here to shoot a biography of him or something?"

"Something like that." Holly felt stupidly unprepared for the question. Well, dammit. She'd only been a producer for about thirty-six hours, and she didn't have her hook yet. Was it always the hero or was it the hill of beans angle? Once she knew where she was going with this piece, it wouldn't be so hard to get there.

For the moment, though, her professional frustration took a back seat to her growling stomach, which was probably why she noticed all of a sudden that she wasn't standing in an ordinary kitchen. This place was a culinary palace with its six-burner stainless-steel stove, monstrous exhaust hood, double wide glass-fronted refrigerator, and marble-topped island with a canopy of hanging pots and pans, none of which appeared purely decorative.

"What a fabulous kitchen," Holly said.

Ruth Reese's mouth defrosted just a bit. "Thank you. This was my fortieth birthday gift from my husband. He did most of it himself."

"It looks professional." Actually it looked like a glossy spread in *Better Homes and Gardens*.

"We had a consultant come down from Dallas for the design work, but Dooley did all the installation." The woman's eyes warmed a few degrees. "Do you cook?"

"Sure," Holly said, then tempered her answer with "Well, not exactly. I would if I had the time, though. And a kitchen like this." She pictured her own cramped galley kitchen in the sublet with its harvest gold stove and dinky refrigerator that usually contained little more than a bottle of ketchup, a squeeze mustard, and a couple yogurts that always expired a few days before she got around to them. "I subscribe to *Bon Appétit*," she added almost wistfully.

Cal's sister offered a tight smile that seemed to indicate that she was a longtime subscriber if not a frequent contributor to the magazine. "I envy you living in New York," she said, picking up a large pottery bowl, curling her arm around it and wedging it against her hip as she began to stir its contents with a wooden spoon. "With so many wonderful restaurants, how do you ever choose?"

Holly, in her honesty, was about to say she merely flipped a coin. Heads for McDonald's. Tails for KFC. Then she reminded herself that she was here not as a lowly, underpaid production assistant but as a big deal, hot-shot, full-fledged producer who could presumably afford to eat out. "It isn't easy," she said, which wasn't a total lie.

Her gaze strayed to the glass-fronted refrigerator and a prominently displayed half-gallon of orange juice. "I wonder if I could have a glass of juice," she said.

"Sure. Help yourself." Ruth pointed her spoon across the room. "The glasses are in the cabinet over the wine rack. Cal said he'd be taking you to Ellie Young's this morning, so I'm making some zucchini and walnut muffins for you to take along."

Holly's stomach vocalized again at the mere mention of the muffins, but this time the sound was closer to a purr than a growl. Maybe it wasn't so bad being back in Texas, after all. Maybe the state had changed in the twelve or so years she'd been away. The not-so-great state she had left behind was choked with dust most of the time. Its kitchens were full of chipped metal cabinets and pearly gray Formica with cig-

arette burns and linoleum floors that never came clean
beneath a thousand coats of wax. There were no zucchini
muffins in her Texas. There were soggy pancakes, white
bread with clots of margarine, greasy bacon with translucent
waves of fat, fried Spam, and people always yelling at each
other or at her.

As if on cue, she heard a heated exchange of male voices
outside the open kitchen door. Suddenly the screen door was
wrenched open, a vaguely familiar voice yelled, "Yeah, and
you can tell the son of a bitch I said that, too," and her hero
appeared in the doorway. When he saw Holly, his scowl
immediately flared into a smile.

"Morning," he said. "How'd you sleep last night?"

"Pretty well, thanks."

It occurred to Holly that she must've been more tired than
she realized the night before because she didn't remember
that Calvin Griffin was so damned good looking. She
recalled the beautiful blue eyes, but had somehow completely missed the finely carved nose just beneath them. He
even seemed taller this morning. Ah-ha! She spied the tan
toes of a pair of boots peeking from the worn hems of his
jeans. He *was* taller.

And she was standing there taking him in like a judge at
a beauty pageant. Good grief. Her eyes snapped up to his
face. If he realized he'd been under such intense scrutiny, his
expression didn't betray it.

"Have you met my sister?" He gestured toward the sink.
"Ruthie, this is Holly . . . uh . . . uh . . ."

"We've met," his sister said. Holly couldn't help but
notice the change in the woman's demeanor. She stood
stiffly, and suddenly looked as if she'd been sucking lemons
all morning. "What time is Ellie expecting you, Cal?"

"Whenever we get there," he said.

Ruth Reese made a little clucking sound of disapproval with her tongue and her mouth got lemony again.

The exchange struck Holly as closer to one between a much-put-upon mother and a shiftless son than an exchange between siblings, both of whom were well within reach of forty. Interesting. Her "hill of beans" theory surged ahead by half a length.

"I'll bet you're hungry," he said to Holly over his shoulder as he opened the refrigerator door.

"Well . . ."

"I'm making my zucchini and walnut muffins for you to take to Ellie's," Ruth said, using punishing strokes now with her wooden spoon. "They'll be done in about half an hour. I really don't have time to be fixing anything else for breakfast. Dooley will be wanting his lunch pretty soon."

"Orange juice will do for me," Holly said, opening an overhead cabinet and standing on tiptoe to reach for a small glass.

"Here." Cal was right behind her. Actually he was right *against* her behind. His body heat radiated into her as he reached past Holly's fingertips to snag two glasses, and she swore she could feel a distinct warmth from his belt buckle on her spine.

The orange juice was a necessity now because her throat had suddenly gone dry. Cal poured them each a glass, and Holly drank hers without stopping to take a breath, telling herself that she'd only reacted to the nearness of the man because it had been so long since a member of that species had been that close to her. It hadn't been personal. Just visceral. Hoo, boy, had it been visceral.

"More?" He was looking at her as if she'd just wolfed down an entire gallon. His own glass was still half full. Or half empty, depending on whether or not he was a born hero or a hill of beans kind of guy.

"No, thanks." She carried her glass to the sink, where Ruth took it, rinsed it thoroughly, then popped it into her state-of-the-art, stainless-steel dishwasher.

"Cal, there's time to show the lady around outside," his sister said as if she wanted to get rid of them both. "I'll call you when the muffins are done and then you can head on into town."

He shrugged. "She probably doesn't want—"

"No, I'd love to," Holly said. If Calvin Griffin couldn't take a hint, at least she could.

He gestured toward the door. "After you."

Outside, it wasn't just the heat that sent Holly reeling, but a combination of both extreme heat and brutal light. It was like being pounced on by a big yellow animal. For a moment, she almost couldn't breathe. When Cal drawled, "It's gonna be a scorcher," she could only give him a weak smile in reply.

Texas. She was deep in the heart of it now. The hot, relentless heart she'd struggled so hard to escape.

Their stroll to the barn and corral was a distance of several hundred yards, but Holly felt as if she were being sucked back in time to the ragged little ranch where she'd grown up. The same harsh sun beat down on her. The same dust covered her shoes. The mesquite and the prickly pear and the occasional live oak could have been the same as the ones that made up the tattered landscape at her parents' place in Sandy Springs.

A man's voice floated out from the depths of the barn, and Holly could have sworn it was her father's voice.

Hollis Mae, you get back in here and muck this stall out

*right. I don't care if you are reading. Reading'll keep. This
shit won't.*

Her father had lost his right foot to a land mine in Viet
Nam a few years before Holly was born, and although he
could get around well enough on the prosthetic foot, he had
used it—oh, how he had used it—as an excuse for everything from his inability to run the ranch properly to his black
moods and his general lack of success. He had hoped for
brawny sons to do what he couldn't or wouldn't do around
the place, and all he got was a wisp of a girl whose nose was
always buried in a book. He let her know, over and over, in
a million ways, that he counted her among his disappoint-
ments.

Dashed dreams. That was what her father had been all
about. Bobby Ray Hicks had left Sandy Springs in 1968
with a big grin on his face. Holly had actually seen that grin
in the clipping from *The Spectator* that her mother kept in a
shoebox along with the letters he'd written her, his brand-
new bride, from Viet Nam. In his cramped penmanship that
was half cursive and half print, Corporal Hicks talked about
his future in the Army. They'd get the hell out of Texas, he
wrote, and they'd see the whole damned world.

It hadn't happened. What they'd seen was a succession of
VA hospitals and then it was back to Sandy Springs, where
Bobby Ray Hicks promptly got drunk and ripped down the
red-white-and-blue banner across Main Street that wel-
comed him home a hero.

Maybe, Holly thought, that's where she'd gotten her athe-
ism, hero-wise.

A voice that wasn't anything like her father's sounded
close beside her. Holly turned and had to shade her eyes to
bring Cal Griffin into focus. "I'm sorry. Did you say something?"

"I was introducing you to Lucifer." He pointed toward a holding pen where an enormous black bull was scratching an ear against a post. "I said if anybody deserves to be on Hero Week, it's that big guy. Four years on the rodeo circuit and nobody ever stayed on his back longer than a couple seconds."

"I'm impressed," she said. The mention of Hero Week reminded her that she'd been here nearly twelve hours and had yet to begin her job. At this rate, she wouldn't get home for a month. "So, you grew up here?"

"Well, I was born and raised here." He chuckled softly. "I guess you could say I grew up in the Marine Corps."

"Was that always a dream of yours? Being a Marine?"

Holly was making a mental check in the Born a Hero column when Cal said quite simply, "Nope."

"Oh." Back to the hill of beans.

"What about you?" he asked. "Did you always dream of being a producer?"

"As a matter of fact, I did."

He leaned against a fence post and crossed his arms. If he'd been wearing a Stetson, this would have been the moment when he would have nudged up the brim. "I thought most little girls dreamed of being movie stars or ballerinas or brides."

Holly clucked her tongue. Where was this guy from? Mars? Oh, wait. It was Texas. "I guess you don't know very many little girls, Mr. Griffin."

"Cal," he corrected. "I was just trying to rile you a little. How long have you been a producer?"

She honestly would have liked to see the look on his face if she answered truthfully *oh, about two days*. But before she could reply with some variation of the truth, he broadsided her with another, far more personal question.

Reaching out to touch a lock of her hair, he asked, "Was your hair this color when you were a little girl? God, it's pretty."

Holly wasn't sure if it was the delicate touch of his fingertips or the soft sound of his voice or the way his incredibly blue eyes were searching her face, but suddenly something had her heart moving up into her throat and then bungee jumping down to her stomach. Her hair? She couldn't have said just then whether it was blond or brunette.

Whoa. Talk about up close and personal.

She cleared her throat. It was all she could do not to fan herself when she said, "You know, I'm the one who's supposed to be asking the questions here."

"Okay. Ask away. But you're going to be pretty disappointed in the answers."

"So, you don't think of yourself as a hero?"

He laughed so loud it startled her. Even Lucifer the bull stopped scratching his ear and turned his head their way. But before Cal Griffin had a chance to tell her just how he did think of himself, his sister yelled to him out the back door.

"Cal, the muffins are done. I just called Ellie and told her to be expecting you in about ten or fifteen minutes, so you'd best get a move on."

♥

Cal tried to imagine what his hometown must look like to a stranger. Honeycomb was basically a wide spot on the blacktop that supplied the needs of ranchers and farmers within a thirty- or forty-mile radius. Not much had changed since he'd left two decades ago.

The false-fronted buildings still needed paint. The pickups parked in front of them all sported rifles across their windows and American flags on their bumpers. The Long-horn Café was still serving their heart attack special, a sixteen-ounce rib eye with hash browns and biscuits and gravy on the side. Ramon's had been called Desert Pete's when Cal was in high school, but it had still been home to Honeycomb's wretched refuse, including one Calvin Griffin, Sr. And now it looked as if Junior just might be taking the ol' man's place.

After he dropped his passenger off at Ellie's, his duty to the White House would be done. He was going to take his little gold star for cooperation, slog through another lousy workout on the track, and then settle in at Ramon's for a long, liquid afternoon. It was the only sure way he knew to make his troubles disappear.

He glanced to his right at the trouble in the passenger seat, and once again felt a discernible jolt, a pronounced quicken-ing south of the border. It had been a long nine months since his libido had run underground, then all of a sudden last night—bam!—it had surfaced at Gate 44 at the Houston International Airport. The good news was it was back. The bad news was the woman who was responsible for its improbable return.

Last night, at first glance, he had this Holly figured for a type he was pretty familiar with—early thirties, single, on a fast upward track. A highly motivated woman two thousand miles from home who probably wouldn't decline a brief encounter of the sexual kind, especially considering there was little else to do in Honeycomb since the movie theater closed in 1984.

But then she'd declared her disbelief in heroes, obliterat-ing any notion that Cal might have had about brief, unen-cumbered sexual encounters. This Holly was as complicated as her hair was curly, as candid as her clear green eyes, as unexpected as any slug fired from an M16, and nearly as unsettling.

Like so many of his colleagues, he'd gotten used to easy pickings. Some women would do anything for a guy wearing a gun. Most women, at least in Cal's experience, maintained an almost desperate belief in heroes. And, although he never pretended to understand the qualifications, he didn't exactly turn his back on the benefits. Even with Diana, there hadn't been much of a challenge. Of course, her belief in heroes hadn't extended to fallen ones.

If this Holly had come along at a different time in his life, he'd have relished the chase. But at the moment his own personal challenges were foremost on his agenda. And if he was completely honest with himself, he wasn't up to the challenge of a beautiful, hard-won woman right now or willing to risk rejection.

Holly Hicks was off limits now. He'd just have to take his newly discovered libido elsewhere.

"You'll like Ellie," he said as he turned off Main Street onto Washington Avenue. The founding fathers of Honeycomb named the cross streets for American presidents, but only got as far as Jefferson before they ran out of roads. "That's her house over there on the right."

"It's huge," Holly said. "It must be over a hundred years old."

"Probably." The house sat, as it had forever, under the cool shade of its surrounding oaks. It looked just the same as it had when Cal was a boy. Hell, probably the same as when his grandfather was a boy. "Ellie's great-grandfather had all those limestone blocks hauled overland by mules from Missouri or someplace. He didn't trust ships. Or so the story goes."

"Interesting," she murmured.

"I'm sure she'll tell you all about it. She's the town historian, or something like that." He swung into the driveway and pulled up in front of the wide steps that led to the big wraparound porch just as the door opened and three-hundred-pound Ellie Young stepped out. Cal killed the engine.

"Welcome!" Ellie called. "Howdy, y'all. Welcome!"

For such a big woman, she came down the porch steps with surprising agility and grace in her long denim skirt and tan, hand-tooled boots. Ellie was Cal's age, but the extra weight and her graying hair made her appear much older. Well, at least it had before Cal had aged quite a bit himself in the past few months.

"Hi, darlin'." He stepped around the T-bird and wrapped his arms around her soft bulk. "I've brought you warm muffins and a real, live, paying guest. Sorry we're late."

Her gray head snapped back. "You're not late. For Lord's sake. Ruth always wants everybody to travel on her itinerary. Any time you got here was fine by me. Now introduce me to this little television lady from New York."

Cal gestured to his passenger. "Miss Ellie Young, meet Holly Hicks."

While the two of them chatted, he retrieved the suitcase and the laptop and her other luggage from the backseat, and carried them up to the front door. For a minute he was almost tempted to ask Ellie if she had another room available. That way he could avoid most of Ruthie's tongue lashings, plus just walk the long block to the high school track and Ramon's. Then he looked at Holly Hicks' lithe little body and her pretty face, and decided he really didn't need to spend any more long nights with just a wall or two and his newly awakened longings between them. One night had been quite enough.

"Holly, I'm leaving you in good hands," he said, stretching out his own to say good-bye.

Her hand was tiny, but strong in his. Her nails were on the short side, unpainted, unglossed. Sexy in their natural state. So different from Diana's acrylic talons.

"Thank you, Cal. I'll be in touch with you in a couple of days with those questions."

"Fine." He didn't want to let her go, but he did. "That ought to give me plenty of time to come up with some interesting answers."

"Stay, Cal, and help us with these muffins," Ellie said.

"I would, Ellie, but I've got a couple appointments."

He didn't bother to tell her they were with old Bee at the track and then with a certain Dr. Heineken at Ramon's.

♥

Ellie Young's house was as huge and welcoming as the woman herself. It was furnished with an interesting mix of antiques and comfortable contemporary pieces. Except for the pair of longhorn horns mounted above the big stone fireplace in the library, it might have been a country home in Connecticut or a fancy hunting lodge in Maine.

Holly counted at least a dozen rooms on the ground floor alone, each one of them reminding her of a museum. Every horizontal surface, from tabletops to mantelpieces to shelves and even the top of the concert-sized grand piano, was covered with framed pictures and knickknacks and memorabilia, and every object seemed to have a story that Ellie was only too happy to tell.

"That's probably more than you ever wanted to hear about my great-great grandfather," the woman said, smiling rather sheepishly as she returned an ancient, heavily engraved pistol to its bed in a velvet-lined box. Augustus Young, Ellie's ancestor, had apparently used the weapon with much success and without regard to race, religion, or gender. "People tell me I spend way too much time in the past, but what's a historian to do?"

"It's fascinating," Holly told her in all sincerity. "And I'm sure I can use a lot of this information as background for my story."

"You work for the VIP Channel? Is that what Ruth told me?"

Holly nodded.

"I've watched pretty near every one of those biographies. I especially enjoyed that month-long series on the presidents. So, you did some of those?"

She nodded again. Well, she wasn't really lying. Not exactly. Her hostess hadn't asked if she'd produced them. Ellie asked if she "did" some of those biographies. What Holly did was tons of research, coordinate a slew of production schedules, and edit several of the final scripts, particularly the Millard Fillmore segment which nobody else wanted to do.

Her stomach growled again, as if to change the subject.

Ellie laughed. "Well, here I am, going on about things that happened a hundred and fifty years ago while you're starving to death, you poor little thing. Come on. Let's take those muffins of Ruth's out back and make quick work of them. How do you like your coffee?"

"Black, please."

"Atta girl."

It was only a bit after ten in the morning and the temperature was probably already ninety-five degrees, but the huge oak trees around the house helped to keep them reasonably comfortable as they sat on the flagstone patio in the back yard with Ruth's muffins and Ellie's cast iron black coffee.

Holly couldn't have chosen a better place to stay. Ellie knew everyone and everything about Honeycomb.

"I went to school with Cal," she was saying. "From kindergarten all the way through high school."

"Was he a good student?"

"Yep." She took a few sips of her coffee. "When he wasn't raising hell, that is."

"Really." Holly leaned forward. "What kinds of hell?"

Ellie narrowed her eyes. "I'm not sure I should be telling you this. I wouldn't want you to get the wrong impression."

"Well, I'd like to know the whole story in order to do it right." Holly didn't add that her personal curiosity was piqued, as well. So, Calvin Griffin had been a hell raiser in high school, one of those wild, golden boys who never cast Hollis Mae Hicks a second glance. An inexplicable ripple of disappointment went through her, and once more she remembered why she didn't want to be back here in Texas, the place where her reputation as a dork was probably engraved on a chalice somewhere.

Ellie took the last bite of her third muffin, chewed inscrutably a moment, then sipped her coffee. "Here's what I'll do," she finally said. "I'll make a list of former classmates, teachers, neighbors, people like that. People who go back a long way with Cal. Then if anything not-so-flattering comes to light, I won't be responsible. I like the man too much to say anything that might be considered detrimental."

"That'll work," Holly said. She'd been planning to ask the woman for a list like that anyway. "I'm not here to do a hatchet job on him, you know. The story is scheduled for Hero Week. I don't know if his sister told you that."

"Oh, yeah. She told me."

From Ellie's tone, and judging from her own experience this morning, Holly guessed Cal didn't exactly top his sister's list of personal heroes. She definitely wanted to look into that.

"I'll go write that list," Ellie said, "and then I'm going to have to leave you. I'm giving a talk at the Kleberg County Historical Association this afternoon. Come on upstairs, Holly honey, and pick out a room."

♥

The room Holly chose was a Victorian delight, papered in huge white cabbage roses on a deep pink background. The big hand-carved walnut bed was covered with a white spread crocheted by Ellie's grandmother. The *Gone With the Wind* lamp had belonged to old, shoot-em-up Augustus himself.

There were two tall windows with wavy glass, and between them a small door that opened onto a rusty fire escape. Ellie had told her she could use it as her private entrance and exit, if she wanted, then she'd laughed when Holly asked her for a key.

"Honey, this house hasn't been locked a minute since it was built. I wouldn't even know where to look for a key if I needed one."

Was that comforting or terrifying? Holly, who'd spent the past few years behind safety chains and triple locks and dead bolts, couldn't quite decide.

Left to her own devices then, she unpacked, located her cell phone at the bottom of her handbag, then clambered up on the high bed and called her office. She had to wait a full five minutes for Cheryl, Mel's secretary, to track him down.

"Hey, kid. How's Texas?" His gruff, three-pack-a-day voice had never sounded so good.

"It's right where I left it," she said. "Big and hot as ever. What's going on in the office?"

"Nothing," he growled. "Maida started her vacation early, and Arnold's pissed so he's not coming in today. What a way to run a station, huh?"

Holly laughed.

"So, how's your hero?" he asked.

"Sexy."

Good God. Where had that come from? It was as if Mel had said, "Hey, kid. Let's free associate. Color."

Blue.

"Eyes."

Blue.

"Calvin Griffin."

Sexy.

Thank God her boss chuckled at her unprofessional remark. "Sexy, huh? Hey, Maida's going to love that. The word is that they're having trouble getting more than a word or two out of Neil Armstrong, and that NYPD hostage negotiator is turning out to be a heroic pain in the butt."

"Griffin's very cooperative," she said.

"That's because you know how to get a story. These other idiots . . . well, don't get me started. So, where are you staying?"

Holly flopped back on the pile of soft pillows at the head of the bed. "A bed and breakfast in beautiful downtown Honeycomb. I wish you could see this room I'm in, Mel." Her gaze drifted around the room as she spoke. "The wallpaper's bubble gum pink with humongous white roses. The bed's comparable to an ark, and the bedspread's handmade, almost seventy-five years old." Holly snapped up to a sitting position. "God, maybe I shouldn't be sitting on it."

"I'm sure it's okay. So Texas isn't so bad after all, huh?"

"Well . . ."

"How's your story going?"

"Great. I met Griffin's sister this morning. He's living with her."

"Wait a minute. I thought he was married."

"He is."

"So, where's his wife?"

After Holly hung up a few minutes later, she stared at one of the dinner plate–sized white roses on the wall. Good question, she thought. Just where *was* Cal Griffin's wife?

Chapter Five

Later that afternoon, Holly stood on the sidewalk in a measly square of shade provided by the awning over the drug store, riffling her fingers through her damp cork-screwed curls. The thermometer on the bank's sign said 103, which probably put the humidity at two thousand. Holly hated Texas all over again.

Mel couldn't have been more wrong about her knowing the territory and speaking the language. She was as out of place here as she had been in Manhattan three years ago when she'd stepped off the bus from Albany. Actually she was more out of place now. Back then in New York, if she kept her mouth shut and didn't gawk too much at the tall buildings, people couldn't tell she didn't belong. Here in Honeycomb she might as well have had PERFECT STRANGER tattooed on her forehead.

Nobody in town was talking. Not about Calvin Griffin anyway. At least, not to a perfect stranger. She'd approached three of the people on Ellie's list this afternoon. Bobby Brueckner, the balding bank manager, claimed he was too busy with Friday afternoon receipts and reconciliations, although Holly hadn't noticed anybody putting money in or taking it out of Honeycomb Savings and Loan while she was there. Nita Mendes, on the other hand, was legitimately busy in her beauty shop on this Friday afternoon and suggested Holly come back Tuesday when things were slow. Tuesday. That was four long, hot days away.

The final non-talker had been Hec Garcia in Ye Olde Print Shoppe, who smiled rather cryptically and said his mother had taught him if you can't say anything nice, don't say anything at all. End of interview.

Holly squinted up at the cloudless sky as if she were seeking celestial guidance. As an interviewer, she didn't seem to be aggressive enough. At least she didn't seem to have the correct approach. People loved to be interviewed, didn't they? People jumped at the chance to see themselves on TV, whether it was wearing silly stuff on their heads and two-tone paint on their faces at football games or providing solemn but useless commentary after a crime or a catastrophe.

Maybe she should say she was from *60 Minutes* or *20/20*. Maybe nobody in Honeycomb had ever seen the VIP Channel. No. Wait. Ellie Young had. But even gabby Ellie didn't want to go on record.

Holly pulled the list of prospective interviewees from her handbag, perused it once more, then looked at the clock on the bank. It was four-thirty. Five-thirty in New York, where the workweek had already wound down and the weekend officially begun. If she were home, she'd probably be elbowing her way out of the train at the Lexington Avenue station right now, hotfooting it down 59th, grabbing something to eat, hoping to be in her robe in front of her two TVs in order to catch most of the local news on at least two major networks. It was how she spent most Friday evenings, barring the occasional date that turned out badly, making her wish she'd stayed home with her TVs.

For a moment, she considered going back to Ellie's and flipping on the big-console TV she'd seen in one of the rooms downstairs, but decided that getting a news fix wasn't going to help her get any closer to her story here in Honeycomb.

Muttering a curse, Holly crammed the list back into her handbag. The hell with it. If nobody wanted to talk to her this afternoon, she'd opt for local color. She was going to find someplace to sit and have a bite to eat and something cold to drink. She eyeballed the street, instantly dismissing the Longhorn Café with its banner telling her that Friday promised all the fried catfish she could eat for $6.99.

As far as she could tell, that only left the asphalt-shingled dive in the middle of the block. Ramon's. Worst case, she'd have a beer and pretzels, then climb her fire escape and call it a day.

When she stepped through the door, the darkness nearly blinded her for a second. The chilled, recycled air was rank with booze and peanuts, and Patsy Cline was wailing somewhere in back by the pool table. God Almighty. Holly took a deep breath and headed toward a vacant stool at the end of the bar where a kid who looked almost young enough to be her son was drying glasses.

"Hey," he said after she'd managed to hoist herself onto the tall stool. "What can I get for you?"

"Is there any chance I could get some kind of sandwich?"

"Sure. No problem." He stepped a few feet to his left and bent to open a small refrigerator. Its light washed over his face. "I can give you ham or . . . ham."

"I'll take ham," Holly said, smiling, already feeling better.

"One ham sandwich, coming up," he said. "What can I get you to drink?"

Holly gazed at the assorted neon signs that decorated the place. A cold beer sounded so good, but it would make her way too sleepy to get any work done after dinner. "I'll have a diet cola," she said.

A moment later the young bartender set a tall, ice-filled glass in front of her and deftly poured the soft drink so that not a drop of foam spilled over. "You're not from around here, are you?" he asked her as he poured.

It was the nicest thing Holly had heard all day. "No," she said. "I'm from New York."

"Cool." Without inquiring what a nice, obviously sophisticated, big-city girl was doing in a dump like this, he began fixing her sandwich, a process which amounted to slapping square pieces of processed meat onto square slices of soft white bread.

Holly sipped her drink. The only other person sitting at the bar was a blonde who looked like a permanent fixture down at the other end. There were people in the back of the room, but it was so dark she could only distinguish their shapes. Every minute or so, there was the thunk of a billiard ball falling into a pocket, followed by a delighted whoop or a disgruntled curse.

It reminded her of the place in Sandy Springs where her parents used to go every Saturday night. What was it called? Joker's? No. Wait. Jester's. That was it. She could remember the boot heel of her daddy's good foot hooked over a rung of a bar stool, and how her tiny mama's feet never touched the floor once she was perched at the bar. In some ways it seemed a million years ago, but in others it seemed like just last week. Even the same song—*Crazy*—was playing on the jukebox back then.

Plus ça change, plus c'est la même chose. That was about all she could remember from the French course she'd taken her sophomore year in college, hoping it would help eradicate her twang. It didn't. All it did was lower her grade point average. The more things change, the more they stay the same.

Man, wasn't that the truth. Holly fished in her glass for a diamond-clear chunk of ice, then popped it into her mouth. Fourteen years spent heading to New York, and here she was back in a crummy little bar in Texas, drinking diet cola, sucking ice, feeling as if she'd never left. She half expected the ghost of Bobby Ray Hicks to limp in and tell her she was expected home right quick to do her chores.

Just then, in the bottle-lined mirror that backed the bar, she saw the front door open and bright daylight cut briefly into the perpetual midnight of the tavern. A man ambled in. Holly couldn't distinguish his features, but his Stetson and outsized belt buckle and slim-legged jeans all branded him pure cowboy.

"Here's your sandwich, ma'am." The young bartender plopped a paper plate in front of her. He had stuck frilly green cellophane toothpicks into each sandwich half, and put a fat hot pepper on the side.

"Thanks," Holly said. "It looks good."

"You need anything to put on it? Mayo? Mustard?"

"Mustard, please. Dijon, if you have it."

"Dee—what?"

"Never mind. Plain ol' mustard'll do me just fine." She couldn't believe those words had come out of her own mouth. And not just the words themselves, but the twang that had accompanied them. After less than twenty-four hours. Dear God. What was she going to sound like in a week or two?

"Hey, now. Don't that look good?" The newly arrived cowboy slung his dusty denim butt onto the stool beside hers. "Rick, fix me up one of those, will you? Hell, make it two. But gimme a beer first."

He tilted his hat back, gave Holly's elbow a nudge, and grinned. God's gift to all the women south of the Nueces River. "Can I buy you a beer, honey?"

"No, thank you."

Holly picked up her sandwich and turned away from him. She had barely swallowed the first bite when he moved closer, his arm fully in contact with hers.

"You're not from around here, are you?" he asked.

She took a sip of her cola to wash the sandwich down. "No."

"Yeah, I didn't think so. I'd've noticed you, for sure. The name's Tucker Bascom." He stuck out a dirt-creased, callused hand. "People just call me Tuck."

Oh, God. Why was it so easy to say "buzz off" in New York and almost impossible to do it here? Holly ignored his hand in favor of another bite of her sandwich.

"I bet I can guess your name," he said, oblivious to the subtlety of her brushoff.

From the opposite end of the bar came a female drawl. "She don't want nothin' to do with you, Tuck."

"Shut up, Patsy," he growled. "Nobody's talkin' to you."

"Thank God," the woman said.

The cowboy lifted his bottle of beer, knocked back half of it, then turned toward Holly again. "You're almost done with that cola, honey. Rick, bring this little lady a light beer. On me."

The young bartender raised an eyebrow at Holly. "Ma'am?"

She shook her head.

"Aw, come on now, Jennifer or Jessica or . . . wait. I bet it's Tiffany. Am I right?"

Holly leaned forward across the bar. "Could I have a plastic bag or something to put the rest of my sandwich in?" she asked Rick. "And a can of diet cola to go?"

"Tiffany! Darlin'! You can't leave me like this. Why, hell, we've just met and . . ."

A pair of shoulders wedged between Holly and the cowboy. "Take a hike, Tucker. The lady's with me."

There might have been a time when Holly would have taken great umbrage with this game of *Got Testosterone?*, when she might have snapped to her would-be rescuer, "Thanks, but I can handle this myself." But this wasn't one of those times. She'd never been happier to see anybody than she was to see Cal Griffin right now.

He had wedged between them so he was facing Holly, and while he told the cowboy to get lost, his beautiful blue eyes were trained on Holly's face. Blue? Surely she could do better than that. She searched for a more descriptive word. Azure, perhaps. Heavenly. Celestial. That was close. Silly, but for one heart-stopping second she was wishing she really were "with" him.

Tucker grumbled, "Well, now how the hell was I supposed to know that," as he slid his beer and then himself several stools away. He glared at Holly in the mirror, but didn't utter another word.

"Thank you," she said softly.

"You're welcome. I've got a table in the back." Cal picked up her paper plate. "Come on. You can finish your sandwich back there."

♥

This was one time Cal didn't mind having the reputation of one mean son of a bitch. Tucker Bascom, if he'd half tried, could probably have wiped the floor with him this afternoon.

"Thanks again," Holly said, settling in her chair across from him. "What a jerk."

"It wasn't that I didn't think you could handle him yourself. I just got tired of his mouth." He pointed to her glass of melted ice. "Do you want another one of those?"

"Actually . . ." Her green eyes twinkled even in this dim light and she angled her head toward his beer. "I wouldn't mind having one of those."

"Rick," he called out.

"Yessir?"

He held up two fingers.

"Coming right up, Mr. Griffin."

Cal settled back in his chair, content just to sit there and to gaze at Holly's face. Still, he'd taken her away from Tucker, hadn't he? A little follow up was necessary. He used to be pretty good at this kind of thing. Hell. He used to be good at everything.

"So, how'd you and Ellie get along?" he asked. "Did she talk your ear off?"

She smiled as she lifted her hands to hook a myriad of curls back on both sides. "Nope. I've still got two of them. See?"

What he was seeing were two perfectly formed, delicate shells, two pale and complicated whorls, and he couldn't remember when a woman's ear had struck him as so erotic, so absolutely sexual. He shifted in his chair, glancing over his shoulder to see if the kid was on his way yet with the liquid reinforcements.

"I enjoyed talking to Ellie," Holly said. "My room is incredible. The bed and breakfast was a good choice, Cal. Thanks."

She picked up her sandwich and bit off a dainty corner, which wasn't all that sensual, but then her pink tongue peeked out in search of a dab of yellow mustard in the corner of her mouth, and Cal's throat almost closed at the sight. He turned his chair sideways, parallel to the table, thinking it might help if he wasn't looking at her head on.

"Have you come up with any interesting answers for my questions yet?" she asked.

"Depends on the questions." He drained what was left in his bottle, then handed the empty to Rick, who had just arrived with the new one.

"Sorry about what happened up there, ma'am," the kid said to Holly.

"That's okay," she told him. "It's not your fault. You make a great ham sandwich, by the way."

"Yeah?" The kid's face nearly glowed in the dark. "Thanks. I appreciate that."

Cal sampled the fresh, cold brew. The first swallow out of a full bottle was always the best. Probably comparable to the first pull on a lit cigarette. Good thing he'd never smoked.

Young Rick headed back for the bar, and Holly asked, in her half Eastern seaboard, half chili pepper voice, "So, are you ready for my first question?"

He wasn't, but what the hell. This was what the White House wanted. "Shoot," he told her affably. "Gimme your best shot."

"Where's your wife?"

Cal gritted his teeth as he dragged his thumbnail through the center of the label. Hell. If he'd known she was going to ask about Diana, he wouldn't have been such a willing volunteer.

"My wife? Right this minute?" He consulted his watch. "Well, let's see. She's probably just putting on her earrings before leaving for dinner at the Bombay Club with her divorce lawyer."

He thought he'd sounded relatively casual, even carefree, but from the look on Holly Hicks' face, he decided his devil-may-care tone may have fallen a bit short.

"Oh," she exclaimed, blinking, apparently as startled by his answer as he had been by her question.

"You probably ought to scratch Diana off your list of possible interviewees," he said, wishing he hadn't answered her in the first place. He should've just said no comment. Even the White House wouldn't fault him for that.

"What happened?" She shook her head and then waved her hand in the air between them as if to erase the question. "No, I didn't mean that the way it sounded. It's too personal. This must be a fairly recent development."

"Not exactly." He turned his chair back in order to face his inquisitor directly. "Look, Holly. Damn. I shouldn't have said anything about her, and I'd really appreciate if you didn't put any of this in the program. You're right. It's too personal. Way too personal. I don't need my dirty laundry hung out for a million people to see on cable TV."

"Sixteen million," she mumbled, her eyes downcast.

"Excuse me?"

"I said we have a viewing audience of about sixteen million households. Give or take a million."

"Great. That's just great." Cal took another swig from his bottle, wondering if it was too late to call Janet Adcock to renege on this whole deal. He'd been happy, sinking into helpless oblivion these past few months. Well, no, he hadn't been happy, but . . .

"You need to keep in mind, Cal, that this piece is going to be featured on Hero Week," Holly said. "Naturally we'll be highlighting that aspect of your character."

He responded with a snort.

"Really," she said in an effort to convince him. "And I am sorry. Sincerely. About your wife, I mean. I think I saw her on *Larry King* or *Geraldo* or somewhere not long after the assassination attempt. She's beautiful."

"She has a beautiful face. That's all." He wished he'd never seen it. Actually he couldn't remember Diana's face all that well at the moment, not while he was looking at a headful of blond curls that almost jingled and a pair of green eyes that fairly crackled with intelligence and curiosity even in the dim and dingy lighting of Ramon's. Now *that* was a beautiful face. He couldn't help but grin.

"So, how'd a non-believer such as yourself get roped into Hero Week in the first place?" he asked her.

Her lips slid into a smile as luscious as it was inscrutable. "Just lucky, I guess."

Holly Hicks turned her full attention to her sandwich then, allowing Cal to drink his beer in the relative silence of a bar gearing up for a Friday night. Ordinarily he enjoyed watching the pick-ups, the put-downs, and the near explosions at the pool table from a secluded corner. Watching others' troubles helped take his mind off his own. But he wasn't in the mood for barroom drama tonight. Not other people's anyway.

He found himself gazing across the table and wondering what it would be like to hold this Holly in his arms. To kiss her. Just once. A slow, deep, Saturday night to Sunday morning kiss. She'd probably taste like . . .

Like a ham sandwich, he told himself, forcing his libido back underground where it belonged.

"When you're finished," he said, "I'll walk you back to Ellie's."

"Thanks." She cast an apprehensive glance toward the bar where Tucker sat sullenly nursing a beer. "I'd appreciate that."

"No problem." Cal grinned as he tilted his bottle in her direction. "Hell. What good's a hero if he can't help a damsel in distress?"

♥

It was a shock, stepping out into bright daylight, after sitting so long in the near dark of the bar. Holly had to stare at her watch a minute before she could even read the time. Five-forty. Six-forty in New York. She took a few steps, only to feel Cal Griffin's hand curve around her upper arm.

"You're going the wrong way," he said.

She pivoted, smiling, hoping he didn't take her for a complete dolt. She never got lost in New York. She just detoured a lot.

Releasing his grip on her arm, he set off down the sidewalk at a comfortable pace. Most men, the taller ones anyway, walked too fast for Holly. She always felt like a dachshund trotting along beside its master. But Cal Griffin's stride was just right. Even better, this Texan didn't mosey or amble or sashay. He just walked. That was nice. Holly almost wished they had farther to go than down the street and around the corner to Ellie's.

"How long are you planning to be in town?" he asked.

"It depends," she said.

"On what?"

"On how quickly I can convince people to talk to me about you. So far, nobody's been willing."

His pace slowed a bit. "Who've you talked to?"

She pulled her list from her handbag. "Well, let's see. The first was the way-too-busy Bobby Brueckner at the bank."

"Bobby," he said with a chuckle. "He'll probably tell you I could've been a world-class pool hustler if I hadn't been diverted into an inferior career. Who else?"

"Um." She squinted at her list. Ellie's handwriting wasn't all that easy to read. "Nita Mendes."

"Oh, shit."

"What?" Holly glanced up at his face. Well, at his jaw-line, actually. It seemed a bit tense. For a hero. She almost giggled. "What's Nita Mendes going to tell me?"

"If that's who I think it is, she used to be Nita Padilla. We, uh, had a thing for each other for a couple months in high school. Nothing heroic, I guarantee."

"Ah. The old drive-in movie scenario."

He came to an abrupt halt. "She told you about that?"

Now Holly did giggle. "No. She didn't tell me anything. She was too busy doing hair and nails. But just about every-body in South Texas has some sort of drive-in movie sce-nario, don't they?"

Cal started walking again. "I guess. I'll tell you mine if you'll tell me yours."

"Oh, no. I'm the interviewer here. And why do you keep insisting I'm from South Texas?"

"Aren't you?"

"Yes, dammit. But it's not supposed to show anymore."

He slanted a little grin her way. "I won't tell anybody." His hand covered his heart. "I swear. Who else wouldn't talk to you?"

"Hec Garcia, who said his mama told him if he couldn't say something nice, not to say anything at all."

"Ah."

"You don't sound surprised," she said.

"I'm not. There was some bad blood for a while between the Anglos and the Hispanics when I was in school. We're all probably carrying a few scars to this day." He held out his arm, turning it over to disclose a jagged, pearly line that extended five or six inches between his wrist and his elbow. "Not too heroic either, is it?"

Holly wasn't even thinking about that. She had witnessed a knife fight once in Sandy Springs, of the same sort Cal had described, between a white boy and a Latino. She could still picture the way the sun had glinted off the blades, the shocking brightness of the blood when one of those blades had found its mark, how her classmates had urged the combatants on. There hadn't been any heroes then, either. Of all the teachers who witnessed the fight, none had been brave enough to step forward and stop it. They had called the cops instead, and the shrill of the sirens stopped the fight before the officers even arrived.

Holly hadn't exactly been a hero either, as she recalled. She'd stood there, shocked by the violence, but calmly registering details while composing an editorial for the school paper in her head.

"No, not too heroic," she murmured.

"Well, here you go," he said, turning up Ellie's drive, gesturing toward the front door.

"Thanks. I'll be fine the rest of the way. I'm going around to use the fire escape on the side."

"Okay." Without another word, he continued across the lawn and around the side of the house, only stopping when he reached the narrow, rusty stairs that rose to the little door on the second floor.

It hadn't looked quite so precarious when Holly had gazed down on it from above. And she hadn't realized that the damn thing didn't go all the way to the ground. The first step was a good three feet high. While she stood deciding how she was going to tackle it, Cal grasped her waist with both hands and lifted her up.

"There you go, Holly Hicks," he said. "I'll stay here to catch you if you fall."

"Thanks."

The iron stairway kind of groaned beneath her feet, and she wondered if anybody had done this in the past fifty or sixty years. She tested each step before she put her full hundred and fifteen pounds on it, all the while not daring to look down, either at the ground below or the man standing there, presumably with his arms out, just in case.

"It's okay," he called up to her. "You're doing great."

"Yeah. Yeah," she muttered. She could hear bits of rusty stair breaking off, hitting the ground like sleet. The same rust clung like dried blood to the damp palms of her hands. Holly sucked in a deep breath and mounted the remaining stairs.

The doorknob was rusty, too. She twisted it, but nothing happened. She twisted it again, this time pushing against the door with her other hand. Nada. She pushed harder. The door wouldn't budge.

"It won't open," she said, maintaining a pretty level tone under the circumstances.

"What?"

"It's stuck."

"Hang on."

The iron staircase groaned again and trembled beneath her as Cal climbed up. There was barely enough room for both of them on the top stair, and Holly experienced another one of those visceral jolts at the physical nearness of him. For a second she forgot to be nervous about the rickety fire escape. But only for a second.

"Are you sure this will support us both?" she asked, her voice not exactly hysterical, but full of obvious and justified concern.

"No. So we'd best not stay on it too long, huh? Move." He elbowed her aside, grabbed the knob and rammed his shoulder into the door, once, twice, before it opened.

"Oh, thank God." Holly scrambled inside, as thrilled to get off the rusty stairs as she was to put some distance between herself and the sensual vibes emanating from Calvin Griffin.

But when he didn't follow immediately, she stuck her head back out the door. Cal was brushing his hands on the legs of his jeans, then all of a sudden he stopped and grabbed onto the railing. His knuckles turned white as pearls. So did his face.

"Are you okay?" she asked.

"Yeah. No. I . . . uh . . . dizzy. I shouldn't have looked down."

She reached out. "Here. Take my hand. It's just two little steps and you'll be inside."

He didn't respond. Holly wasn't even sure if he had heard her. His lips were compressed so tightly that the corners of his mouth were white as chalk.

"Cal," she said sharply, truly alarmed for him now. "Take my hand. That's it. Come on." She had to pull him the final foot or so. "There." She sighed and closed the door behind him.

Making his way a bit unsteadily toward the bed, he

grasped one of the fat, carved posts, then stood there a moment with his eyes closed.

"Better?" she asked.

He nodded. After a minute, he opened his eyes and gazed slowly around the room. "That's some wallpaper," he said with a weak chuckle.

"You're obviously not a man with Victorian sensibilities," she said, relieved that he felt well enough to criticize the flowery pattern. "Why don't you sit for a minute. I'm going to the bathroom just down the hall to get you a glass of water."

She was gone for more than the minute she promised. First she had to rid herself of the cola and the beer. Then, while she washed her hands, she noticed what a mess her hair was, so she finger-combed it back into submission. Then she had to hunt for a glass or a cup, and finally found some dinky paper ones in the cabinet next to the sink. She filled two and carried them back to her room, where Calvin Griffin, hero, was stretched out on her bed, apparently sound asleep.

Or dead.

Chapter Six

"Dooley."

Aw, damn.

Dooley Reese battened down his eyelids and dug his head deeper into the pillow. Seemed like he'd only just fallen asleep.

"Dooley!"

Ruthie was shaking his shoulder now and tugging at the covers. God bless it.

"What?" Dooley sat up, struggling awake, his heart beginning to gather speed. "What's wrong? What the hell time is it?" It was still pitch black in their bedroom.

"It's a little after five. Cal didn't come home last night."

Cripes. He thought the barn was on fire or one of the bulls had leapt a fence. He rubbed his eyes and sighed. "So?"

"So?" Ruthie's voice climbed to a higher register, one that was almost painful this early in the morning. "So, I'm worried sick."

"Your brother's thirty-eight years old, honey. He hasn't had a curfew in over twenty years. And even when he did, I don't remember him ever abiding by it."

She sat on the edge of the bed. "This isn't about any curfew, Dooley, and you know it."

"Honey . . ."

His wife brushed away his well-meaning hand. "And don't tell me I'm overreacting, either," she snapped.

Dooley knew better than to tell her that.

He'd loved this woman, with her sharp tongue and her good heart, since the first day he saw her in first grade, and nearly twenty-four years of marriage hadn't diminished his affection a bit, but Ruthie had been hell on wheels for the past couple years. What was it about the Griffins, anyway? They tended to get mired in their difficulties.

Ruthie's personal blues set in when their son, Colby, went off to college. But then, once she got accustomed to her empty nest, she started feathering it with new carpets, new drapes, a whole new set of dishes—godawful yellow ones, although she insisted they were "saffron"—and a slew of brand-new pots and pans.

Along with the new utensils, she started taking her cooking seriously. Always a good cook, she was suddenly determined to be a great cook. She gave up her soap operas for cooking shows on television, and she quit reading mysteries in favor of cookbooks. The word "cuisine" infected her vocabulary. She planted an enormous herb garden, and she cooked up a storm, which sounded good in theory, but often left Dooley craving meat and potatoes after long stretches of soufflés and quiches and way-too-small portions of veal or salmon.

It was about two years ago, after a scare with a lump in her breast, that she started talking about her own restaurant. Dooley never knew it had been her dream since childhood. How could he have known? She never told him. He couldn't read her mind, something he considered both a blessing and a curse. But the lump that turned out to be merely a cyst had scared him even more than it had scared her. And if it was going to take a restaurant to make her happy, well, then, they'd figure out a way.

She wasn't just talking about opening a nice little place in Honeycomb to compete with the Longhorn Café, but Ruthie was thinking along the lines of a nice little place in Houston or Dallas. Lord help him. Dooley had put in the new kitchen for her last year, hoping maybe that would satisfy her, but it had only fueled her dreams.

When Cal got shot, everything went on a back burner for a while. But now that her brother seemed better, Ruthie was antsy again. Now Cal had apparently stayed out all night and she was fit to be tied. The more she loved a person, the madder she got at them.

"I just don't think you ought to worry about him so much," Dooley told her now.

"Well, if I don't worry about him, who will? Not that la-di-da wife of his, that's for certain."

"Cal's well rid of her," he said softly. He and Ruth had driven all the way to Dallas last year in order to meet the woman Cal seemed so smitten by. Diana acted like they'd just tumbled off a turnip truck. When she asked him what he did for a living and he told her he raised the best rodeo stock in the country, all she'd said was, "I went to a rodeo once during my Urban Cowboy phase. That brought it to an end, needless to say."

Needless to say, Ruth and Dooley both thought Cal could do a whole lot better, but he'd married the woman anyway for reasons of his own.

"What if he wrecked his car?" Ruthie was a worst-case-scenario kind of woman. "What if he's lying in a ditch somewhere bleeding to death?"

"We'd have heard, honey."

"What if he got in a fight with one of those no-good ranch hands who hang out at Ramon's?"

"We'd have heard about that, too."

"That brother of mine is killing me with worry." She groaned. "I swear. I'm almost sorry I ever said he could come home."

Dooley bit his tongue in order not to remind her that half of "home" belonged to Cal. Their mother had left Rancho Allegro to them both in equal shares. Ruthie tended to forget that most of the time since she was the one who lived here, or as she sometimes put it, "the one who got stuck here while he went off and followed his dream."

Ruthie could be difficult, especially lately when it came to her dreams. But Dooley loved her dearly. And he had a natural patience. It probably had something to do with the fact that he'd worked with big, ill-tempered animals most of his life. Not that his wife was big and ill-tempered. She was small. Petite, you might even say. But lately she'd been damned moody.

"Let me take a shower, honey," he said, "then we'll make a couple calls. You got any of those good muffins left over from yesterday?"

A tiny smile cracked her somber face. "Did you like those muffins?"

"Best I ever had." He leaned forward and kissed the top of her head. "You go put the coffee on, sweetheart, and then we'll decide what to do about Cal."

♥

When Holly opened her eyes, the first surprise was that she wasn't in her own bedroom in New York. The second surprise was the big white roses on the bubble gum pink wallpaper. And the third surprise—the real lulu—was that she wasn't alone in bed.

Oh, God. Cal Griffin had looked so peaceful last night that she hadn't had the heart to wake him up. She'd sat in a chair with Mel's laptop balanced on her knees, making notes about interviews and possible shooting locations, until the light from the computer was the only illumination in the room. For a little while, she'd put her head back and closed her eyes, but the chair was way too uncomfortable for sleep.

She'd looked longingly at the bed. Her bed. It was queen-sized, big enough for two, she decided. Besides, the way Cal Griffin was sleeping, chances were good that Holly would wake up long before he did, so he'd never know she'd been there. And so what if he did? It was *her* bed. And a comfortable one, it was, since she must've slept right through the night.

She turned her head to the right now in order to read the time on the little clock on the nightstand. Six-thirty. Then she turned her head to the left.

When she'd first glimpsed him at the airport, behind his dark glasses, Cal Griffin had looked every bit the stern, stone-faced Secret Service agent. He'd matched her expectations perfectly. But on closer inspection, that wariness of his had turned to a kind of weariness. Well, the man had been shot, for heaven's sake, and his wife had apparently left him. Little wonder he looked weary.

At the moment, though, he looked merely peaceful. The downward curve of his lips had relaxed to a smooth, neutral line. His complexion seemed darker than the day before, but Holly ascribed the change to the faint whiskers that shadowed his cheeks and jaw. His hair was a bit rumpled, too. Kind of sweet. How odd to be so intimate with someone she didn't really know at all. In a week or so, though, she'd probably know this man inside out, and then she'd never see him again, asleep or otherwise.

Somewhere in the house a phone began to ring. She wondered if Ellie was home to answer it. After a moment the ringing stopped only to be replaced by the sound of Ellie's voice. It was indistinct at first, but then as it grew more and more clear, Holly realized that the woman was approaching the door to her room.

"No," she was saying. "Last time I saw him was yesterday when he dropped off the little television gal. He said he had an appointment."

Ellie sounded increasingly irritated. "Well, I don't know about that, Ruth. It's what he told me. Just that he had an appointment. It wasn't my business to ask him where or who with. No, I don't know if Miz Hicks saw him later. If you want to wait a minute, I can knock on her door and ask her. It's awful early, you know, Ruth. All right. All right. Just a minute."

When the phone had begun ringing, Holly had turned toward the door, but now she turned back to the man on the other side of the bed.

His eyes were open and suddenly he didn't look so peaceful anymore. Just the opposite, in fact. Tension shaped his mouth again. His jawline was taut, almost grim. A muscle ticked in his cheek.

Ellie knocked. "Miz Hicks? Holly? Are you awake? I hate like the devil to disturb you, but I've got Ruth Reese on the phone trying to locate her brother."

"Busted," Cal muttered.

"Are you here?" Holly whispered.

He shook his head, then pressed a finger to her lips. "Give me two seconds before you answer," he said. "And thanks for the best night's sleep I've had in months."

He leaned forward, reached out his hand to skim her cheek with his fingertips and then to hook a few curls behind her ear. It felt just like the prelude to a kiss.

Holly's breath stalled in her throat. A kiss? She closed her eyes. Cal Griffin was going to kiss her? She was going to let him do it? That certainly seemed to be the case. But when she opened her eyes a moment later, Cal Griffin was already halfway down the rusty fire escape.

Ellie knocked again. "Miz Hicks? Holly?"

"Yes." Holly remembered how to breathe, thank God. Now if she could only do something about her rampaging heartbeat. "Yes, I'm awake. Just a moment, please."

♥

From the bottom rung of the fire escape, Cal hit the ground running. In ten seconds he had rounded the corner of Ellie's house, jumped the boxwood hedge that bordered her drive, taken the porch steps in two's, and then pounded on her front door hard enough to be heard halfway down the block.

He wasn't dizzy. His knee hadn't locked up on him. He wasn't even breathing hard, which was nothing short of a miracle since he'd barely moved this fast since pushing Randolph Jennings through the hotel door and out of harm's way. Just why he was moving so fast wasn't exactly clear to him, but it had something to do with an instinctive need to protect

Holly Hicks' reputation. Whether or not the woman deserved such a chivalrous gesture didn't seem to matter.

If nothing else, he owed her for the first good night's sleep he'd had since he'd been shot. Not only that, but this morning he felt better than he had in a long, long time. Hell, it was the first morning in months he hadn't been hung over.

Ellie opened the door, the phone still in her hand. "Well, speak of the devil," she exclaimed. "Morning, Cal. Here. Ruthie's looking for you." She thrust the handset at him, then rolled her eyes. "Good luck."

"Thanks," he murmured before offering a cheerful, if somewhat defensive "Hey, Sis" into the phone.

He followed Ellie into the house while Ruthie gave him a thousand lashes with her razor-sharp tongue. Where had he been all night? Why hadn't he called? Didn't he realize she'd be worried sick, imagining him dead in a ditch somewhere? Was he doing this on purpose just to make her miserable? When he could get a word in edgewise, Cal told her that he'd slept in his car rather than drive home after one too many beers.

"Well, that's a first," she said, segueing smoothly into a tirade on the derelicts who frequented Ramon's, himself included.

Ellie tapped him on the shoulder. "Coffee?" she whispered. Cal nodded.

"What are you doing at Ellie's so early?" Ruth asked.

Good question. He hadn't framed an alibi yet, so he responded with the first excuse that came into his head. "I'm taking Holly Hicks out for breakfast."

"I hear she's been asking a lot of people a lot of questions," his sister said in the same tone she might have used if she'd said *I hear the woman murdered both her parents with an axe.*

"Yeah. I guess that's part of her job. Asking questions."

"Well, I just hope she doesn't get answers that are going to embarrass us."

He mumbled noncommittally. As far as he was concerned, embarrassment was pretty much a given with this Hero Week deal. For him, anyway.

Ellie put a steaming mug of coffee in his hand and he sipped it while Ruthie went through a litany of Griffin embarrassments, including their father's penchant for alcohol and loose women, Cal's hell raising in high school, his brief, misguided marriage and his current state of limbo. He was getting like Dooley, he thought. Allowing her complaints to go in one ear and out the other without having much effect in the middle other than to induce a dull throb. When she finally hung up, Cal had a full-fledged headache.

While Ellie poured a topper into his mug, she shook her head. "That sister of yours has a terrible tongue," she said, "but she means well, Cal. She worries about you."

"That she does," he said with a beleaguered sigh. It was what he'd come home for, after all. Somebody to worry about him. Somebody who loved him enough to worry.

"So you're taking Holly to breakfast?" Ellie asked.

He nodded. "That was the plan. Is she up yet?"

"She's up." That unique blend of East Coast cool and hot chili peppers sounded just behind him.

Cal turned slowly, forestalling an attack of vertigo, but the sight of Holly Hicks alone almost made him dizzy. Her snug jeans and tee of yesterday had been replaced by a soft pink bathrobe that clung in all the right places. Until this moment he'd merely thought of her as tiny. Now the word "luscious" came to mind. With her face scrubbed clean of makeup and her hair damp from the shower, she was the very definition of "natural beauty." Unlike him, he thought, as he ran a couple fingertips across his unshaven jaw.

"Morning," he said as if he hadn't seen her in hours, as if he hadn't almost kissed her just a few minutes ago. Right now he wished he had. "If seven's too early, I can come back."

"Seven's perfect," she said. "I'm starving. It'll just take me two minutes to get dressed. Where are we going?"

Ellie laughed. "Take your pick. The Longhorn Café or the Longhorn Café."

♥

The Longhorn Café lived up to its name. It was quintessential Texas with horns and antlers decorating its shellacked knotty pine walls, along with horseshoes, branding irons, and Lone Star flags. The branding iron motif was repeated on the brown and beige curtains and on the greasy laminated menu.

Cal had been strangely quiet on their walk from Ellie's, leading Holly to suppose that he wasn't a morning person.

"What do you recommend?" she asked him, peering over the top of the menu.

"Anything but the biscuits and gravy," he said, "unless you enjoy walking around all morning feeling like you've just eaten wet concrete."

She gave a little shudder. That was how she'd felt every morning for her first sixteen years after eating her mother's biscuits and gravy. "Maybe I'll just have a bagel and coffee."

A blond waitress in a brown and beige uniform that matched the curtains stopped at their table. "Coffee, y'all?" she asked, holding out a full glass pot.

"Please," Holly said.

"You're up bright and early, Cal," the woman said while she poured the hot brew. "How're you feeling these days, hon?"

"Great," he answered without much enthusiasm.

His expression seemed neutral enough, but Holly sensed it was just a mask, not so different from the one he wore professionally. The waitress, whose nametag read CORAL, appeared to accept his answer as gospel, however.

"Glad to hear it," she said. "I'll be right back for your order. We've got some real nice-looking cherry Danish today."

When she was gone, Holly took a sip of her coffee, then asked, "How *are* you feeling these days?" She dispensed with the "hon."

"Great," he said again, this time a bit more defensively.

Holly wasn't buying it, not in her capacity as a journalist nor as the woman who'd watched this man slumber so peacefully the night before only to have worry return once he opened his blue eyes. "You haven't been sleeping well, I gather."

Those eyes fixed firmly on her face. "I did last night."

"So I noticed." She couldn't fight off a foolish grin or the slight flush she felt burning across her cheeks.

God, what a juvenile reaction for a thirty-one-year-old woman. She needed to start thinking like a producer instead of some silly, starry-eyed kid. She reached for her water glass and took several cooling gulps. And anyway the man had fallen asleep on her, hadn't he? How flattering was that?

"You should have kicked me out last night," Cal said, "but I'm grateful that you didn't."

Holly shrugged. "No big deal." Well, it wasn't, after all.

"I didn't have the heart to wake you. But I'm grateful you made such a dashing exit this morning."

"I figured you would be."

Holly got lost for a second in the crinkles at the corners of his eyes just before Coral re-appeared, plucking a pencil from her blond beehive. "Okay, what'll it be, folks?" she asked.

"I'll have a bagel and orange juice," Holly said.

"Sorry, hon. No bagels. We used to have them on the menu, but nobody ever ordered them. How 'bout if I bring you one of those nice cherry Danishes before they're all gone?"

"That'll be fine," Holly said, all of a sudden craving a golden-toasted, butter-dripping bagel more than anything in the world. Or one with lox and cream cheese like the ones Mel brought to work every once in a while. Her stomach twisted with hunger and homesickness.

Cal ordered the Danish, too, and after Coral sashayed back to the kitchen he grinned across the table and said, "You're not in New York anymore, Dorothy."

She laughed. "Do I look that disappointed?"

"Well, your face fell an inch or two. It's still a really pretty face, though."

Cal Griffin thought she was pretty! The unprofessional part of her began to melt like ice cream down the side of a cone, while the professional in her went all stiff and thin-lipped. What did pretty have to do with anything? The two attitudes clashed with a little cluck of her tongue as she reached into her handbag for her notebook and a pen.

"I had intended to do a few collateral interviews before officially interviewing you, but I guess it doesn't matter all that much," she said, pushing aside her cup and saucer, then flipping open the notebook to a clean page.

Now who looked disappointed? Ha! Now whose face fell several inches but still managed to look really, really handsome?

"I didn't realize this was an interview," he said.

"Well, why waste time?"

She sat up a little straighter, and with her pen poised above the blank page, Holly wracked her brain for a good opening question, one that wouldn't make Cal Griffin uncomfortable, one that would lead innocently and irrevocably to meatier questions and astonishing replies. A Barbara Walters kind of question. God help her, she couldn't think of anything at the moment except the way those soft whiskers darkened his strong jaw and the way that little muscle jerked in his cheek and how the color of his eyes reminded her of a Siamese cat she once had named Murrow in honor of Edward R.

"If you could be any kind of vegetable," she blurted out, "what would you be?"

He laughed, then rolled those deep blue eyes toward the ceiling. "What kind of dumb question is that?"

"It's not a dumb question."

"Yes, it is."

Holly gripped her pen and stared at him belligerently. This never happened to Barbara Walters. "There are no dumb questions," she said. "Only dumb answers."

"Right," he said, just as Coral approached their table. "Well, let's get one."

"Here's your Danish, hon," the waitress said, sliding a plate in front of Cal.

"Coral, darlin'," Cal said, "I've got a question for you. If you could be any kind of vegetable, what would you be?"

"Broccoli," the woman said without missing a beat while she set the other Danish on the table.

"See!" Holly yelped.

Cal glowered at her. "What do you mean 'See'?" He looked up at Coral and snarled, "Why the hell would you want to be broccoli?"

She shrugged. "I don't know. It was just the first vegetable that popped into my head. It's a really dumb question, Cal. Can I bring y'all anything else?"

"No, thanks, darlin'." He flashed a fairly smug grin across the table at Holly. "I rest my case."

Putting her pen down and closing her notebook with a solid thump, Holly said, "You're just not into the spirit of the interview." She reached for the Danish and took a bite.

Across the table, her companion didn't begin eating, but rather leaned back in his chair and crossed his arms, all the while aiming a smile at her that struck Holly as inappropriately amused if not slightly arrogant. Okay. So she wasn't Barbara Walters. Maybe it was the vegetable part of the question that didn't quite work, she thought. Maybe she should have asked what kind of dog he'd like to be.

He was still giving her that nasty grin, so she swallowed the food in her mouth, then took a sip of orange juice. "What?" she demanded.

His head cocked a bit more to the left, slanting his grin. "What kind of vegetable would you be?"

She thought about it a minute, and the more she thought, the more she wanted to laugh. Dammit. Nobody in their right mind wanted to be a vegetable of any kind. "All right. All right. You win," she said finally. "It was a dumb question. There. Are you satisfied?"

"Reasonably." He sat forward and picked up his Danish. "How many people have you interviewed?"

"Hundreds," she lied. "Why?"

"Just curious."

They finished their meal in silence, and then—after a brief tussle over the check, which Holly won, by God—they walked out into the warm sunshine.

"What are your plans for the day?" Cal asked her.

"I thought I'd just wander around town and get some ideas for backdrops for camera shots. That sort of thing." She was sorely tempted to ask if he'd like to join her, but decided she really shouldn't be distracted. She needed to focus on Honeycomb itself, not Honeycomb's favorite or least favorite son.

"Okay. Well, I guess I'll head back out to the ranch. Thanks for breakfast."

"You're welcome."

She tried not to feel sad or disappointed as she watched him walk away from her down the sidewalk. This was business, not pleasure, after all. She wasn't here to have fun. She tried, too, not to think about those long, obviously powerful legs heading in the opposite direction or the way the worn, sky blue denim of his jeans hugged that oh-Lordy just-right butt.

When he was a hundred or so feet away, he stopped and turned slowly back toward her.

"Zucchini," he called.

"Excuse me?"

"The vegetable I'd want to be. Zucchini." Then he laughed and walked away.

Holly laughed, too, then shook her head, wondering how she was going to get *that* image out of her head during the next week or so.

Chapter Seven

After Cal left, Holly sat in the little park next door to the bank. In New York the space would have been called a pocket park, and chances were good that it would have been decorated with eccentric sculptures and whimsical benches and brightly painted playthings, all of them covered in graffiti, of course, but still more appealing to the eye than one gnarly-rooted mesquite bush, a picnic table stained with bird droppings, and a rusty swing set with a broken seat.

It was already hot at nine o'clock, and she had to shade her eyes in order to read the list of names that Ellie had written for her. She'd struck out on three interviews yesterday, four if she counted Ellie. This morning's attempt to interview her hero had been a joke, at best. Still, after thinking about it, Holly was grateful it hadn't been worse. It only occurred to her after Cal walked away that you didn't ask the victim of a serious head injury what kind of vegetable he'd like to be. God. How insensitive was that? What had she been thinking? What was wrong with her?

"Nothing," Holly muttered. Absolutely nothing was wrong with her, for heaven's sake. "You can do this, Hollis Mae Hicks. You know you can do this."

Well, of course, she could! She'd produced hundreds of pieces—thousands!—over the years. The fact that they were all in her head didn't detract from their quality one bit as far as Holly was concerned. She had put together everything from hard-hitting exposés of political hacks and military morons and industrial sleazebags to poignant vignettes, little jewels of journalism that would make even Charles Kuralt weep with envy. Compared to all those pieces, a straightforward biography of Calvin Griffin, hero or not, ought to be a piece of cake. A slam dunk. A breeze. A walk in the damned park.

As if propelled by her own thoughts, Holly began pacing from one side of the little park to the other, careful to avoid the tangled roots and the low limbs of the mesquite bush. She'd wasted far too much time already. It was time to commit to a hook, and her instinct at the present was to go with the hill of beans theory, to make the Calvin Griffin story one of overcoming low expectations in a less-than-enriched environment. Given a few twists of fate, Honeycomb's hero might just as easily have taken a bullet in a gang fight or a bank robbery as he had in saving the life of the President of the United States.

Now all she needed to do was to sit down with Mel's laptop, hammer out a solid plan for this production, and then follow through with it. With her hook firmly in mind, her interviews would just naturally improve. Holly grabbed up her handbag and strode along Main Street on her way back to Ellie's.

She was just about to turn the corner onto Washington when something caught her eye through the vacant lot that sat between the barber shop and the saddlery. Over the weeds and broken bottles and paper trash, about a block to the south, Holly saw sunlight glinting off a turquoise Thunderbird convertible parked next to what appeared to be a running track.

It was Cal Griffin's car, she was certain. After all, how many classic turquoise convertibles could there be in a town this size? Or any town, for that matter? When they'd parted, Cal had told her he was going back to his sister and brother-in-law's ranch. Obviously he'd changed his mind.

In that instant, Holly changed her mind, too. Rather than return to her room, she decided to wander over toward the track, which she presumed was part of the high school. It wouldn't hurt to take a look at her subject's alma mater before she worked up her list of shooting locations. And if she just happened to encounter her subject in the process, well, so much the better.

As she got closer, she noticed that the track formed the perimeter of a football field, which was torn up at the moment, no doubt ready to be re-seeded or somehow revamped for next year's season. They loved their football in Texas, and Honeycomb probably wasn't any different from Sandy Springs or any other town in that regard. The phys ed budget in her high school was double that of any other department. She'd written more than a few nasty editorials on the subject for the school paper.

Cal Griffin wasn't anywhere in sight, so Holly walked toward the grandstand and perched on a bench in the first row, almost as if she were the first spectator to arrive for a big game. She could see the back of the school itself, and decided that she hadn't been too far off the mark when she'd imagined it would be a one story Texas-Danish modern building with tan bricks and plenty of glass. Probably hot as hell inside, too, she thought, remembering her own school while she looked at the air-conditioning units that stuck out of every third or fourth window.

The feeling of déjà vu was nearly numbing. Not that Holly had spent much time in the grandstand at Sandy Springs High, however. She'd watched *20/20* instead on Friday nights, usually with her mother stomping in and out of the living room, making disparaging remarks about her social life.

She wondered if Cal Griffin had been on the team here. It was easy to imagine his muscular physique in a football uniform with rippling, thigh-hugging spandex. After all, just because she hadn't gone to the games didn't mean she didn't appreciate some of the finer aspects of the sport.

She wondered if the knife fight Cal had mentioned had taken place after a Friday night homecoming game when tempers tended to flare. Or maybe Cal and Hec Garcia had come to blows over Nita Mendes, the beautician. In her imagination, Holly conjured up a bonfire and two crowds gathered at each of the goal posts—the Anglos on Cal's side and the Hispanics on Hec's, and nobody in the middle asking, "Can we all just get along?"

But maybe the fight hadn't happened here at all. Maybe Hec Garcia lay in wait for Cal in the alley behind Ramon's. Or . . . oh, brother. Maybe it had been Cal who'd lain in wait for an unsuspecting Hec. If that had been the case, Holly really didn't want to know. She'd have to write a memo to Arnold and Maida, requesting that her package be scheduled for Hooligan Week, instead.

She heard a footstep to her left, and turned just as a voice said, "You must be the little TV gal, waiting on Cal."

The man who spoke was tall and lean and pure Texas from the crease in his straw Resistol to the dusty tips of his Tony Lamas. His sand-colored mustache failed to hide a warm and engaging smile.

"I'm Dooley Reese," he said, extending a hand. "Cal's brother-in-law."

Holly put her hand in his solid, enthusiastic grip. "I'm Holly Hicks," she said. "I met your wife yesterday."

"She told me." He lowered himself onto the bench beside her, nudged the brim of his hat upward, and drawled, "Hero Week, huh?"

"That's right." She gazed back at the track that circled the football field. "I saw Cal's car and thought my hero just might be around here someplace."

"He is," Dooley said.

"Excuse me?"

"Right over there." The man pointed toward a small stand of oaks halfway between the track and the school building, where Holly could see one arm and one leg, both covered with gray sweats. "He's taking a little break from his work-out, I reckon."

Holly reckoned she'd looked right at him at least twice without ever "seeing" him. If Cal had seen her, he obviously hadn't felt compelled to greet her or acknowledge her presence in any way. A little tic of disappointment registered somewhere inside her.

"Does he do this every day?" she asked.

"Yep."

"Getting in shape for going back to work, I suppose."

"Yep."

Holly smiled as she made a mental note to cross Cal's monosyllabic brother-in-law off her list of potential on camera interviewees. "Any idea when he plans on going back?" she asked.

"Nope."

She almost laughed. On second thought, maybe she ought

to film Dooley Reese. A few well-placed yeps and nopes would add a certain *je ne sais quoi* to her production.

Across the field just then the figure in the gray sweats levered up off the ground, gazed for a long moment toward the two spectators in the grandstand, and then began walking—not ambling or moseying or sashaying, Holly was happy to see—toward them. A black dog that looked part Border Collie and part just plain dog shambled along by his side, sniffing the ground and every now and then glancing up at Cal's face as if to ask, "Everything okay? How're we doing here?"

"I didn't know Cal had a dog," she said.

"He doesn't. That's ol' Bee, the high school mascot. He kinda belongs to everybody in town."

"Bee." Holly repeated the name. "As in honeybee?"

"As in yellow jackets," Dooley said. "That's the name of the football team. For years the kids used to spraypaint yellow stripes on Bee before games until some new young English teacher made a big fuss about animal rights and so forth. Ol' Bee never seemed to mind it, though." He shook his head, chuckling. "Guess he never knew he had rights."

"I guess not."

"That dog's taken a real liking to Cal."

Holly was about to wave to ol' Bee and his pal, but Dooley stopped her with a light touch on her hand. His voice was low, close to a whisper. "I like him, too, Ms. Hicks, which is why I'd hate to see some TV program make him out to be a washed-up nobody."

She blinked, sincerely shocked by the man's statement. "I have no intention of doing that."

"I hope not. You talk to enough people around town and you'll find out soon enough that the only person who thinks Cal's still got a future in the Secret Service is Cal himself."

"He doesn't?" she asked, blinking again. That wasn't the

impression she'd gotten. She assumed Cal would be back at work, probably by the time her piece appeared on Hero Week.

Dooley shrugged. "It'd be a miracle."

Holly was eager to ask him more, but the man who was apparently in need of a miracle was just a few steps away from them right now. Close enough for her to react to the astonishing blue of his eyes. Her heart seemed to skid to the right an inch or so.

"Good morning," she said, feeling a silly and unwelcome grin slide across her lips. "Again."

"Morning," he replied, then looked at his brother-in-law. "Hey, Dooley. What's up?"

"I need to ask a favor of you, Cal."

"Shoot."

"Your sister's been after me all week to take her up to Corpus Christi so she can try out some new restaurant there, so we're taking off around noon. We'll probably spend the night there and be home around noon tomorrow."

"Okay," Cal replied. The word was part simple acknowledgment and part implied question. *So, why are you telling me?*, he seemed to be asking.

Holly knelt down to pet Bee's thick black coat while Dooley responded above her.

"Well, there's just one little hitch. Ruthie forgot that some real estate agent's supposed to stop by with a prospective buyer sometime this afternoon. It's not altogether certain. Just a maybe. But we can't get in touch with the guy to confirm it, and I'd hate for Ruthie to stay home and then not have them show. You know?"

"Yeah, I know," Cal said. "I wouldn't want to be within a hundred yards of Ruthie if she got stood up."

"Yeah," Dooley added with a small sigh.

Holly, remembering her cool reception yesterday morning in Ruth's stainless-steel kitchen, silently concurred while she continued to pet Bee. She wouldn't want to find herself on Ruth Reese's bad side either.

"We'll be home, like I said, till noon or so," Dooley said. "Can we count on you to be there after that? Just in case this fella does show up and has any questions."

"Sure. No problem."

Holly had begun to pick burrs out of Bee's thick coat when Cal's hand drifted across the dog's back and collided with hers.

"Sorry," he said softly. "You don't need to bother with those cockleburrs, Holly. He'll just pick up a hundred more this afternoon."

"I don't mind," she said just as Bee's wet pink tongue took a swipe across her cheek. "You like the attention, boy. Don't you?" She scratched his ears. "Yes, you do. Don't you, Bee?"

"Ol' Bee never had it so good," Dooley murmured above her. "Well, I'm gonna be going. Thanks, Cal. I owe you one."

"No problem."

"Oh, and listen," Dooley added in a voice that wasn't quite so affable all of a sudden. "I'd just as soon you didn't say anything too discouraging to this real estate fella. You know. Like the last time."

A rumble sounded deep in Cal's throat, menacing enough to make the dog turn his head in that direction. There was more than a little irritation in his voice when he said, "I'm not going to tap dance and hand out free soda and popcorn, if that's what you're expecting, Dooley. You know how I feel about this sale."

Her curiosity piqued by the exchange, Holly stood up in

order to hear better. Things were definitely heating up in Heroville.

"Yeah, I know how you feel," Dooley said. "And you know damn well nothing'll come of it. Ruthie's just dreaming a little bit. That's all. Let her dream. It doesn't do any harm."

Cal responded with an inconclusive shrug.

Dooley gave an irritated twitch of his mustache, then nodded at Holly and touched the brim of his hat. "It's been a pleasure, Ms. Hicks. I hope to see you again."

"Thank you. Same here. Have a good time in Corpus Christi."

"I plan to," he said, then turned to leave the grandstand, calling back over his shoulder, "No later than twelve-thirty, Cal. Okay?"

"Got it."

Holly knelt down to snag a few more burrs from Bee's neck, and after a moment said, "I get the impression you don't want your sister to sell the ranch."

"You do, do you?" Cal squatted down.

"Uh-huh. What did you do to discourage the last real estate agent?" she asked.

"It was more misdirection than discouragement." He grinned. "The guy wound up in the next county."

She laughed. "I don't suppose your sister appreciated that."

"Not much." His expression soured briefly before he smiled again and lifted his hand. "Here. Hold still. You've got a couple burrs in your hair."

"Oh, that's . . ."

"Hold still," he commanded.

Not only did Holly's head hold still, but so did her heart

as Cal's fingers deftly combed through her hair and extricated the sharp little objects from curl after curl.

"There." He chuckled softly, his fingers just grazing her cheek. "You can open your eyes now."

She hadn't even realized they were closed while all of her senses were focused on his touch. How embarrassing. "I should probably be getting back to Ellie's," she said.

"What are you doing here at the track?"

"Just taking in the sights," she said, not adding that he was one of them. "You went to school here, right?"

"Yes, ma'am," he drawled.

"Did you play football?"

"No." He cocked his head. "Why?"

"Oh, just . . ." *Your great bod. The way those damp gray sweats cling and curve and, well, bulge.* "You strike me as very athletic. I mean, you'd have to be, considering the requirements of your job."

"Yeah, well . . . I didn't play football," he said in a tone that clearly signaled the end of that particular discussion.

"I was just curious." She plucked a final burr from Bee's neck, flicked it away, then endured one last wet lick across her face before she stood up. "Guess I'll head back to Ellie's."

Cal got up, too. Not with the ease and grace of an athlete, but with obvious difficulty, accompanied by a grimace and a muted curse. She nearly winced watching him, then thought about what Dooley had told her a little while ago. *The only person who thinks Cal's still got a future in the Secret Service is Cal himself.*

Holly clenched her teeth, aware of the question any Journalism 101 student would ask right now, knowing she ought to ask it, and fighting not only her professional instincts but her personal curiosity as well in order not to take advantage of this man's obvious vulnerability at the moment. She could almost imagine a microphone in her fist, directed first at herself as she intoned, "There are a lot of people who don't think you'll make it back, Cal. Would you care to comment on that?" and then angling the mike toward Cal for his response.

"Come home with me," he said.

"Pardon me?"

He lifted his hand to extract another burr from her hair. "I said how about coming home with me this afternoon."

She was so surprised by the invitation, so pleased, so distracted by his touch and her reaction to it that she didn't know what to say. Her invisible microphone sort of melted in her hand like an ice-cream cone, and there was nothing in her head to replace the question she'd decided not to ask. Yet. So, she didn't speak exactly. Her little sound bite was closer to a gulp. "Why?"

"I don't know. Why not? You can snoop around the alleged hero's childhood home. Look at high school yearbooks. Go through old photograph albums. Don't you people use things like that? Or you could just keep me honest if the real estate guy shows up."

"I had planned to spend the rest of the day working," she said, "but that's not a bad idea, actually. The yearbooks and the photograph albums, I mean. I had intended to ask you or your sister about those sometime soon anyway."

"Well, there you go," he drawled as he reached down to scratch Bee's ears. "Why don't I come by Ellie's for you around noon?"

"Great. Okay. It's a date."

Holly wished she'd bitten off her tongue rather than say those last three words. Waving her hand in the air, wishing she could erase them, she said, "Well, you know what I mean. It's not a date. Not a *date* date. It isn't a date at all. I guess if we had to call it something, if we had to come up with a word, you know, for this afternoon, appointment would be a good one. Or engagement. No, forget that."

God. She could hear herself babbling. She was standing there, having an out-of-body experience, watching herself chatter like a squirrel and wave her hands like an idiot while she conducted a monologue on semantics and while Cal Griffin's smile grew wider and whiter, and his eyes turned an almost Bahamian blue in their sensuous nest of crows' feet and crinkles.

"Go on," he said, crossing his arms.

"Go on?"

"Keep talking," he said. "I'm waiting for you to get to the part where you explain what the definition of 'is' is."

She sucked in a breath, let it out slowly, and spoke with all the clarity and precision she could muster. "I'm extremely reluctant to mix business with pleasure."

"I can see that, Ms. Hicks," he said, laughing as he stepped down from the grandstand and headed back toward the track with Bee at his side. Then he called over his shoulder, "I'll see you at twelve. And don't worry. I won't give you any more pleasure than you can handle."

Holly sighed. Oh, God. That's what she was afraid of.

♥

Well, he still talked a pretty good game, Cal thought as he changed out of his damp sweats in the men's room at Ramon's. He wouldn't give her any more pleasure than she could handle. Yeah, right. Provided his performance anxiety didn't get in the way.

He hadn't even dared to resume his workout on the track

until Holly had walked away for fear of tripping over his shoelaces or feeling his knee lock mid-stride, sending him sprawling, or taking a distant second place to an arthritic mutt in the quarter mile. On the other hand, maybe he should have just gone ahead while she was in the bleachers watching. His biography could probably do with a little comic relief.

It was a date, dammit. She knew it as well as he did, no matter how she tried to cover it up with synonyms and semantics. And unless his injured brain was misreading her signals, Holly Hicks was as attracted to him as he was to her.

All of his fine intentions of avoiding her seemed to have gone up in smoke this morning while he was picking cockleburrs from her warm hair. He'd stood there wanting to sink his hands up to his wrists in those vibrant curls, wanting to sink himself into her lithe little body, wanting to drown himself in her the way he'd been drowning himself in booze these past few months.

Once he was dressed, Cal realized he still had an hour before it was time to pick Holly up. He stashed his gym bag behind the bar.

"Ready for a beer, Cal?" Ramon asked, and since the dark-haired, barrel-chested barman considered it a rhetorical question, he was already reaching for a cold Heineken when Cal said, "Let me have a club soda on ice, will you, Ramon?"

The man leaned toward him across the bar, cupping a hand to one ear to shield it from a ninety-decibel Alabama tune. "A what?"

"Club soda on ice," Cal repeated, louder this time.

Ramon stared at him a second, as if he barely recognized him, then asked, "You okay?"

"Yeah. I'm okay," he answered irritably. "Just pour me a goddamned seltzer, will you?"

"Hey. Okay, man. Coming right up. You want a twist in that? Lemon or lime?"

"Fine. Whatever. Anything but a fucking umbrella."

Cal straddled a bar stool while he waited for his drink. If things worked out the way he hoped, it was going to be a long day, spent in the company of the little hero hunter, Holly Hicks, and he didn't want to start out with one foot already in the bag. Maybe later in the afternoon he'd kick back with a beer. Maybe they'd have dinner at the ranch and maybe then he'd pull a bottle out of Ruth's built-in wine rack and . . .

"Here you go. One club soda with a lime twist. And no umbrella." Ramon slid a cocktail napkin in front of him and centered the clear, sparkling drink upon it. "Hey, man. As long as you're here, you mind taking a look at a fifty-dollar bill for me? Some guy asked Rick for change last night, and this fifty just doesn't look right to me."

"Sure. Let me see it." Cal took a sip of the club soda while Ramon pulled the bill from beneath the change drawer in the cash register.

"See what I mean," the barman said, handing the bill to Cal. "It's a phoney, right?"

Cal handled the limp, bleached paper with its frayed edges and taped tear. Bleaching and damage were often good ways to disguise a counterfeit, but in this case the defects were simply because the bill was old. As far as he could see without a magnifying glass the edges on this one were crisp enough and there was still a little life in ol' Ulysses' eyes.

"It's fine," he said, handing it back.

Ramon didn't look convinced. "You sure?" He glared at the currency and kept turning it over in his hands.

"Well, if you want a second opinion, take it over to Bobby

at the bank and have him check it out. He's probably got a UV light or an iodine pen."

"Yeah. I just might do that."

While Ramon tended to other customers, Cal sipped his seltzer, vaguely enjoying its sharp bite on the back of his tongue, but wishing it were a beer. The neon clock told him he had another forty-five minutes before it was time to pick up Holly. At the moment it felt more like forty-five years. He was about to go through a day stone cold sober, something he hadn't done since coming home almost six months ago.

That thought alone was enough to make a man want a drink.

Even a hero.

Chapter Eight

I thought Cal would be home by now," Ruth said, frowning at her good watch while she paced from one end of her kitchen to the other. "Dooley, are you sure you told him we wanted to leave for Corpus around noon?"

Her husband was half-standing, half-sitting, with one hip slanted on her marble-topped island. He looked so good in his western-cut gray tweed jacket and dark gray slacks. He'd even put on a regular tie, one of the dozens she'd given him over the years, silk Repps and paisleys and pin dots that rarely saw daylight and didn't do much but flap on his closet door whenever he opened it. She knew he'd put on the tie to please her, and she was trying hard not to slide into a foul mood that would sour the rest of the day.

"I told him twelve-thirty, babe." Dooley checked his watch. "It's just a few minutes past twelve. He'll be here."

She snapped on the cold water at the sink and filled a glass. Her throat was so dry and tight she could hear herself swallow. "I don't know why I let these things upset me," she said. "I never used to."

"Worst that can happen, honey, is that the real estate fella will bring his client back some other time."

"You're right."

She said it, but she didn't believe it somehow. The worst that could happen was she'd never have her restaurant. There would always be something—Cal being late, a no-show realtor, Dooley not getting the price he wanted for a particular bull, Colby totaling his truck and asking for a loan, her own doubts and hesitations—coming between herself and her dream.

None of her friends had dreams. At least none that required such a substantial investment of capital. Ardith Voss had just gotten herself a web site to sell her patchwork totes and purses, but what was that? A couple hundred dollars at the most? Julie Caldwell, inspired by Oprah's book club, was working on a Master's degree in literature and trying to write a novel of her own.

Ruth had considered a smaller dream. Writing a cookbook perhaps or marketing her balsamic beans. But it struck her as settling. And she didn't want to be an author or an entrepreneur. She wanted to be a restaurateur.

The therapist she'd seen in Kingsville a few months ago hadn't helped at all. Ruth had made the appointment without telling Dooley, and she'd driven up there hardly even knowing why she was doing it except that it seemed to be the thing to do when things just weren't working out. The woman seemed nice enough. They'd talked for a while, sitting in matching flame-stitched wing chairs, sipping Earl Grey tea, and then the psychologist had asked, "What do you want?"

"My own restaurant," Ruth had replied.

The woman put her cup and saucer down, closed her eyes a moment, then leaned forward and whispered, "What is it you *really* want?"

That was when Ruth was pretty sure she needed a financial planner more than a therapist.

God bless it. She wasn't depressed. She wasn't in the throes of a mid-life crisis or suffering from some perimenopausal hormone imbalance or empty nest syndrome or anything else. She wanted her own restaurant. Just a little place with crisp white linens on the tables, substantial silverware, fine crystal, and comfortable chairs.

She wanted to prepare Trout Meuniere and risotto alla Milanese, have it served by competent, if not elegant, waiters, and watch her customers close their eyes with pleasure as they ate. She longed for her skills to be enjoyed and appreciated by gourmets instead of people who were polite but would've preferred an eight-ounce rib eye, a baked potato, and tossed salad with creamy Italian dressing.

It wasn't as if she wanted the moon. Not a full moon, anyway. Just a sliver. It was such a tiny dream when all was said and done. Except not for a woman living in Hell and Gone, Texas, where, even if she could afford to set herself up in competition with the Longhorn Café, she couldn't turn a profit what with the cost of trucking in fresh vegetables and seafood.

All she wanted was a chance. Before it was too late. Before ill fate or bad luck or a bullet struck her down and took her dream away, the way it had with Cal. Well, she didn't know if he'd ever actually dreamed of being in the Secret Service, but she was convinced he wasn't going back.

"We'll have a good time in Corpus," Dooley said, straightening up, his head just missing her eight-inch omelette pan hanging from the rack above him. "We'll get a room with a Gulf view." The slight, suggestive lift of his eyebrows and sexy slant of his mustache made her smile. Even after all these years.

"I love you, Dooley Reese. Have I told you that today?"

He opened his arms to her. "Seems to me you did, but it'd be nice to hear it again, darlin'."

♥

Even Holly had to admit it was a gorgeous day with a sky that was nearly sapphire and big white clouds billowing across it. Okay. Maybe she did miss Texas skies. She was willing to concede that much. And maybe blasting down the road at sixty miles an hour in a convertible with Santana streaming from the radio and the wind whipping her hair did have all the overtones of a date, including the easy smile of the guy at the wheel and the way his right arm was draped over the seatback in her direction as if anticipating a "slide over, baby" turn. But this wasn't a date.

It wasn't.

Well, even if it was, she refused to let it distract her from her purpose.

The story.

"Tell me why you don't want your sister to sell the ranch," she yelled over Santana and the wind.

Cal disengaged his arm from the seatback to turn the radio down. "You mean other than the obvious?"

"Which is . . . ?"

"Me winding up homeless."

"Don't you have a place in Washington?"

"I had a place. A condo in Bethesda. Now it's my ex-wife's."

Holly wasn't sure about the propriety of a follow-up question, but she was insanely curious about his divorce, or more exactly about the brief marriage that had preceded it. *Why had they even bothered?* she wondered.

"I'm not so much trying to prevent her from selling it," he said. "I'm just buying a little time for myself. Who knows? I might wind up retiring here someday and buying out her share."

Retiring? Just as Holly was fashioning a follow up to that, something a bit more professional than "What do you mean, retiring?", a car appeared in the distance. The large green SUV was pulled over on the side of the road and two men stood beside it, one with his arms crossed while the other gestured west over miles of mesquite.

Cal's foot came off the accelerator. "Looks like a real estate agent to me," he said. "What do you think?"

Judging from his malicious little grin, Holly thought Cal Griffin was about to send another prospective buyer on a wild goose chase. This was going to be good. And much as she despised Texas herself, who was she to stand in his way if he wanted to retire here? More power to him.

"I'd say you're right," she answered with an evil little grin of her own. "He strikes me as moderately aggressive and fairly confident at the moment."

His expression turned positively devilish. "Not for long," he said as he slowed and brought the T-bird to a dusty stop a few feet behind the SUV.

"I'll be right back," he said, opening the door and swinging his legs out of the car.

"Need some backup?" Holly asked.

He cocked his head and those blue eyes fairly twinkled. "Sure. How good a liar are you?"

"On a scale of one to ten?"

He nodded.

"A fifteen," she said. "I'll just follow your lead."

She joined him at the front of the car. He clasped her hand

in his, and together they moseyed up to their unsuspecting victims.

"Afternoon," Cal drawled. "You fellas taking a look at the Griffin place?"

The taller of the two stuck out his hand. "We sure are. Chuck Bingham of Bingham Properties. And you are . . . ?"

"Tucker Bascom," Cal said without missing a beat. "And this is my wife, Charlene."

"Howdy, ma'am." Chuck gave the brim of his hat a snap before he reached for Holly's hand.

"Howdy," she said in return, managing not to choke on the word.

The realtor gestured to the shorter man who was wearing a pair of pleated khaki Dockers, a navy Polo shirt, and not boots, but Docksiders on his feet. "This is Gordon Brown, my client."

After another little round of howdy's and pleased-to-meet-you's, Cal casually inquired, "You raise cattle, Gordon?"

"Me? Oh, no. I'm from Chicago. I represent a group of investors who hope to put together a ten thousand–acre parcel for a hunting lodge."

"Ah." Cal nodded. Rather sagely, Holly thought.

"Y'all live around here?" Chuck asked.

"Down the road a ways," Cal said.

"We run a goat ranch," Holly said, figuring it was her turn, and then, when Gordon appeared intrigued, she elaborated. "Actually we raise dairy goats. Angoras. We milk them by hand in order to make Feta cheese."

"Fascinating," Gordon said.

"I had no idea," Chuck added.

Cal simply gazed at her, clearly awarding her the floor, or the pavement in this case.

"Feta," Gordon murmured. "Isn't that the Greek cheese?"

"That's right. My father's Greek. He started the ranch forty years ago right after he married my mama. She's Creek."

Gordon blinked. "Excuse me?"

"Creek," Holly said. "Native American?"

"Oh, yes."

"It's too bad about the titanium here," she said, apropos of nothing, letting her gaze wander westward.

The realtor cleared his throat. "The what?"

Holly curled her arm through Cal's and leaned against him. "Why don't you tell them, hon?"

Without a second's hesitation, he clasped the baton, so to speak. He didn't even blink. The man was magnificent.

"Well, the Air Force *said* they cleaned up after that canister got loose in '96. They *said* nothing would leach into the soil. They *said* . . ."

"Wait." Chuck held up a hand. "What canister?"

"The titanium," Cal said. "From when the hatch blew on the C-130 making that emergency landing at the Naval Air Station in Kingsville."

"When was this?" Chuck asked. Behind him, Gordon said, "Titanium? Isn't that radioactive?"

" '96, wasn't it, Charlene?"

"Thereabouts. It was '97 when the goats lost all their hair."

Actually, Chuck was doing a pretty good job controlling his hysteria, she thought. She, on the other hand, was almost drawing blood from the insides of her cheeks not to mention the mounting urge to pee in her pants.

"Your goats lost all their hair?" Gordon exclaimed.

"Sure did," Cal drawled. "The ones who lived, anyway."

Hearing that, Gordon glanced off warily at the surrounding landscape.

"Well, speaking of goats," Holly chirped, "we'd best get back to ours, sugar." She pulled Cal by the arm. "Pretty close to milking time."

"I'd like to find out more about this incident," Chuck said with some urgency. "You mentioned the Naval Air Station in Kingsville?"

They were almost back to the T-bird. Cal called back, "Yep. But you won't find out squat. They'll only tell you it never happened. Same for the plutonium canister that came through the skylight at the high school in Honeycomb. That never happened either. Well, so long. Nice meetin' you gents."

He opened the door for Holly. Under his breath he said, "Get in. Jesus, woman. Greek and Creek. I'm going to lose it in about two seconds."

♥

Five minutes later back in Ruth's cathedral of a kitchen, Cal poured two tall glasses of orange juice, then drank half of his while Holly was in the bathroom. He hadn't laughed like that in nine months. Maybe not in his entire life. Ruthie, if she ever found out about this afternoon's incident with the realtor, would kill him, slice and dice him and put him in a blender, but it would be worth every painful second. Even now he couldn't stop grinning.

She was something else, this little Holly Hicks. Texas in a martini glass with a twist of Manhattan. A margarita in a goblet from Tiffany & Co. A chili pepper in silken skin. Smart as a whip and playful as a kitten.

He felt goofy, wearing this grin. Like a kid, instead of a

man who should've known better. Like a man who once again had a semblance of control over events in his life. When she walked into the kitchen, his heart kicked in a couple of extra beats.

"That was fun," she said, taking the glass he offered her. "We make a pretty good team."

"Here's to you, Charlene." He angled his own glass toward her in a toast. "Where'd you learn to lie like that?"

"I'm a writer," she said. "It just comes naturally. And it's not really lying. It's just . . . oh, I don't know. Improving on reality."

"You'd be great undercover."

Her green eyes sparkled, her mouth curved deliciously and her strawberry blond curls almost jingled. "Really?"

"Really," he said. "You're a natural."

"I loved your disclaimer from the Navy. That's what sold them."

Cal shook his head. "Nah. It was the goats."

They started laughing again.

"That poor man from Chicago," Holly said. "He's probably halfway to Houston by now in search of a Geiger counter." She reached out her hand to touch his arm. "I wish I could be a fly on the wall when Chuck makes his call to some poor baffled admiral in Kingsville."

Just that moment Cal felt a little like a fly on the wall himself, watching two happy people, seeing the perfect moment when the man would draw the laughing woman close, lift her chin, and study her mouth for a moment before he kissed her. If he did, he probably wouldn't need to come up for air for a week.

"Can she?" he heard Holly ask. He realized it was the tail end of a question he hadn't even heard.

"Can she what?"

"Your sister can't possibly discover that it was us, can she?"

He shrugged.

Her mirth subsided. It was like watching someone sober up. "Well, if she does find out, tell her it was my idea. I won't be around to suffer the fallout."

The mere mention of her temporary status here seemed to close the lid on their little joke. It wasn't really a date, after all. It should have been, he thought.

"You probably want to take a look at some of those photo albums," he said.

"And don't forget the yearbook. I'd love to use a shot of you when you were two or three, and then your senior picture. They're pretty standard footage in a show like this."

Cal finished his orange juice and put the glass in the sink. "Well, let's go take a look," he said, even as he thought he'd changed beyond all recognition, on the inside anyway, from the images she was about to see.

In his room, the sofa bed greeted them, all tidily made and tucked in tight after Holly had slept in it two nights before. He kept forgetting he'd slept with her last night, the first night of deep, dreamless, restorative sleep he'd had since the assassination attempt. Nice as it was, he wished he hadn't wasted the entire night just sleeping.

"What's in all these boxes?" she asked, pointing to the wall where they were stacked like sandbags in a World War I bunker.

"My worldly goods," he answered. It made him sound like such a Sad Sack that he immediately laughed. "Junk mostly. If you want my high school yearbook, you've got your work cut out for you, kid. It's someplace in there."

"You want me to just start hunting?"

"Sure. Be my guest."

Cal reached under the bed for one of his ten-pound weights, then sat doing a series of curls while he watched Holly open the first box that Diana had paid some movers to pack up and ship out of her life. He wondered if his ego was in one of them, dried and pressed between the pages of a book, or balled up like an old moth-eaten sweater.

"Watch out for booby traps," he muttered. "My ex-wife packed those."

♥

At the moment, Holly felt less like an intrepid journalist and more like a furtive spy as she dug her way through Box Number Two. The first box had held a mildly interesting assortment of corduroy throw pillows, bath towels in a dark slate gray, and a white terrycloth bathrobe with an intriguing splotch of pink nail polish on one of the lapels. She knew it was nail polish because she'd sniffed it.

From his seat on the edge of the sofa bed, Cal had asked, "What are you doing?"

"Trying to figure out how a man gets 'Love That Pink' on the lapel of his bathrobe."

She couldn't tell if the resultant sneer on his face was from the effort of lifting the weight or a fairly clear memory of how the enamel stain had been acquired.

"Don't sniff my clothes," he said. "That's pretty sick, don't you think? What are you—part bloodhound?"

"God, maybe I am," she said, folding the robe and laying it back in the box. "Haven't you ever noticed how different men's things smell from women's?"

"Pheromones," he said, changing the barbell to his other hand and bracing his elbow on his leg.

"No. It's more than that. And it's more than just cologne

and perfume. Men's things always smell like sawdust and shoe polish and autumn leaves."

"I never noticed."

"Oh, I did. I used to live with a man in Cincinnati . . ." She continued despite his raised eyebrow. "And some mornings after he'd left for work, I'd open a couple of his dresser drawers, not to snoop, but just to breathe in that masculine fragrance."

"What happened to him?" he asked a bit sourly.

"Well, it was more what happened to me. I got downsized to a station in Columbus, and that was the end of that."

After that she'd gone on to the second box, which held more slate gray bathtowels, an ancient boombox, and several shoeboxes jammed with cassettes. If she'd expected to find the collection heavy on Country and Western, Holly was very wrong. Not a picker or a twanger in the lot. It was jazz for the most part. Dave Brubeck. Charlie Parker. Wynton Marsalis. One box contained classical tapes. Beethoven and Mozart and Brahms. Oh, my.

"No yearbook yet?" Cal asked.

"Not yet." Holly tugged open the flaps on Box Number Three. "More towels," she said. "You must've taken a lot of showers."

"The gray ones?"

"Uh-huh."

"Those were a wedding gift from President Jennings and the First Lady, I think."

"Oh, wow," she breathed, lifting the top one carefully, almost reverently, from the box.

"They're towels, Holly, for chrissake."

"Well, still . . ." She pressed the thick terry fabric to her nose only to hear Cal growl, "Will you quit smelling my stuff!"

She put the towel back, then eased her fingers more deeply into the box. "What's this?" Pulling out a framed picture, the first thing she noticed was that the glass was cracked. The second thing she noticed was Cal's handsome face and those deep blue eyes, so full of pleasure and warmth. Although he was looking directly at the camera, it was easy to tell that his thoughts were solely on the woman who stood within the circle of his arms. The lovely Diana, with her lion's mane of lovely hair and—what do you know? —her long nails painted "Love That Pink."

"What's that?" Cal asked.

Holly cleared her throat. "I think it's a wedding picture."

He stretched out his free hand. "Let me see it."

"It's broken," she said, reluctant to hand it over for some odd reason.

"No kidding."

"The glass, I mean."

He wiggled his fingers. "Let me see."

Holly handed it to him with a sigh, and then watched him as he gazed at it. There was no wistfulness in his expression. There was no anger, at least none she could detect. If she had to find a word to describe his visible emotion, it would have been regret. Ah, but what Cal Griffin regretted was a mystery still to be fathomed.

While he contemplated the photograph, she poked around in the box some more—touching the Presidential towels, which impressed the hell out of her even if they didn't make much of an impression on Cal. She ran a finger across the script of the monogram, which was a large G flanked on each side by the smaller letters, D for Diana and C for Calvin. Now *that* was being married, having your initials entwined with someone else's on forty-dollar bath towels. From the President, no less.

"It's a halfway decent frame," he said. "Sterling, probably. Do you want it?"

Holly shook her head. She'd never be able to look at the silver rectangle without seeing the striking couple originally inside it.

"Okay." He turned to his left, then smoothly lobbed the photograph into the wastebasket beside the blue recliner, sinking a perfect three-pointer. The broken glass broke a little more, making a tinkling sound in the metal receptacle.

"Oh." The tiny cry broke unbidden from her throat.

"Where's that yearbook?" he asked, suddenly sounding impatient. "Did you find it yet?"

"No," she said. "Not yet."

He set the heavy weight down with a thump, then turned his wrist to look at his watch. "You hungry?"

Was she? Up to her elbows in Calvin Griffin memorabilia, Holly hadn't even thought about food. But now that she did think about it, she was famished. "Starving."

"Okay. You press on with the hunt, and I'll go make us a couple sandwiches."

"Sounds good." She closed the Presidential towel box, shoved it aside, and reached for Box Number 4.

♥

Two dozen boxes, two peanut butter and jelly sandwiches, and a quart of lemonade later, Cal said, "You might be better off checking for a copy of the yearbook at the high school or the library."

She didn't seem to hear him. Or if she had, she was ignoring his suggestion. Christ. You'd think the woman was searching for treasure in King Tut's tomb the way she carefully handled and inspected every artifact of his life. Towels seemed to hold as much interest for her as retired shoulder holsters, busted handcuffs, and outdated credentials. His boyhood collection of matchbox cars intrigued her. The battered Frisbee with the USMC eagle, globe and anchor might have been made of platinum for the cry of delight it elicited.

As far as Cal was concerned, it was all pretty depressing. The things he'd kept over the years for their sentimental value no longer touched him now. It was as if they'd belonged to somebody else—some other little boy who saved his allowance for minuscule '55 Chevys and '65½ Mustangs, some other gung-ho recruit on leave at Laguna Beach, some other fool who'd married and been showered with monogrammed towels.

He did enjoy sitting and watching Holly, though, so he didn't object when she said, "Just two more boxes. I won't bother if you're tired of all this."

"Go ahead," he said, and then before he even knew his mouth was still open and operative, he added, "I like watching you, just being with you."

Her eyes widened, and she took in a quick little breath, as if she were about to reply, but then she waved her hand and swallowed whatever it was she'd been about to say.

Cal couldn't help but grin. "I didn't say it was a damn date, Holly. I said I like being with you. In a professional manner of speaking."

"Well, in that case, I like being with you, too." She smiled and turned back to the wall of boxes.

Did she? Did she like him? Or want him? Up until nine months ago, he never would have questioned a woman's attraction to him. That was a given, like the sun coming up in the east and the proverbial bear shitting in the woods. If her smile had been one of affection or relief, Cal couldn't quite tell. But now that he'd begun, he forced himself to press ahead.

"Maybe we should try a date sometime," he said with a chuckle, "since we get along so well professionally."

"Maybe."

"Or we could call this a date, and then we'd have our first one practically out of the way."

She threw a glare over her shoulder, but Cal could see the green light of possibility in her eyes. That would have to do for now. He was content to savor the possibility of Holly Hicks rather than risk her rejection.

♥

It wasn't a date, but whatever it was went on until late that evening. Holly never did find the yearbook. Instead, in the very last box, she found a small leather jewelry case, where—among assorted medals, old coins, cuff links, and studs—she saw the separate halves of a gold wedding band.

"I wondered where that went," Cal said, looking into the velvet-lined box over her shoulder.

Holly picked up one half circle, then gave a surprised little yelp when its rough edge bit into her fingertip.

"Let me see that." Cal took both halves and ran his finger across the ends. "I thought maybe I'd lost it last September, but they must've cut it off in the emergency room and given it to Diana."

"It could probably be soldered together again," she said.

"Why?" He dropped the pieces back into the case.

He'd seemed a little blue after that, so to cheer him Holly had suggested they take a walk, maybe keep their eyes peeled for traces of titanium. While they walked, they laughed as they relived their victory over the evil agents of real estate. It was nice, strolling pasture after pasture beside him, and when she stumbled over an exposed mesquite root and he reached for her hand, it felt natural somehow and Holly didn't pull away.

Then the walk blended into a beer to cool off, and the cocktail hour moved seamlessly into the dinner hour when they defrosted some of Ruth's fabulous leftovers and opened a bottle of wine and chatted like new friends if not old. It was midnight before she knew it.

"I had fun today," Holly said when Cal parked the T-bird in Ellie's dark driveway.

"Good." He was quiet a second, just staring ahead through the windshield, and then he said, "You know, if this were a date, I could kiss you good night."

A part of her just wished he'd grab her and do it. The other part responded, "But it's not a date."

"Yeah," he said with a sigh. "Well, then, this isn't a kiss."

And it wasn't. It was heaven. Pure, unadulterated, genuine heaven. Well, Heaven South. Pure, unadulterated, genuine and hot. How he turned and gathered her so smoothly, so completely in his arms was a mystery. One moment she was on the passenger side of the car, and the next she was in his arms, against his chest, practically a part of him. His mouth was as sure and competent as the rest of him, and while his kiss just took her breath away, she was vaguely aware of wine, Calvin Klein cologne, and wisps of sawdust and shoe polish and autumn leaves.

My God.

If she kissed him back, she wasn't aware of it. A tiny moan throbbed in somebody's throat, and it could have been hers but she wasn't quite sure. Somebody's heart was crashing against her ribs, but it wasn't clear whether it was inside or out. Hers or his. All she knew for certain was she could have stayed there all night, all week, forever. She could have made a career out of being kissed like this.

Then, because her eyes were glazed, it took her a moment to realize it was over, the kiss that wasn't a kiss, and that Cal was smiling at her, his face a few inches from hers.

"Good night, Holly Hicks," he whispered. "Thanks for the best day I've had in a long time."

He walked her up to Ellie's front door, and thank God he didn't not kiss her again because Holly's knees couldn't have stood it.

Inside, she leaned against the door, listening to the rich rumble of the T-bird's engine followed a moment later by what she could only describe as a sort of juvenile squeal of the tires as the car turned out of the driveway and roared up the street. And somewhere, over the engine's roar and the loud laying of rubber and the pounding of her heart, she was certain she heard a high-pitched y*ee-hah*.

Hollis Mae Hicks was back in Texas, and she was in big trouble.

Chapter Nine

The next morning Holly woke to church bells and sunshine sifting through lace curtains. She sighed and stretched while her gaze drifted like a drowsy bee from cabbage rose to cabbage rose, while her mouth slid into a dopey, dreamy smile that seemed to originate somewhere in the vicinity of her toes and work its way up the length of her body. That kiss, that incredible, heart-stopping, flag-waving, soul-searing kiss was still reverberating through her.

She'd never known a man like Cal Griffin.

She hadn't known that many men, period. Men had never been a priority in her life. They were ships passing in the night on the great ocean of her career. Holly almost laughed out loud. Okay. So it was a melodramatic metaphor, but it was true all the same. If she twisted the metaphor a bit, men were icebergs looming up every so often, scraping her hull, threatening to sink her. Or they were blips, faint ones mostly, on her radar screen. She simply didn't pay much attention to the opposite sex.

She didn't even date in high school, where her reputation as The Brain was an obstacle far too difficult for any boy in Sandy Springs to tackle. In college, she hadn't dated all that much before she spent her senior year with Jeremy James, a pipe-smoking grad student, a poet with a seductive voice and a way with words and an innate need to be waited on hand and foot, which had made it fairly easy for her to leave him in the end. Her only other serious affair had been with a colleague in Cincinnati, but when it came time to choose between Bryan and her dream, there had been no choice. It was somewhat comforting to know that Bryan would have done the same, and Holly moved on to Columbus with a sigh and no regrets.

After that, it seemed the farther east she traveled, the greater the number of jerks she encountered, along with morons, animals—those were mostly cameramen, for some odd reason—vanilla ice-cream anchors, cardboard cutout anchors, obsessive-compulsive weathermen, and frogs who wouldn't turn into princes no matter how many times they were kissed. Icebergs. Blips. The nicest man she'd ever met in the business was Mel Klein, who was old enough to be her father and still totally, grouchily in love with his wife of twenty-eight years.

Since men had never mattered to her all that much, neither had their kisses. There was something else about that kiss last night, something she meant to remember, some unique blend of . . .

Holly blinked now as one of the cabbage roses she was staring at seemed to take on some very suggestive features, morphing into a voluptuous, erotic, petaled organ almost worthy of Georgia O'Keeffe. My God. It was her second day in this room and just now she was noticing how sexy the wallpaper was? She hadn't really even thought about sex in the past two or three years, and here she was suddenly besotted by a kiss and surrounded by Victorian genitalia printed on a pink bubble gum background.

It was probably time to get up and take a shower, she decided. She sat up and cast a baleful glance at the laptop, its battery quietly re-charging from the outlet on the wall, its keyboard resting in the darkness of the closed case, all its little circuits and synapses just priming themselves for her powerful presentation of Calvin Griffin's life story, and right now all she could think about was Calvin Griffin's mouth, the tiniest most erotic touch of his tongue on her lower lip, the faint taste of red wine and the scent of leather and soap, and how her stomach was reeling again, just cartwheeling, at the memory of his kiss.

And it wasn't just the kiss that had turned her on so. It was the man himself. Once they'd started talking yesterday afternoon at the ranch, they hadn't stopped. Cal was funny and smart and far more sophisticated than she'd given him credit for. At one point, she even had to remind herself that he was a Texan, not someone whose roots were on the eastern seaboard, particularly in Washington or New York.

To her amazement, he knew Manhattan better than she did after her three years there. And when he described a wonderful little Italian bistro in SoHo and said the next time he was in town he'd take her there, Holly found herself almost believing it for a moment despite what Dooley had said about Cal's returning to the Secret Service.

Yesterday's interlude with her hero *was* a date. There was no denying it. And she had never done anything quite so stupid, so misguided and unprofessional, in her entire life. Holly flopped back down, reached back for the pillow and plopped it on her face so she couldn't see the stamens and pistils and velvet petals practically throbbing on the wall.

Why hadn't they sent her to Ohio to do the Neil Armstrong bio? She knew Ohio like the back of her hand. She spoke the language there. She could have used that wonderful Moon footage and woven that "small step, giant leap" theme through her story like a golden thread.

In Ohio, she would've been safe with the notoriously media-shy, reticent astronaut. Neil Armstrong wouldn't kiss a producer in the middle of her job!

He wouldn't have the bluest eyes in all creation. He wouldn't look like a minor god who'd just jogged down from Olympus in wet gray sweats. He wouldn't laugh with her, tears streaming from both their eyes, about lost titanium canisters, Greeks and Creeks, and hairless goats. The pieces of Neil Armstrong's life wouldn't be packed and stacked in two dozen boxes in a sad spare room. He wouldn't have a shattered wedding photo or a sawed-off wedding band that just about broke her heart.

If they'd sent her to Ohio, she wouldn't be waking up to erotic wallpaper.

And—oh, dear God—if they'd sent her to Ohio, she would've been able to shake her hero's hand when her job was done and walk away without a second thought, without a glance over her shoulder, without a single twinge of sadness or regret.

That wasn't going to happen now.

♥

Resting his leg after a tough half mile, Cal looked down at Bee, whose wet salt-and-pepper muzzle rested on his thigh. It wouldn't be such a bad job, he thought, being the town dog. The pay wasn't great, and there were certain indignities like outdoor plumbing and the occasional painted yellow stripes, but all in all Bee had a pretty good deal. He ate outside the back door of the Longhorn Café, got plenty of exercise for a guy his age, and still apparently had his way with Honeycomb's ladies, judging from the number of black-coated puppies around town.

"I don't suppose you ever dream about herding sheep across the moors, do you, Bee?" he asked. "Or taking first in breed at Westminster?"

The dog's bluish, cataract-clouded gaze lifted momentarily and his tail thumped twice on the ground.

"Yeah. I didn't think so." He settled his hand on Bee's neck, tipped his head back against the tree trunk, closed his eyes, and finally allowed his mind to go where he had forbidden it to go all morning.

That had been some kiss last night. Sudden and sweet and as sensual as anything in his memory. He had reached across the car seat, pulled Holly against him, and claimed her mouth, all accomplished even before he'd worked up the courage to do it. If he'd thought about it overlong, he'd have been paralyzed.

Maybe the reason it was kicking around in his head so much this morning was because it *was* just a kiss. When was the last time he'd stopped at a simple kiss? Probably '78 or '79 when he was still in junior high, and then he hadn't stopped willingly or graciously or of his own accord. Maybe his entire system had short circuited without the attendant climax, without the obvious conclusion to the natural chain of events that a kiss always put in motion. Maybe his bodily fluids had backed up and he was being slowly poisoned from inside.

Maybe he should get a grip.

Bee lifted his head, sniffed the air, then relaxed again with a soft, contented moan. Cal felt like moaning, but not out of any kind of contentment. Whatever moved a wolf to howl at the moon had its hook in him, too.

Just a kiss, and yet it had wreaked more havoc in his system than a night of no-holds-barred sex ever had. He knew why, too. Any fool would. He was crazy about the little producer from New York with her bright green eyes and her strawberry curls and the undertones of Texas in her speech. She was quick-witted and warm, and he couldn't remember ever wanting a woman more than he wanted Holly Hicks.

There must've been something really wrong with him, Cal thought, for marrying a woman he hadn't wanted half as much, and that was *before* his brain injury. God only knew what sort of scrambled, half-assed decisions he was making now.

"What decisions?" He voiced the words so loud, so unexpectedly that they surprised him as much as Bee, who struggled to sit up and was now looking around for the human to whom Cal must've spoken.

He hadn't decided anything. Not about Holly, anyway. Not about anything.

He hadn't decided to get divorced. That had been Diana's unilateral conclusion, apparently arrived at as she hotfooted it out of the hospital after witnessing one of the three or four seizures he'd had in ICU before his condition stabilized. "It was just so . . . so . . . horrible," she'd told him. No kidding. "You should've seen it from the inside, babe," he'd replied.

He hadn't decided on a year's medical leave. That had been the dictum from higher-ups in the agency, and he'd felt insulted that they thought it would take him anywhere near that long to come back. Now, of course, he was grateful for the time. That year of medical leave would be up in September.

That's when he'd make decisions, three months from now, after he passed or failed the fitness tests at the federal training facility in Georgia. If he failed . . . well, that was that. If he passed, but not with scores high enough to put him

back on protective duty, then there would be other decisions.
Did he want to ride into the sunset on a desk, for instance?
Right now the answer was no. But it wasn't a firm decision.

As for Holly . . . If anyone had asked him if he needed a
green-eyed, curly-haired, infinitely kissable woman to com-
plicate all his equations right now, he would've said no. Neg-
ative. Absolutely not.

But nobody had asked, had they?

Jesus. She'd really blindsided him.

He muttered a gruff curse that caused Bee to lift his head
again. Cal sighed. "You ready for another half mile, fella?"

Bee was less enthusiastic about the second turn around
the track, so he wandered off into the infield where he lifted
his leg on the goalpost, and then headed toward town, leaving Cal to sweat it out on his own under the broiling sun.

He was pulling up in front of the grandstand, checking his
watch, berating himself for the dishonorable, downright
embarrassing time of eight minutes twenty-eight seconds for
a lousy half mile, when he heard three sharp rifle shots cut
through the Sunday morning quiet.

♥

With her hair still dripping from her shower, Holly trotted
down the stairs, but when she saw Ellie standing out on the
front porch, she detoured from her original destination, the
kitchen.

Her hostess was standing with her arms crossed beneath
her ample breasts, above her ample belly, staring in the direction of Main Street. She was so involved in her own thoughts
that she started when Holly said, "Good morning, Ellie.
What's going on?"

"Oh. I didn't even hear you come out, honey." She angled

her gray head toward the center of town. "Seems we've got an incident."

"An incident?" Holly looked in the direction of Ellie's gaze and saw the flashing lights of a police cruiser. "What's going on?"

"You didn't hear the shots?" Ellie asked.

She shook her damp head. "I didn't hear anything. I was in the shower. What shots? What's happening?"

"Well, if I had to guess, I'd say it's Kin Presley going on a rampage again." She clucked her tongue. "It happens once or twice a year. He was due."

Holly's journalistic ears pricked up and her nose for news began to twitch. "Really? Some guy goes on a rampage a couple times a year? Any particular reason?"

"Oh, sure. It's all because of Trisha."

"Trisha?"

"His wife. She flirts and fluffs around town until Kin can't stand it anymore, and then he does something crazy. One of these days it'll end badly."

Ooh. Maybe today! It was horrible, but Holly was a journalist to the marrow of her bones. She never hoped for catastrophes or "incidents," for disasters or dire events, but when they happened, she just couldn't help feeling a profound rush. And that's what she wanted to do right now. Rush toward Main Street.

"Hm," she murmured, attempting to sound as cool and dispassionate as any good journalist ought to be, not wanting her hostess to think she was a ghoul or an ambulance chaser. "Well, I think maybe I'll just wander over there and watch the fireworks, if there are any."

"Shoot. I'd come, too," Ellie said, "but I'm waiting on a call from my Aunt Grace to see if she wants a ride to church. You be careful now, honey, you hear? Don't get too close."

"I won't," Holly called over her shoulder, heading down the driveway, trying her best to keep from breaking into a ghoulish, ambulance-chasing run.

She picked up her pace along the residential block of Washington in the dappled shade of its big oaks and sycamores, then skidded around the corner onto Main and into blistering sunshine.

♥

Cal scowled at the big plate-glass window of the Longhorn Café from his vantage point behind the open passenger door of Deputy Jimmy Lee Terrell's cruiser. He'd been hunkered down there for the past ten minutes, trying to inject a bit of common sense into the situation before somebody got hurt.

A little authority was a dangerous thing for Jimmy Lee. The 5'7" deputy was usually quite literally in the shadow of Honeycomb's big, ham-fisted police chief, Vernon Bates. The duo gave a pretty good impression of Mayberry's finest, with Jimmy Lee perfectly cast as Barney Fife. But Sheriff Andy was on vacation in Alaska at the moment, and Barney was squatting down behind the open driver's door now, his service revolver drawn, using his damn bullhorn when a shout was all he needed to make contact with Kin Presley, barricaded with his runaround wife and a few unlucky customers inside the café.

Jimmy Lee had recently attended a seminar in San Antonio on Suicide by Cop. At this point, he was more than willing, even eager, to oblige the poor, cuckolded son of a bitch.

The last thing Kin had yelled was that he'd hand over his hostages in exchange for a car with a full tank of gas.

The wiry deputy lifted his bullhorn and boomed back. "It's not the policy of the Honeycomb P.D. to negotiate."

"Jesus, Jimmy Lee," Cal groaned. "Give the guy a fucking vehicle and get this over with."

"If I need federal intervention, Cal, I believe I know how to go through the proper channels." He shot a glare across the cruiser's front seat. "You're not even carrying, are you?"

"I usually leave my Uzi at home when I work out."

The deputy's eyes widened. "You got one of those babies back at the ranch? I'd sure like . . ."

"What about it, Jimmy Lee?" Kin yelled out. "How about it? You gonna get me that car?"

Then, just as the deputy was reiterating the Honeycomb P.D.'s stance on hostage negotiations, Cal caught a glimpse of blond curls out of a corner of his eye.

Jesus H. Christ. Holly was coming down Main Street, slipping cautiously from doorway to doorway along the block, apparently oblivious to the fact that each doorway was a clean shot from the window of the Longhorn across the street. The closer she got, the cleaner each shot became. What the hell was she thinking? Every muscle in Cal's body tightened. Every nerve ending snapped. The headache he'd been coaxing to the back of his brain sallied forth in all its splendor as he placed a hand on the door's armrest and pushed himself up.

"What are you doing, Cal?" Jimmy Lee exclaimed. "Get down. Get down."

Just what *was* he doing? Cal wondered as he walked across the street to the barbershop doorway where a certain strawberry blonde was trying pretty unsuccessfully to make herself one with the aluminum siding.

Her green eyes were about the size of crab apples as she watched him approach.

"I think I've done something pretty dumb here," she said, her voice wavering with false bravado. "Something amazingly stupid, actually, and I'm not exactly sure . . ."

No shit, Sherlock.

"Do what I tell you to do," he said, dispensing with any preliminaries or good cheer, positioning himself between her and Kin's rifle while he swung slowly around in order to keep an eye on the window and door of the café as well as the cruiser with its flashing lights and flung-open doors.

Behind him, Holly's response was immediate and smart. "Okay," she said. "Tell me."

"Try the door. If it opens, get inside, lock it behind you, then go to a back room, away from the street."

He heard her jiggling the knob and swearing softly. "It's locked," she said. "Oh, God. I can't get it open."

"Okay," he said, keeping his voice absolutely level while he watched the barrel of Kin Presley's rifle poke out the café door once more. "We'll just go to Plan B."

Cal dragged in a deep breath and nudged his headache farther back in his skull. And just what *was* this Plan B? His assessment of the situation so far was that it wasn't lethal, but he knew only too well how things could go sour in the blink of an eye, with the twitch of a finger on a trigger, with a single inept word from an angry spouse or a deputy going for glory.

He didn't have any authority here, but by God, with Holly in jeopardy now, he had reason enough to take charge of the situation. There weren't too many options. He could screw around and try to find an open door for Holly on this side of Main, or he could just bring the whole incident to an end right now. All his training and experience screamed, "Shut it down."

"Plan B?" she gulped.

"Just do what I tell you to do, Holly."

"Okay."

♥

Oh, man. Well, of course she'd agreed to do whatever Cal told her. He was the expert here, after all. She wasn't stupid, despite the fact that she had stupidly blundered into the middle of a hostage situation. But Holly thought Plan B would involve getting *away* from the situation, not walking *toward* it.

"Stay close behind me," Cal had told her. "I mean close as in inches and completely behind me. Keep your eyes on the spot right between my shoulder blades. Do not even think about peeking around my shoulder to see what's going on. You got that?"

"Okay, but . . ."

"Don't argue. Just do it."

His voice was so level and calm, he obviously knew what he was doing. Right? His blue eyes had burned with such determination that she had to trust him. Didn't she?

He'd told her to stay close, and she was doing her best, practically plastering her boobs against the middle of his back, measuring her stride to fit his as they crossed the street, but even so, managing to step on the heels of his running shoes every now and then.

"Watch it," he growled.

"Sorry."

As instructed, she was keeping her gaze on the gray sweatshirt fabric between his shoulder blades, but in her peripheral vision she could see people peeking out of doorways up and down the street, then quickly ducking their heads back.

Dammit. She wished she had a camera. The most exciting drama in her life, and she was *in it* instead of *all over it* like a proper journalist. She wished she had grabbed her tape recorder or a notebook. She wished she could see something other than the damp gray spot on Cal's back.

"How many hostages are inside?" she asked.

"Dunno," he snapped, still moving forward.

"Any idea?"

"Ssh," he hissed.

Holly was attempting to curb her curiosity when the deputy's bullhorn boomed. "Step out of the street, Cal. I repeat, step out of the street."

That wasn't such a bad idea, actually. Cal obviously didn't think so, though. He just kept walking toward the Longhorn Café.

Then he stopped, and Holly ran right into him.

"Kin," he called out. "It's Cal Griffin. You can take my car. Let all those people walk out the door, and then I'll hand over the keys."

To their right, the bullhorn squawked. "You don't have the authority to—"

"Put a sock in it, Jimmy Lee," Cal growled.

Directly ahead, from behind the door of the café, a voice called out. "The Thunderbird?"

"That's right. It's parked right out here."

Holly didn't see it, but neither could Kin.

Now she heard the door creak open and the hostage-taker ask in a sort of baffled tone, "You're letting me take your T-bird?"

Cal reached slowly into the pocket of his sweatpants and came up with a set of keys, which he jingled. "Yep. Let those people all come out and I'll give you these. The tank's three-quarters full and the last time I had it on the highway, I had the needle up to one-twenty."

"I'm taking Trisha with me," the man said.

"Trisha comes out with the rest," Cal responded calmly. "Otherwise, no deal."

"Lemme think about it."

"You've got two minutes," Cal told him.

"Two minutes," the deputy croaked on the bullhorn.

Silence descended upon Main Street. Holly could almost hear herself sweat. The sun was throwing knives at the top of her head, so she leaned forward, pressing her forehead against Cal's back.

"How're you doing back there?" he asked quietly.

"Fine," she said, "for an imbecile."

He felt him chuckle. "This'll all be over in another minute."

"One way or another," she groaned.

No sooner had she said those words than Holly heard the door of the café open. She recognized Kin Presley's voice when he called, "They're comin' out, Cal. All of 'em. Just like you said."

"Here we go," Cal murmured.

"Oh, thank God," Holly breathed. "Should I . . . ?"

"Stay behind me, just like you are."

Then she could hear the quick footsteps of the newly released hostages as they hastened out the door, and their voices tumbling over one another.

Hurry up now, sugar.

Thank you, Jesus.

That durn fool.

Watch the door now.

"Let's go, folks," the deputy ordered via the now thoroughly unnecessary amplifier. "Keep moving. Let's go. Let's go."

Holly leaned a little to her right and glimpsed them around Cal's upper arm. She recognized Coral, the waitress with the blond beehive. If this were New York, there would be a slew of reporters waiting to pounce on these people. She only hoped, since she couldn't play journalist herself, that some enterprising young scribe from the *Honeycomb Gazette* was appropriately positioned with notebook and pen in hand.

"That's all of 'em, Cal," Kin Presley called. "Gimme those keys. And tell that idiot Jimmy Lee to keep back."

"Stay with me now," Cal told Holly under his breath as he started forward again. "Stay close."

"Oh, God," Holly gulped. "What now?"

"Shove the rifle out on the sidewalk, Kin," Cal called to the man still inside, "and I'll turn over the keys."

"You said the hostages, Cal. You didn't say anything about the rifle," the man yelled.

"No rifle, no T-bird," Cal said.

"Aw, hell. Okay."

A moment later she heard the rough clatter of a firearm on the sidewalk. Then, with Holly still plastered to his back, Cal stepped forward to kick the weapon out of reach.

Kin Presley stomped out the door muttering, "You ain't really gonna give me those keys, are you?"

"Nope," Cal drawled.

"I didn't think so. Well, hell. Just tell Deputy Dawg over there to keep his pistol packed, will you? I don't trust Jimmy Lee any farther than I can throw him."

Holly, feeling relatively safe now, peeked out from behind Cal's back in time to see the erstwhile hostage-taker and T-bird driver hold out his arms, hanging his head and proferring his wrists for handcuffs, as if he'd been down this road before.

"Jimmy Lee," Cal said to the approaching deputy. "Kin's turning himself in and he wants to make a call to his attorney. You make sure he has access to a phone, you hear?"

"I believe I know the law, Cal," the deputy said with a sneer as he slapped a pair of cuffs on Kin, and then gave his prisoner a shove toward the cruiser. "Get in the car, you lame brain."

It was at that point that half the town surged forward in their Sunday best and bathrobes, to shake Cal Griffin's hand and pat him on the back, gradually but effectively moving Holly farther and farther away from him, the way a strong tide moves a swimmer farther and farther from the beach. She didn't really mind. It gave her a moment to catch her breath, to think about what had just happened.

Her knees had begun to tremble a bit in a delayed reaction to events, so she sat down on the curb in front of the barber shop.

Rufus panned the street, and the tape in Holly's head started rolling.

On a Sunday morning in Honeycomb, Texas, rifle shots rang out along with church bells. What could have been a tragedy was averted when a tall man in gray sweats . . .

No. Wait.

. . . when a hero in gray sweats . . .

Taking his cue from her script, Rufus zoomed in on Cal, who at that precise moment turned, head and shoulders above the crowd, and found Holly with his heavenly blue eyes.

Her heart did a sort of half gainer within her chest. Then all of a sudden she was dizzy. She was hot as hell, melting, and she could hardly breathe. The tape in her head started *thwap thwapping* and her vision blurred.

Chapter Ten

It was the damnedest wallpaper Cal had ever seen. When he'd first looked at it on Friday in a blur of vertigo, he thought he'd never see it again. But then he'd awakened to the big, white, man-eating roses yesterday morning, and now here he was again, back in the nineteenth-century floral nightmare on Ellie's second floor.

When the dust had settled on Main Street a while ago, Holly had passed out cold. Whether it was from the heat of the day or residual terror, he wasn't sure. She'd been pale as a fish and her skin had felt clammy so, over her weak protests, he'd carried her back to this godawful room, laid her on the big four-poster bed, and put cool washcloths on her forehead and neck.

While she rested, Cal sat on the hardwood floor rather than ruin Ellie's little flowered armchair with his damp sweatclothes. He sat, stared at the white-petals-on-bubble-gum wallpaper, and wished this whole hero business would just go away.

In spite of the non-violent outcome, the drama at the Longhorn Café had been a debacle in Cal's eyes. The cardinal rule of law enforcement may have been take control of the situation, but there was nothing in the rule book about being a hot dog. Which was what he'd been this morning. A real, prize-winning, ballpark frank. In hindsight, he knew he could have hustled Holly down the street to safety, well out of harm's way. Why the hell hadn't he done that?

He'd already come up with one reason, which was that he'd wanted to keep the little producer close to him, as close as his own skin. It wasn't such a strange reaction from someone trained to be a protector. It might have been egotistical, but it wasn't out of bounds.

The other reason, though . . . the one that kept cropping up, only to be shunted aside. The one that kept knocking on his consciousness like a very unwelcome guest. The reason he didn't want to think about had something to do with this hero business. And someplace in the back of his brain Cal was ashamed to think he'd handled the situation the way he had this morning in order to impress the producer of Hero Week, to show her he wasn't some useless, washed-up Fed, some has-been who'd be collecting a pension pretty soon.

Someplace deep inside him, Cal suspected that he'd wanted to be Holly's hero, and he'd kept her in harm's way longer than necessary to accomplish his objective. That was why all the kudos and congratulations out on the street this morning had just about turned his stomach.

Just as he was coming to this less-than-heroic conclusion, Holly sat up on the bed, still holding the compress to her forehead. He was glad to see her color had come back.

"You must think I'm the biggest wimp in all creation," she moaned.

"No, I don't. Are you feeling a little better now?"

She nodded, tentatively at first as if she were testing her head, and then with guarded enthusiasm. "A lot better, actually. Thanks for playing white knight to my dumb damsel in distress."

"Aw, shucks, ma'am. It was nothin'." That was the right response, wasn't it? That's how John Wayne would've responded, his eyes downcast, lifting his beefy shoulders in a shrug and toeing the ground with sincere humility. Then The Duke would've promptly changed the subject, which is what Cal proceeded to do.

"Do you like Latin music?" he asked.

Holly, intelligent woman that she was, seemed to sense a diversion. She set the compress aside, then shifted so she was sitting cross-legged on the big bed like a curious little girl not about to be denied. She cocked her head to one side, jutting out her chin. "You don't want to talk about what happened this morning?"

"Not particularly." Attempting to rise from the floor like a guy who didn't have a bad leg and bum knee and hit-and-miss balance, Cal thought he probably looked like his own grandfather. He tried not to sound like him when he said, "I'd rather talk about tonight."

"Tonight?"

"Yeah. Tonight. A little salsa, a little mariachi, a little whatever it is they're playing around here these days. What do you say? There's a roadhouse not too far from here. Are you game?"

Uh-oh. Apparently not, he thought, watching her lips thin and her forehead furrow. Well, hell. He wished now he'd never asked her. He wished he were dead. He'd rather face a firing squad than this woman's polite, well-meant, articulate rejection.

"Sure," she said as her frown transformed itself into a smile. "Why not?"

Why not? All of a sudden, Cal could think of about a hundred and twenty reasons, beginning and ending with the powerful physical attraction he felt toward her. And somewhere on the list was the minor, but nevertheless significant detail that he was still a married man, even if he did have divorce looming in his future, along with possible unemployment.

Her grin turned sassy as hell and utterly delicious. "This would be an official date, right?"

"Right." He couldn't help but grin back. "Our second, technically. Does that make a difference?"

"No. Just checking." She unwound her legs and scooted off the bed. "It's always good to clarify these things up front. Plus . . ." Now she was sauntering toward him, a devilish glint in her green eyes. "I'll be glad to get all this dating out of the way so I can get my head back to business."

Despite the fact that his heart was ramming his ribcage, Cal managed to sound cool. "Distracting you a little bit, am I?"

"A lot."

By now she was standing less than a foot away from him, her hands on her hips and her pretty face tilted up to his. For all intents and purposes, she looked like a woman who wanted to be kissed. But Cal, former D.C. Don Juan and West Wing Lothario, didn't trust his instincts anymore.

He took a cowardly step back, in the direction of the door. "How 'bout if I pick you up at seven o'clock?"

"Perfect."

"Okay then." He reached out his hand and connected with the doorknob. "See you at seven."

He left the rose-papered room so fast it wouldn't have surprised him if his Reeboks had laid rubber on Ellie's polished oak floor. After that, he detoured around the central block of Main just in case some Sunday morning stragglers

felt compelled to congratulate him again. When he reached
the T-bird at the high school, it wasn't even noon yet. That
gave him a little more than seven hours to recover his once
legendary cool and to sharpen whatever remained of his
instincts where women were concerned.

♥

Holly lay back down and draped the damp compress over
her entire face, not because her head hurt, but because she'd
just behaved like . . . like . . . a lap dancer or something. She
certainly hadn't acted like herself. Cal had looked at her as if
he no longer even recognized her just before he beat a path
down the hallway and the big staircase and out of Ellie's
house.

It must've been temporary insanity, Holly thought. She'd
been lying here, recovering from heat prostration or hero
fever or whatever it was that had struck her down, when suddenly she'd decided the only way she was going to get her
mind off Cal Griffin was to surrender to this overwhelming
attraction she had for the man. Trying not to think about him
was a little like visiting the observation deck of the Empire
State Building and trying not to think about jumping. It was
like a dieter trying not to think about Pringles and Sara Lee
and M&Ms.

So, when he'd suggested the date, Holly had leapt on the
invitation. It just seemed so logical, so brilliant, practically
inspired. She'd immerse herself in Cal Griffin tonight. She'd
think about him, focus exclusively on him, breathe him,
savor him, maybe even kiss him. She'd pig out on the man,
and then she wouldn't be hungry anymore, and she could get
her mind back on business, where it belonged.

Otherwise . . .

Her cell phone gave a little chirp in the depths of her handbag. Holly flung the damp compress aside. Now who in the world was calling her on a Sunday?

The word "hello" had hardly cleared her lips when she heard Mel Klein's gruff voice.

"We've got a problem, kid."

Mel often worked on Sundays when there was no one in the office to disturb him or, as he put it, to get in what was left of his hair, so the timing of the call didn't really surprise Holly. But a problem?

"Oh. What?" she groaned, climbing back onto the big bed. If there was a problem, it could only be one thing. "They've decided to give the piece to somebody else, right? They hired another producer. I knew it. Damn. I knew it was . . ."

"No. Whoa. Slow down. Where'd you get that idea? You're still producing it, Holly."

Thank God. "Well, then, what's the problem?" she asked. Or maybe she should have specified *the problem in New York*, because she already knew the problem in Texas. At the moment, her hero story was all hero and no story.

She could hear the springs in Mel's chair squeal as he leaned back and growled, "We just found out late Friday that the History Channel is putting together something similar and planning to run it the first week in October."

"A biography of Cal Griffin?" she asked.

"No. A hero series."

"Featuring Cal Griffin?"

"No," he said. "I don't even know who they're featuring, but it doesn't make any difference. Hero, schmero. Bottom line is we're moving our series up a full three weeks in order to . . ." He chuckled. "Well, we're gonna head 'em off at the pass, to use your language, kiddo."

"That's not my language, Mel." Holly rolled her eyes in exasperation. "I've never said that in my life."

"I was just twitting you, kid. Listen. Here's the deal. I need you back here no later than Thursday afternoon with all your production notes. We've lined up Wesley Cope to host Griffin's segment . . ."

"The Country and Western singer?"

"Yup," he said while another chuckle rumbled in his sarcastic, city-slicker throat.

Holly hardly knew which bit of information to react to first—the sudden three-day deadline or the fact that a man notoriously long on looks and hair but short on brains would be hosting her piece. The deadline. Definitely, the deadline.

"Thursday afternoon! Mel, that doesn't even give me three whole days to wrap things up," she exclaimed, as if wrapping up were all that was left to do, as if she *had* anything to wrap other than her arms around her hero.

"Sorry, kid. That's the deadline I'm working with on this end. We'll need the polished shooting script by the end of the following week, and then you'll go back for the actual shooting with Wesley Cope over the Fourth of July. You might want to go ahead and pin down your interviews with that in mind. Will Griffin be there over the Fourth? Do they have anything special going on in town? A parade? Fireworks?"

"I haven't the vaguest idea." Holly thought about the events of that morning, wondering if that was enough fireworks for Mel. She wouldn't be able to use any of that in her piece, unfortunately, because of her own involvement.

"Have you managed to spend much time with him?" Mel asked.

"Griffin? Oh . . . yeah. A few hours here and there."

"Have you nailed him yet?"

Holly sat up, blinking. Had she nailed him? "Excuse me?"

"Have you got a decent hook for your story?"

"Oh. Sure." That kind of nail. Not that there was anything hanging on it yet. "It's coming right along."

"Good. Okay. Well, I'll see you Thursday afternoon, kid. Cheryl will get your ticket. You might want to check back with her tomorrow or Tuesday."

"Okay. See you Thursday."

Holly broke the connection, then sat there envisioning her career as a small skiff being captained by the Tid-E-Bol guy, going around and around in ever-decreasing circles, about to disappear in one gigantic flush.

♥

Ruth and Dooley got back from Corpus Christi at two o'clock Sunday afternoon. The new restaurant—*Ma Maison* —where they'd dined the night before hadn't been any great shakes in Ruth's opinion. The upholstered chairs and the quilted tablecloths had been an interesting touch, but overall the décor, the excellent service and a fine wine list hadn't made up for the fact that the chef, Paul somebody, supposedly from Paris by way of New Orleans, was a disaster.

His veal was overcooked, its texture reminding Ruth of the thin sole of a bedroom slipper. His pasta was at least two minutes past *al dente*—even Dooley agreed that the linguine was pretty near mushy—and his salad of field greens, roasted beets, and walnuts was overwhelmed by the Feta. Upon leaving the restaurant, Ruth had felt quietly smug, as well as newly inspired to open her own place.

Corpus was now on her list of possible sites not only because of the dearth of fine restaurants, but because she and Dooley had so enjoyed the view of the Gulf through their wide balcony door. That view had been inspirational, too.

She couldn't even remember the last time they'd made love twice—in moonshine and then again at sunrise.

Still, it was good to be back at the ranch. She always liked coming home. Not that she ever went away all that much. As she stepped down from the pickup, she could hear the phone ringing inside the house.

"Let it ring," Dooley said, catching her in his rangey arms as she came around the front of the truck. He nuzzled his soft mustache into her neck while his hand slipped beneath her shirt. "Let's go back, Ruthie. Right now. This minute. Let's jump in the truck and drive back to that motel room."

"Dooley Reese!" She laughed, and briefly considered her husband's proposition before she frowned and said, "Let go now. I've got to answer the phone."

"Cal's home." He angled his head toward the Thunderbird parked just in front of their truck. "Let him get it."

"You know he won't."

"Then let the damned thing ring."

"I can't do that." She pushed gently out of his embrace, and then began tucking in her shirt as she headed around toward the rear of the house and the kitchen door. Her herb garden hadn't suffered in her absence, she was happy to see. She'd forgotten to ask Cal to water it, but he wouldn't have remembered anyway.

Her kitchen always made her smile when she first entered, whether it was first thing in the morning or arriving back home after being away, even for an hour or two. She grabbed the phone on what must have been its twentieth ring.

"Mrs. Reese? This is Chuck Bingham of Bingham Properties."

"Oh! Good morning, Mr. Bingham. Or I guess I should say good afternoon. Were you able to get by the ranch yesterday?" Damn. She wished she'd had a chance to talk to Cal about the man's visit. She felt at a distinct disadvantage, not knowing who the prospective buyer was or how he'd reacted to the ranch yesterday.

"Yes, we did. And I think I have some very good news for you," the realtor said.

Ruth's heart felt like a fist surging up in her throat. Was this it? Was she finally going to have the money to finance her dream? She could hardly breathe. "Well, that's wonderful," she said, trying not to sound too eager.

"My client's interested in the entire fifteen hundred acres . . ."

Damn. Her calculator was on the desk in the living room, and she wasn't on the portable phone.

" . . . and he's willing to go as high as two hundred thirty-three dollars per acre."

Ruth blinked. Two hundred thirty-three? She didn't need a damn calculator to confirm that it was less than half the six-hundred-dollar-per-acre figure she had in mind. She swallowed the anger and disappointment that were rising in her, told herself this was business and that the man was simply opening negotiations. She needed to be cool and clear-headed.

"I'm willing to listen to a higher bid, Mr. Bingham," she said, pleased with her tone. Friendly but forceful. A steel door, but one that was still open.

"That's as high as he's willing to go," Bingham said. "In all honesty, Mrs. Reese, I think it's a very generous offer in light of the problems at Rancho Allegro."

"What problems?"

"Well, you know." He laughed nervously. The man sounded like a jackass. "That business with the titanium. You know. The dead goats. All that."

"The titanium." Ruth's voice was flat now and sour as

curdled milk. Her foot began to tap on the floor. "Dead goats. You must've talked to my brother yesterday."

Across the kitchen Dooley walked in the door, all smiles, while the realtor was replying, "Your brother? No. No, I don't believe I did. I spoke with a Mr. Bascom, one of your neighbors, and his wife. They stopped to chat while we were looking at the northern acreage of the ranch. Oh, and by the way, Mrs. Reese, I wonder if you have Mr. Bascom's phone number. My client wanted to make him an offer on his Thunderbird."

Ruth slammed the phone down so hard she nearly broke it.

"What's going on, honey?" Dooley asked.

"Calvin Griffin!" she screamed. "If your gun is in your room, you better hide it from me."

♥

Cal glanced at the maple dresser, where his holstered semi-automatic was stashed with his socks and underwear, and then with his head still braced against the back of the sofabed, he closed his eyes. He'd been anticipating some sort of explosion ever since he heard the truck roll into the driveway just as the phone began to ring. He had answered it himself an hour earlier, just in case Ruth and Dooley had a problem on the road and needed his help, and he'd politely informed good old Chuck Bingham that he had the wrong number. The realtor, obviously unconvinced, had been phoning every ten minutes since. Such aggressive phoning could only mean one thing, Cal decided. Titanium and dead goats to the contrary, Chuck wanted to make a deal.

God help him. He didn't want to trample Ruthie's dreams, but he just wasn't ready to sell his half of the ranch. It wasn't out of any particular loyalty to family history, or because he didn't have anything else, any place else in the world to call his own. It was mostly because he simply didn't trust himself to make irrevocable decisions right now. He'd been thinking about that ever since leaving Holly's room this morning.

Why taking the producer to a roadhouse tonight struck him as an irrevocable decision, he wasn't sure. Coward that he was, he'd called Holly half an hour ago to cancel their date, but nobody answered the phone at Ellie's. Now he was wishing he'd jumped in the car and driven into town to tell her personally. Then he wouldn't have to face the furious woman who was just now stomping into his room.

"You did it again, didn't you?" his sister screeched. "I can't believe it. You did it again."

"Hey, Sis. How was Corpus Christi?" he asked, hoping to re-channel her anger so they didn't have to have the sell-the-ranch discussion right now.

"Don't you 'hey, Sis' me, Calvin Griffin, after you promised Dooley you'd behave and then gave the real estate man some cock and bull story about plutonium and dead animals."

"Titanium," he said, suppressing a grin.

Ruth threw up her hands. "I don't care if it was uranium or arsenic in the well water. You flat-out lied to the man and I'm so damn mad I can't see straight."

"Well, Ruthie darlin'." He laughed softly, sadly. "I can't think straight so I guess that makes us quite a pair."

Cal could see the blue flames in her eyes lower to a simmer. The anger was still there, but her expression softened. So did her voice. "I just wish . . . oh, I don't know. I'm not trying to sell the ranch out from under you, Cal."

"Then don't," he said. "Give me a little more time to get myself together, and then we'll work something out."

"I'm forty-two years old," she said, shaking her head, bearing an almost eerie resemblance to their mother all of a sudden. "I don't have that kind of time anymore. This restaurant is important to me. It's all I want."

"I know that, Ruthie."

"And yet you're doing everything in your power to prevent it," she said. "That's just not fair."

"Did Bingham make you an offer?"

"It was insulting," she said. "A joke, thanks to you and your silver tongue." Her eyes narrowed. "He said you were with your wife. Did you bring a woman back here yesterday?"

Ah. She had reverted to Sergeant Ruth of the Sex Police. This facet of his sister was far easier to deal with than Ruthie the Restaurant Dreamer. "Two women," he said. "Twins. We did unspeakable things in every room but the kitchen."

Luckily she didn't have anything in her hand to throw at him. Just a searing blue glare. "I'll bet it was that woman from New York. That producer person. And I'll bet you let her snoop all over the house."

"Actually she only snooped in here, through my boxes." He gestured to the stack beside her. "We were looking for my high school yearbook."

"Well, it's not in those boxes. I can tell you that right now." Ruth sniffed. "It's on the bookshelf in the living room, right next to mine, right where it's always been. Mama kept them side by side."

The phone rang again, and Ruth gave a little start. "I hope it's not that idiot calling to insult me with another low offer," she said, cocking her head toward the hallway as the ringing stopped. "Dooley must've answered it."

They both listened to Dooley's soft drawl as it drifted

down the hall. It was a short conversation, comprised mostly of *yeps* and *nopes* and a final *okey-doke* before he hung up.

"I'll bet it's Bingham wanting to come back and look at the place again," Ruth said, her voice rising with hope. "And if that's the case, Cal, I want you to tell him you were just pulling his leg yesterday with all that nonsense. You hear me?"

Before Cal could answer, Dooley appeared in the doorway.

"Who was that on the phone?" Ruth asked.

"It was for Cal."

Her mouth curved down in disappointment. "Well, he was right here, Dooley," she snapped. "Why didn't you . . . ?"

"She didn't want to talk to him."

"She?" Cal asked, sitting up.

"It was that little New York gal," Dooley said. "She said she's sorry but she won't be able to see you tonight."

Cal shook his head. "Okay. Thanks, Dooley."

So much for irrevocable decisions. But now that he didn't have to make one, it was somehow all he wanted to do.

Why the hell was she breaking their date?

Chapter Eleven

Holly switched off her phone. There. That was that. She'd broken her date, and now she could concentrate fully on her story. And she would—just as soon as she stopped feeling lower than the belly of a worm for leaving the message with Cal's brother-in-law instead of speaking with Cal, himself.

She shouldn't have agreed to go out with him tonight in the first place. She wasn't here to have fun, for heaven's sake. Who did she think she was kidding with that "One date and then I'll never think about him again" business? She certainly wasn't here to date the subject of her documentary. There was probably something starred and highlighted and double-underlined in one of her old journalism textbooks about this exact ethical dilemma. She would check that out when she got home.

That was the good news, of course. That she was headed back to New York. The bad news was that it was so soon.

On Thursday.

Oh, God. There was still so much she had to do.

"Holly? You up there?" Ellie called from the bottom of the stairs. "Yoo-hoo."

Holly slid off the bed and went to the door of the bedroom. "I'm here, Ellie. Just doing a little work." Emphasis on little, she thought with some disgust.

"Well, come on down here," her hostess' voice boomed. "I've got a surprise for you."

Uh-oh. If the surprise had the world's most beautiful blue eyes, she wasn't going to be very pleasantly surprised. As far as she knew, though, ol' Blue Eyes was still back at the ranch, where Dooley Reese was probably relaying her cancellation right about now. "Okay," she answered. "Be right there."

On the off chance that it was Cal, Holly checked the mirror before she left the room. She almost wished she hadn't when her hair turned out to be beyond redemption.

Much to her relief, it wasn't Cal standing at the bottom of the stairs, but rather Ellie and three women—a blonde, a brunette, and a redhead. With Ellie's gray hair, the women looked almost as if they were posed for a Clairol ad. She recognized the brunette as the busy beautician and former friend of Cal, Nita Mendes. Holly paused on the staircase, not knowing quite what to make of the little group. Were they a welcoming committee or a mini-mob, ready to ride her out of town on a rail? Should she smile or scream? Walk toward them or run for her life in the opposite direction?

"Holly Hicks," Ellie said, "I want you to meet Carol Duggan, Jen Eversole, and Nita Mendes. We all got to talking after church about you and your program, so I said why didn't these gals come back here for some iced tea and cookies and a little talk about you-know-who."

Holly knew who, indeed. "Oh. This is wonderful! Let me just run back up to my room and get my tape recorder."

♥

Out on Ellie's patio, it didn't take long for the women to warm up to their topic, and after ten or fifteen minutes, nobody was even glancing at Holly's little black tape recorder where it sat between the sugar bowl and the big glass jar of sun tea. They seemed to have forgotten that they were speaking on the record. Or else they no longer cared as one story about Cal instantly sparked memories of another. And another. Holly had already decided the VIP Channel had erred by featuring him on Hero Week. To hear these women talk, Calvin Griffin was far better suited for Heartthrob Week.

Carol, the blonde, hadn't spoken much at all, but now she laughed as she spooned sugar into her second tall glass of iced tea. "All right, well, shit, since everybody's 'fessing up here, I guess I'm gonna have to admit that in our junior year I had a not-so-accidental flat tire out at Rancho Allegro."

"Now how'd you manage that?" Ellie asked while Jen and Nita exchanged knowing looks.

Carol blinked innocently, then replied, "With a steak knife. What I hadn't counted on, though, was that it would be Dooley Reese instead of Cal coming to my rescue. Damn the luck. He'd gone off to Padre Island or someplace for the weekend. It must've been about a hundred and ten that afternoon, but Dooley was so sweet when he changed my tire. Poor thing kept apologizing for not being Cal."

"He and Ruth were probably still newlyweds then," Jen, the redhead, said. "I hardly remember ever being so young."

"And foolish," Carol said.

Jen nodded. "On the other hand, I do remember I used to turn down dates with other guys in the hope that Cal would call and ask me out." She took a thoughtful sip of her tea before adding, "And I sat home plenty of Friday and Saturday nights, too, when he didn't."

"For Lord's sake, girl. Why didn't you just call *him*?" Ellie exclaimed. "I don't understand it. Or was I the only one in our class who subscribed to *Ms.* magazine back then?"

"Yes," all three women answered in perfect unison, after which all four of the former classmates dissolved in laughter.

It was like a class reunion, Holly thought, this unexpected get-together out on Ellie's flagstone patio, sipping from tumblers of iced tea in the deep shade of ancient oaks, the hems of the women's Sunday summer dresses rippling with an occasional breeze while they fanned themselves with little paper napkins that Ellie had brought out with a tray of ginger cookies. It was like a time-out from present-day demands and problems, an opportunity to reminisce, to linger awhile in lost times.

Holly was loving every minute of it. She'd never been to a class reunion herself. She wondered if she'd feel quite this comfortable, sitting on a patio in Sandy Springs with her own classmates, and she tried to imagine having anything in common with Lynda Bryan or Deb Sims or Bethany Watts. Of course, they wouldn't be discussing Cal Griffin, would they? Nor would Holly be hanging on their every word and gesture, telling herself her interest was strictly professional.

"Well, I guess we were all pretty smitten with Cal, if that's the right word," Jen said with a sigh. At thirty-nine, she was the oldest of the group, as well as a three-time grandmother already, a status that Holly found almost staggering considering that the woman was only eight years older than she.

Nita, who still looked about twenty and had the longest fingernails that Holly had ever seen, laughed. "Smitten's good. It sounds a lot better than saying we all had the hots for him."

"And guess who wound up with him most of senior year?" Carol said, grinning. "Nita, you slut."

The beautician's glossy lips curved in an inscrutable smile and her dark eyes gleamed, leading Holly to believe Nita was probably savoring a few memories—maybe the drive-in movie scenario—that she wasn't entirely willing to share.

"You *did* sleep with him!" Jen squealed. The young grandmother sounded like a teenager, and her charm bracelet, bedecked with the birthstones of children and grandchildren, went wild as she clapped her hands. "I knew it. Didn't I tell you, Carol? I just knew it. Nobody ever looks that happy in high school unless . . ."

Ellie, far more matronly than her classmates and the self-appointed mistress of ceremonies this afternoon, cleared her throat. "More cookies, y'all?" she asked, running interference with her silver tray. "I'm not sure this is exactly what Holly came all the way from New York City to hear. Are your ears just about melting, honey?"

"No," Holly said, taking a gingersnap from the tray. "I'm really enjoying this. Honest. Tell me more."

"Yeah, Nita." Carol winked over the rim of her glass. "Tell us all more."

"Well, that's the funny thing." The expression on Nita's face changed dramatically from decadent to wistful, from secretly sensuous to visibly sad. She almost looked like a different person, older, much older, and not necessarily wiser.

"We never did," she said, all of the earlier good cheer gone from her voice. "Oh, I know what everybody thought, and I didn't even mind that people sort of assumed that Cal and I were sleeping together. I thought I was pretty hot stuff back then, you know?"

The beautician blinked back the mist in her eyes. "But the truth is that, in spite of all those steamy nights in the backseat of Cal's mother's old Plymouth or on the couch in my parents' den or wherever, we never did it. We never made love. Not once." A wistful little laugh broke in her throat. "And since we're being so damned honest, it wasn't because I said no, either."

Everyone was quiet for a moment, and Holly wasn't sure if the silence was out of disappointment at a shattered myth or disbelief or a kind of awe at such long-ago restraint on the part of a teenage boy. Whatever it was, though, it was very, very personal. This information was not for an audience of sixteen million. Holly leaned forward and shut off her tape recorder.

"Hard to believe, huh, guys?" Nita summoned up a fraction of a smile.

"Well . . ." Carol and Jen were both obviously at a loss for words. "Um . . ."

Once again, Ellie intervened with a dismissive flap of her hand. "Well, I never listened to gossip back then, myself. Still don't. And for what it's worth, I'd say Cal was a good boy with a bad reputation. And a handsome devil, to boot."

"Nobody's mentioned Hec Garcia," Holly said, assisting her hostess by nudging the conversation in a new direction. "I gather he and Cal got into it once or twice."

They all looked at her—even unflappable Ellie—as if she'd spoken in a foreign language. Way more foreign than New York. Swahili, maybe.

"Well, he showed me that scar on his arm," she said, "and I just assumed there had been some sort of fight."

"Oh, I remember that," Carol said.

Jen leaned forward for another cookie. "A fight? Are you

thinking about that football game against Mendocito, Carol?"

The blonde nodded, and then said to Holly, "But Cal wasn't *in* the fight. He got slashed breaking up the fight."

"Oh." Holly sat back. Hot damn. Hero Week was on again.

"Lord Almighty," Ellie said. "It's after four o'clock already. Jen, didn't you tell me you had to get home to bake a cake or something?"

There was a flurry of movement as the women all looked at their watches, each of them expressing surprise that the past hour and a half had flown so fast. Holly stood, searching for the right words to properly thank each one of them, particularly Nita, for her candor and helpfulness. But then, just as she opened her mouth to speak, she closed it abruptly when she saw Cal coming around the side of Ellie's house.

The good boy with the bad reputation was wearing a conservative light gray suit, a solemn tie, and polished shoes, nearly the same uniform in which she'd first seen him at the airport. He looked professional, thoroughly urban, and absolutely out of place. At the same time his face had never looked quite so handsome, and his eyes had never looked so blue. And Holly's heart had never before gone from zero to sixty in a single, bounding beat.

"Well, now." Ellie laughed. "Speak of the devil, and who should appear?"

♥

Holy mother of . . . !

Ahead of him, on the shady patio, Cal saw what looked like a coven of summer witches wrapping up a Tupperware party. Worse. It looked like a hen party, awaiting the arrival of the cock. Him. He would've turned tail and run if he hadn't thought he'd fall flat on his face.

Jesus. There was Ellie and Carol and . . . What was her name? The pretty redhead? . . . and Nita and last, but hardly least, little Miss Holly Red Hot Chili Pepper Hicks, the date breaker.

He clenched his teeth, stifled a groan, and then put on a smile that said he really didn't give a rip if she went out with him or not. Hell. He was only here to drop off the yearbook Ruth had found. Right? Forget that he had showered and shaved and slapped on enough cologne to devastate a regiment of women over and above one little reneging New Yorker. Forget that he'd even put on the uniform to enable him to feel, if not look, competent and in control.

"Well, look who's here," Ellie said. "Were your ears burning, Cal?"

"Ladies," he murmured, finding it hard to believe a man breaking out in a slick cold sweat could sound even half that cool. His gaze skimmed Ellie and Carol and the redhead and Nita, then came to rest on the date breaker. "Holly."

"Hi," she said a bit breathlessly. Her green eyes were nearly glowing and her mouth twitched into a grin that seemed beyond her control. That pretty face of hers almost blossomed. A person might even call it a blush. Well, if she was so damned delighted to see him, why the hell had she canceled their date? This was probably not the proper time to inquire.

"You're looking mighty fine, Cal," Carol said. "How're you feeling these days?"

"Good," he said. "Better." A lot better, in fact, now that he'd seen the welcoming expression on Holly's face. He sneaked another glance in her direction just to reassure himself it was still there. Oh, yeah.

"We heard about what happened at the Longhorn this morning," Nita said. "It's a good thing you were there to keep Jimmy Lee from killing poor ol' Kin. You ought to move back and take over as sheriff, Cal."

"Too much excitement," he said.

While all the women chuckled, Ellie surged across the flagstones toward him. "What in the world have you got there, Cal?" She pointed to the yearbook he'd wedged under his arm. "That's not an old copy of The *Yellowjacket*, is it?"

With a little squeal, the redhead rushed forward to grab it. Jen! He suddenly remembered her name. She used to be Jen Williams. Or Willman. "Oh, Lord," she said. "I lost my copy years ago."

"Me, too!" Nita exclaimed. "Let me see." The two women nearly had a tug of war over the book.

Meanwhile, Holly moved closer to Cal's side. "Hey, you found it," she said quietly.

"Ruth did." He smiled down at her. God she was pretty with the late afternoon sun flaming in her hair and just teasing the freckles on her face. He caught himself wondering about the ones he couldn't see, and the late afternoon sun seemed to burn hotter all of a sudden. He cleared his throat. "I thought I'd bring the yearbook by and see if I couldn't change your mind about . . ."

Jen whooped just then, winning the tug of war after Nita apparently snapped one of her red talons.

"I can't believe you showed up with this, Cal, right when I have to get back home. Oh, I don't want y'all to go through it without me." She stamped her foot while hugging the book to her chest. "Promise me you won't."

Nita plucked her wounded fingertip from her mouth just long enough to say, "I'm not promising shit, Jen. You broke my nail."

"I did not."

"Yes, you did," dark-haired Nita snarled.

"Well, I'm sorry, Nita. But I still don't want y'all to go through The *Yellowjacket* without me. Okay? It'd just be so much fun to look at it together."

"Then that's just what we'll do." Ellie, ever the mediator, stepped in. "We'll all meet back here after church next Sunday. I'll fix the iced tea. Carol, how 'bout if you bring those good peanut butter cookies of yours? Nita can bring her double chocolate brownies, the ones with the white chocolate chips."

"You got it," Carol said. "This'll be a blast. You come, too, Cal, okay? It's your yearbook, after all."

"Sounds good to me," he answered. "Forget the damn tea and crumpets, Ellie. I'll bring a couple six-packs and pretzels."

Ellie pried the book from Jen's grasp. "I'll put this in a drawer for safekeeping in the meantime."

"Promise you won't look at it until next Sunday," Jen said. "You have to promise, Ellie."

The big woman sketched a cross over her ample bosom, then turned to Holly. "Naturally you're invited, too, honey. Unless you've already heard way more than you ever wanted to know."

"Yes, please come, Holly," Carol said.

Jen laughed. "How could she resist?"

"I wouldn't miss it for the world," Holly replied.

Cal wondered if he was the only one who picked up on the forced cheer in her tone. A quick glance at her face revealed a pinch of worry between her strawberry blond eyebrows, a faint withering of her rosy smile. He suddenly knew why. Aw, damn. She knew she wouldn't be here next Sunday.

After that he was barely aware of what he was saying to his female classmates as they took their leave. He carried Ellie's big tea jar into the kitchen for her while Holly followed, carrying empty glasses on a silver tray.

"I'll help you wash these, Ellie," Holly said.

Much to Cal's relief, Ellie shooed her away from the vicinity of the sink. "No, you won't."

"I don't mind. Really."

"Well, *I* mind," Ellie said. "I enjoy cleaning up after a party. Gives me time to think about what all went on, who said what, and whether or not I had a good time." She laughed. "Get out of here, you two. I expect you've got plans for dinner."

"We do," said Cal at the same moment Holly said, "No, we don't."

The big woman crossed her arms and looked from Holly to Cal. "I think you've got your signals mixed, people. Which is it? Dinner or no dinner?"

"Dinner," Cal said, grasping the little date breaker firmly by the elbow. "Come on."

♥

"Didn't you get my message?" Holly asked once they were out of the kitchen.

For just a second, Cal's baby blues went all shifty beneath their dark and luxurious lashes, as if he were trying to come up with a lie, but then he met Holly's gaze squarely and said, "Yeah, I got it. I just decided to ignore it."

She made a strangled noise, a cross between a growl and a beleaguered sigh that seemed to float above her head like a cartoon *arghh*. "I really can't go out with you this evening, Cal. I'm sorry." Boy, was she sorry.

The sexiest grin she'd ever seen in her life flared across his mouth. "But you're flattered by my persistence, right?"

"Staggered, actually," Holly said in all sincerity. "I'm just not used to . . ."

She stopped in mid-sentence. Just what was it she wasn't used to exactly? Being pursued? That happened on a fairly regular basis. After all, she was reasonably attractive. Her figure wasn't Pamela Anderson's, by any means, but it was okay. Her teeth were straight, and she usually smelled alluring even if she didn't particularly feel that way.

No. The thing she wasn't used to was responding so viscerally to her pursuer. She wasn't used to being turned on by anything other than a well-honed opening sentence of a news piece or camerawork that set the perfect mood for a story. She wasn't used to her heart bashing against her ribs or edging up into her throat and then doing a dizzying back flip straight to the pit of her stomach.

She wasn't used to feeling such intense heat from a man who was moving closer to her that very moment, a man whose expression seemed to mirror her own astonishing desire.

"Not used to what?" His voice was somewhere between a whisper and the purr of a sleepy tomcat.

"I . . ."

It was a good thing that he kissed her just then, otherwise she would've said something incredibly stupid. The kiss wasn't one of those hell bent for leather varieties like the previous evening, but it stopped her heart all the same, especially when his tongue teased the seam of her lips. Just a sample, it seemed to say. An hors d'oeuvre. Wait'll dinner, babe. Wait'll dessert.

Oh, God. Against her better judgment, in spite of all her

protests, and to her everlasting shame—How could she be so weak?—she was going to go.

♥

While Holly was upstairs changing, Cal sat at the kitchen table, sipping iced tea and watching Ellie wash and dry glasses. She'd refused his offer of help.

"I'd've offered you a beer, Cal, but there hasn't been anything stronger than iced tea in my house since Hank Kelleher stopped coming by about six or eight years ago."

"The tea's fine, Ellie." He took another sip to prove it, then before he even knew he was going to say it, he confessed, "Anyway, I'm trying to cut back."

She nodded her gray head solemnly as if she understood all the unspoken implications of those few words. You didn't have to be the town historian to know that Calvin Griffin, Sr. had pissed his life away in Honeycomb's bars and back rooms.

"It's hard, I expect," she said. "You lived a pretty fast and furious life in Washington before you hit that brick wall last year. It might take some time, Cal, but you'll adjust. Whatever happens. You'll find your way."

Having dispensed that little nugget of Lone Star wisdom, Ellie turned back to the sink to concentrate on her glassware, leaving Cal to contemplate the meaning of *whatever happens*. He was beginning to sink into a proper funk when Holly reappeared in a little black wisp of a dress that nearly blew him out of his chair.

"I'm ready," she said.

God help him. So was he.

Chapter Twelve

If Cal had known that Bobby Brueckner from the bank and several other old buddies, along with their wives, would be at El Mariachi, the roadhouse ten miles east of town, he would've taken Holly somewhere else. Anywhere else. Even the Longhorn Café. And if he'd had his former wits about him, he and Holly wouldn't have been snagged the second they walked into the place and then wound up sitting at separate ends of a long red-and-white checkered table that was laden with enormous pitchers of beer and heaping platters of nachos.

The band was too loud—Cubans, he guessed, in shiny black pants, gold cummerbunds, and ruffled yellow shirts—and the glare of the recessed ceiling fixtures on Bobby's bald head at the far end of the table was just about blinding Cal. For a guy so reluctant to talk two days ago, ol' Bobby was sure flapping his gums at the moment. But as much as it irritated him, Cal couldn't tear his gaze away because Bobby was sitting next to Holly, really bending her ear, and the little red hot Manhattan jalapeno in the little black scrap of a dress apparently didn't mind one bit. Not about Bobby exercising his jaw or the fact that there was a half mile of table-cloth between her and her so-called date.

Yeah, well, he'd be kissing her again later, bent ears and all, even if he had to negotiate the half mile obstacle course of table top on his hands and knees. Holly wanted him just as much as he wanted her. He'd seen it in her eyes. They'd turned a deep and sensual jade after he'd kissed her in Ellie's hallway. He'd seen the desire in her glazed expression, and he'd tasted it on her lips. He was sure. Well, almost sure.

He was warning himself about the deficiencies in his judgment of late when Kathy Brueckner, Bobby's wife, nudged his arm.

"Be a sweetheart and pass me that pitcher of beer, will you, Cal?"

He reached out for the heavy pitcher and filled her empty glass to the rim. "There you go, darlin'," he said while adding a conservative inch or so to his own glass. No sense courting impotence with too much booze, he told himself. No sense flirting with failure. Besides, he'd meant what he'd told Ellie about trying to dry out. Bad enough that he was nervous as a virgin on a very first date. A kid who'd been carrying a condom under the flap in his wallet for a long and hopeful year.

Uh-oh.

Shit.

It had been so long since he'd had sex that he'd not only forgotten how to fucking do it, but he'd forgotten the necessary precautions that accompanied the act. He could almost hear a little *pfft* right now, the sound of his plans for tonight going up in smoke. Unless . . .

He looked the length of the table again where Baldy and Curly had their heads together like two goofy conspirators planning to assassinate Mickey Mouse. Was she on the pill?

Was there room enough in that little purse she carried for a diaphragm? Or did Miss Holly Hicks, like so many savvy women these days, carry her own selection of brightly colored, fancifully named square packets? What was it Diana had handed him the night he met her on the plane? Some damned French thing labeled Etna or Vesuvius or something.

Somehow he couldn't picture Holly with a Parisian rubber in her purse, or even a diaphragm, for that matter. This woman wasn't a huntress like his so aptly named about-to-be-ex-wife.

Then, while he was contemplating his pitiful, and now postponed, sex life, Cal suddenly felt a bare foot inching suggestively up his calf. Whoa. What the . . . ?

It would've been nice to think the sensuous foot belonged to Holly, but she would have to be a minimum of sixteen feet tall to have legs long enough to go the distance under this table. Since that was out of the question, highly trained investigator that he was, he took a sip of his beer and gazed casually around his end of the table at the wives of his buddies who were sitting within "playing footsie" distance.

Kathy Brueckner, on his right, was turned away from him, deep in conversation with a waitress. As near as Cal could tell, they were debating the merits of Monterey Jack cheese versus Colby. On his left, Marv Preston's wife, Janiece, a pretty blonde no bigger than the minute hand on a watch, was searching through her handbag just then as if her life depended on finding whatever it was she was looking for. That left only sloe-eyed, big-haired, sequin-and-spandexed Sandy Carter, who was sitting directly across from him.

The exploratory tootsie was approaching his knee as he slowly settled his gaze on Mrs. Bertram "Bud" Carter. Her foot held still, but her brown eyes widened perceptibly while her tongue made a wet pass across her lower lip. Oh, brother.

How long had she and Bud been married? Twenty years at least. Cal had been an usher at their wedding that summer. Jesus, he remembered how hung over he was from the rehearsal dinner. Who the hell knew what made a woman like Sandy run her foot up a guy's leg? Maybe Bud wasn't paying enough attention to her. Maybe she was hitting some kind of mid-life deal, like Ruth, and instead of opting for a restaurant, Sandy was looking for a tryst in a turquoise convertible. Whatever.

It just struck him as sad right then, and not that he was a white knight by any stretch of the imagination, but he didn't want Sandy leaving here tonight feeling lousy about herself. He knew all about feeling lousy. And he'd recently begun to know more than he ever wanted to know about rejection.

"Hey, Sandy," he said, his voice low and not meant to be heard by anyone else. "Is that you in search of a foot rub, darlin'?"

"Could be," she said.

Her toes edged inside his knee now, and Cal would've been a liar if he said it wasn't a turn on. He just wished the foot were attached to somebody else's leg.

"Care to do anything about it?" she asked.

After another sip of beer, he put his glass down and then reached under the table with both hands to plant his thumbs firmly against the sole of her stockinged foot. "How's that?" he asked, pressing hard.

Her thick eyelashes fluttered and Cal could see the moan she was having a tough time stifling. "Oh, God. That's wonderful," she murmured. "Don't stop."

He slid his hands up to her ankle, then dragged his fingers back, pressing hard into the fleshy part of her instep while he watched her head arc back a couple of inches and her dark brown eyes sink closed. "You look just as pretty as you did on your wedding day, Mrs. Carter," he said, keeping his voice low, continuing the massage.

"You're full of shit, Cal." She smiled as she said it.

"No, I mean it. You've still got world-class ankles, too, Sandy. You always did. Hell, I could do this all night. Except . . ."

Her shuttered eyes opened a crack. "Except what?"

With a tilt of his head, Cal gestured down the table. "Except that little strawberry blonde down there would probably kill me if she suspected I found anybody sexy but her. She's a lot stronger than she looks. And as I recall, Bud used to have a lethal left hook."

A small sigh of acknowledgment broke from her pink glossy lips. "You're saying we're just too old and scared to fool around, huh?"

"Well, I don't know about you, darlin', but I'm feeling every minute of my age these days." He grinned. "I kinda wish we'd both thought about playing footsie eight or ten years ago."

Sandy—Mrs. Bertram "Bud" Carter of twenty years, with probably twenty or thirty more to go in that role—fully opened her eyes now in order to roll them heavenward. "You really are full of shit, Cal. You know that?"

He shrugged. He knew it, but he was hoping Sandy wouldn't figure it out.

She gave a conclusive little sigh then as she pulled her foot from his hands. "You're a good man, Cal Griffin, and that strawberry blonde is one lucky little girl."

They both turned their gazes to the opposite end of the table where the lights were nearly dazzling on Bobby's skull as he stood behind Holly's chair, helping her up, and then ushering her toward the dance floor. Holly pitched Cal a woeful little "Mayday" look over her shoulder.

"Cripes," Sandy said with some disgust. "There goes Bobby again, trying to prove he can do the tango. He watched that movie with Al Pacino too many times."

By now, Kathy had turned back from her conversation with the waitress and she took a bit of umbrage at the remark about her husband. "He's not *that* bad, Sandy. Besides, I think it's kind of cute." Chuckling, she nudged Cal's arm. "Still, your date probably wouldn't mind being rescued before ol' Al tangos all over her poor feet."

"That's not such a bad idea," he said, already shoving his chair back. "Excuse me, ladies."

♥

"Ouch." Dammit. Holly hadn't meant to yelp. Not out loud anyway. Bobby Brueckner was so utterly serious about the tango, but the banker-slash-hoofer had just clipped her little toe for a third time, and they'd only been on the dance floor a minute or two.

"Sorry about that," he mumbled, sounding less than sincere, as if it were *her* fault for being clumsy and getting in his way.

"That's okay." Holly stiffened her right arm just a bit so they weren't quite so close. Actually, his beer gut was already doing a fairly good job of separating them. Maybe he just had incredibly big feet. She was beginning to wonder if the VIP Channel had made any provisions for hazardous duty pay. God. She'd been a participant in a hostage drama this morning, and now she was about to have a toe amputated or be trampled to death in a crummy Texas roadhouse.

When Bobby abruptly reversed direction, he got her big

toe—eee-oww!—and she didn't say a word when he made a condescending cluck of his tongue instead of offering abject apologies. Okay. So she wasn't Ginger Rogers or Jennifer Grey. But Bobby wasn't exactly Fred Astaire, and he sure as hell wasn't Patrick Swayze.

"My turn, Bobby."

Cal's voice, as it drifted over the banker's shoulder, sounded like the music of the angels in concert with guitars and blaring trumpets and insistent maracas. *Gracias a Dios. Mil gracias.* A thousand thanks. More. A million.

Bobby's intense grip on her hand evaporated, and the next thing Holly knew she was being enfolded in Cal's arms. It felt a little like going from a bed of nails to the all-encompassing warmth of a duvet. Being in his arms felt so right. Just perfect.

The hand at her back pulled her close while his left wrist curled her hand against his solid chest. "This is purely a rescue operation, babe," he murmured at her ear. "I don't dance. Not anymore."

"Feels like dancing to me," she said, surprised at the sultriness of her own voice. The words came out as purring rather than speech. "Feels good."

He tilted back a few inches to focus his blue, blue eyes on her face. "Yeah?"

"Yeah." Holly couldn't suppress a smile that felt absurdly contented, ludicrously smitten. She didn't even want to fight her feelings at the moment.

Cal's smile was fairly smitten, too. "What do you say we ease on over to the far side of the dance floor, and then make a break for the back door?"

Holly laughed. "You lead. I'll follow."

Making their way across the crowded dance floor turned out to be easier said than done. It seemed that Bobby wasn't the only local aficionado of the tango. They were thumped and bumped from all sides as they moved in the general direction of the kitchen and the back door. Holly didn't especially mind the jostling, though, because every thump and bump seated her more firmly in Cal's arms, against his warm, solid form. Right that moment she would've followed him anywhere—out the back door, across the border, to the moon.

♥

Up until nine months ago, Cal had been, among other things, a professional people mover and crowd threader, using his own weight and forward progress to shift others off balance and out of his way. A human bulldozer with badge and gun. Christ, now he felt like a rat in a maze just trying to reach the edge of the dance floor. As a dancer, he'd never been any great shakes, but he knew how to hold a woman, and judging from the renewed glaze in Holly's expression, he'd succeeded admirably.

Now what?

With his arm around her shoulders, he guided Holly off the dance floor and down the narrow corridor that led past the pay phone and the rest rooms, both of them labeled in Spanish. It took Cal a long moment to distinguish *Chicos* from *Chicas*.

"I'll be right out," he told Holly even as he was pushing the door and congratulating himself on solving the problem about protection. He'd never been in a Texas roadhouse that didn't have a condom dispenser in the men's room. It was standard equipment.

He stepped inside, only to be greeted by the intense odor

of pine and the sight of about half a mile of wide shoulders, all in assorted plaids, lined up at the urinals.

The guy on the far right zipped up and swung around. It was Sandy Carter's husband, Bud. "Hey, Cal," he said, ambling toward the sink.

"Hey, Bud."

Damn. Cal glanced at the dark green dispenser on the far wall and wondered why he'd assumed he'd be alone for this little transaction. He didn't give a rat's ass about his own reputation, but he'd be damned if he'd let everyone within a forty-mile radius know he was making it with the little producer from New York. Instead of heading for the rubber machine, he went to the sink and washed his hands, just so he didn't look like a total jerk.

"So they're doing a TV show about you, huh?" Bud asked from the adjacent sink, glancing at him in the mirror.

"Yeah."

"That's really something, man. Who would've thought it back when we were kids?"

"Yeah. Who would've thought it," Cal echoed. He shut off the faucet and snapped a paper towel from the holder. "See you around, Bud."

Out in the dim hallway, Cal didn't see Holly at first, so he thought maybe she'd decided to use the *Chicas*. He leaned a shoulder against the wall, waiting. He could detour a few miles north on the way home. Holly'd never know the difference. He could stop at a drug store, be in and out in a minute, with no one the wiser.

Then what?

Hell.

Then *where*?

They couldn't very well go back to Ruth and Dooley's, could they? If Ruthie caught them . . . All of a sudden Cal felt like a furtive teenager, looking for a place, any place, to lay his lady. He cursed himself for choosing the T-bird with its bucket seats when he could have had a big '68 Caddy for the same price. Of course, six months ago, when he'd bought the car, sex had been the last thing on his mind. But now . . .

Just then, over the guitars and trumpets on the bandstand, he heard a familiar female voice. A familiar, *strident* female voice. More Brooklyn than Brownsville.

"You *and* the horse you rode in on, asshole."

Cal glanced to his left. Holly hadn't been in the ladies' room after all, but standing only a short distance away, wedged between Tucker Bascom and the wall.

Well, hell. The last thing he wanted to do tonight was confront some half-drunk, bow-legged Romeo who couldn't take no for an answer, so Cal stifled his natural instinct to intervene. Besides, the little chili pepper seemed to be handling herself just fine.

"Aw, c'mon, Tiffany," Tucker moaned.

"Get *away* from me." Holly, only an inch or two above five feet, reached up with both her hands and gave the six-foot, three-inch, inebriated cowboy a shove that sent him pinwheeling backward across the corridor and into the opposite wall.

Cal wasn't one to ignore an opportunity to avoid trouble. He levered off his square foot of wall and reached for Holly's hand.

"Come on, Champ. Let's get outta here."

♥

"I thought you had a thing for rescuing damsels in distress," Holly said, sliding into the T-bird's passenger seat.

"You were doing just fine without me."

Cal laughed as he closed her door and then walked around the front of the car. Holly could have sworn she saw moonlight glinting off his smile. That wasn't possible, was it? Stuff like that only happened in TV commercials. She rubbed her eyes.

"Tired?" Cal asked, settling behind the wheel.

"A little." She wasn't, not really, but he'd asked the question in a certain hopeful tone, as if he might be looking for an excuse to end the evening. "Are you?"

"Nah. I just thought . . ."

Before he could finish, the back door of El Mariachi shot open, slammed hard against the metal siding on the rear wall, and Tucker Bascom stumbled out.

"I want to talk to you, Griffin," he called, pointing across the gravel parking lot. "Wait up."

"Oh, God," Holly muttered. "What is that guy's problem?"

"You, I guess." Cal turned the key in the ignition and the T-bird's engine growled to life, while Holly's immediate instinct was to turn to her right and lock her door, a pretty futile act considering that she was sitting in an open convertible.

"Wait up," Tucker bellowed, advancing toward them.

"Buckle your seat belt," Cal told Holly at the same moment he rammed the gearshift into drive and hit the gas. For a second the wheels merely spun, spitting gravel at the fast-approaching cowboy, but then the tires bit into the ground and the T-bird shot forward, leaving Tucker Bascom flapping his Stetson and choking in a cloud of dust.

The sudden acceleration thrust Holly back into her seat, and she held her breath while the speedometer climbed to ninety and the wind knifed through her hair. Just a minute ago, if she'd had to predict the course of events, she'd have bet any amount of money that Special Agent Calvin Griffin would have sprung from the driver's seat as if he'd been ejected, after which he'd have promptly beat the shit out of Tucker Bascom with a few, select, government-approved moves.

Instead—surprise!—he'd fled.

Of course, she reminded herself that this was the guy who got knifed, not while fighting, but while breaking up an altercation. Her hero. The same guy who hadn't gone all the way with a young Nita Mendes.

And then it occurred to Holly that the reason she had just sneaked out the back door of the roadhouse with Cal was probably for the same reason Nita had sneaked out with him all those years ago. She glanced to her left. At ninety miles an hour, Cal's focus was on the narrow two-lane road, right where it should have been.

Any woman with half a brain and a normal flow of adrenaline would've felt scared to death right now, but amazingly all Holly felt was safe and well-protected. Maybe it had something to do with his gray suit and serious tie. Maybe it was just the way he'd held her on the dance floor, as if she belonged to him.

"You don't think he'll follow us, do you?" she asked over the sound of the wind.

Cal's gaze cut briefly to the rearview mirror. "He already is."

Holly turned to see the flare of two headlights punctuating the darkness behind them. Her sense of safety faltered. "Oh, God. This isn't good at all. What are we going to do?"

Cal didn't answer. He probably thought her question was rhetorical. It wasn't. She wanted to know what the plan was here.

"What are we going to do, Cal, just keep driving? Is that

the plan?" she asked, and then when he still didn't respond she started thinking out loud while looking over her shoulder every few seconds. "You know, if I were writing this scene for a movie, it would definitely be set in a city where we could make a sharp right, nearly hit a woman with a shopping cart, just miss a pushcart, then take a quick left at the end of the block. It might even be fun if it were San Francisco and we were leapfrogging at ninety miles an hour on those steep hills. But this . . ."

She waved her hands in the air for emphasis. "This is Texas, for God's sake, where the roads just go straight and flat for miles, forever. The guy who wins is the one who doesn't run out of gas, right?"

He still didn't answer.

Squinting at the dashboard, Holly was relieved to see that the T-bird had over half a tank. But the lights behind them were coming on fast. Too fast.

"Cal? Seriously. What *are* we going to do?"

"This," he said. "Hang on."

She dug her fingertips into the dashboard. "This" turned out to be some combination of decelerating, braking, and steering that had the T-bird screeching and squealing as it turned 180 degrees at a force of about three Gs. The maneuver practically knocked the breath out of Holly's chest, and the next thing she knew they were going ninety again, but in the opposite direction. With Tucker Bascom's headlights coming right at them.

Before she could let go of a scream of protest, the two vehicles passed with a giant whoosh, the blare of horns, and Tucker's curses blowing back on the wind.

And then Cal hit the brakes and turned the wheel again, and the T-bird went careening off the road—backwards!—

thumped over some rough ground, angled behind a huge mesquite bush, and stopped. Dead.

The only sound then was the whine of the roof as it rose from behind the back seat and came forward over their heads. Cal reached up to latch it on his side, then leaned across Holly to secure the latch on the passenger side and crank the window closed.

"There," he said, settling back behind the wheel.

"There?" Holly's breath had come back. "There what?"

Cal angled his head toward the road, barely visible now through the tangled branches of the mesquite bush. Holly looked in that direction in time to see Tucker Bascom's pickup flying past, back toward El Mariachi. She watched until the truck's red taillights disappeared in the dark.

"He won't be back," Cal said as he reached across the console for her hand. "Don't worry."

"Right."

"You're shaking." He drew her hand to his mouth, softly kissed her fingers.

"Nah. That's just my normal metabolism." Holly was amazed that Cal's palm wasn't the least bit sweaty after their harrowing ride. His hand was steady as a rock.

"Don't worry. Really." He chuckled. "By the time that ol' boy realizes he's not chasing us anymore, he'll be in the next county."

Holly couldn't help but laugh, weakly at first, but then managing an all-out giggle. "That was some pretty spiffy driving, Agent Griffin."

He laughed. "Yeah. And it'll be even spiffier if I can get this vehicle back on the road."

"What do you mean?"

"I mean the reason I turned off here was because the ground looked wet and I figured we wouldn't raise any dust."

"That was pretty quick thinking. I'm impressed."

"Yeah?" He lofted an eyebrow.

"Yeah," she said.

"How impressed?" His voice was low, but even so there was a note of amused challenge in it, and despite the dark confines of the car, she was sure she could detect a sexy little gleam in his blue eyes.

He was waiting for her to initiate a kiss! Her heart sort of levitated into her throat at the realization, and then it dropped to her stomach as she leaned to her left to put an end to the wait.

"Baby," he whispered as his mouth met hers and his arms moved around her, pulling her closer.

It wasn't a kiss at all, Holly thought. It was more like a match stick meeting tinder. Which was she? The tinder or the match? Not that it made any difference. She was burning all the same. Completely engulfed by Cal's hot mouth, his strong arms, his warm hands, the golden beery taste of him, the hot Texas night smell of him.

Holy shit.

She didn't realize she'd spoken out loud until he groaned against her lips, "No kidding. Let's get out of here. I don't know about you, but I'm too old and battered to make love in the back seat of a car."

Holly extricated herself from his embrace so he could reach for the ignition. The engine sparked to life. He slipped the gearshift into drive and stepped on the gas.

The rear wheels spun.

Cal eased off the accelerator and swore.

"Here we go," he said. "Nice and easy."

The tires spun. And spun. And spit wet, sandy soil out behind the car that sank, little by little, deeper and deeper, into the ground.

He snapped the ignition off and slapped the palms of both hands against the wheel before he leaned his head back on the seat and closed his eyes with a sigh that seemed to come up from the soles of his feet.

"We're stuck, huh?" Holly offered not so helpfully.

"Yep."

Chapter Thirteen

By the time Ruth realized it was the actual telephone that was ringing on her side of the bed, and not some dream phone in the dream kitchen where she was supervising a Jamaican sous-chef with a ten-inch blade and the world's longest dreadlocks, Dooley had already reached across her to fumble with the receiver.

He had dropped back down on his own side of the bed then, responding to the caller with muted *yeps* and *nopes*, while the black coil of phone cord that stretched across Ruth's neck was threatening to strangle her.

God bless it. She lifted up the cord and slid out from beneath it. Theirs was probably the only black rotary phone left in the whole state of Texas, but Dooley wouldn't have anything else beside their bed, where he demanded "a real phone," to use his expression. "Not one of those flimsy plastic toys."

As long as she was up, Ruth padded into the bathroom across the hall. What was it she'd been dreaming? Oh, yeah. The Jamaican sous-chef. He had the prettiest caramel skin, hazel eyes with long, long lashes, and the most lovely, melodic voice. She must've seen him on TV, she thought. In a commercial or something. To her knowledge, she'd never seen or heard a real live Jamaican. Not in Texas, certainly. Never in Honeycomb.

How such an exotic young man had gotten into her dream, Ruth didn't have the least notion, but she could only conclude that his unlikely presence was a measure of her frustration over her restaurant. Was her dream ever going to come true?

She studied her reflection in the mirror over the sink, adjusting her mouth slightly to diminish the downward pull at the corners. So this was what forty-two looked like. It wasn't so bad really. Dooley didn't seem to mind the silver that was creeping into her hair or the inevitable sagging fore and aft. Just as she didn't mind that his hairline was sneaking up under his Resistol and the dentist was lobbying hard for extracting a slew of upper teeth.

She'd been Ruth Reese now more years than she'd been Ruth Griffin. A life with Dooley was all she'd wanted at the age of eighteen, when she didn't know how to dream. She'd been a good wife, and together they'd raised a fine boy in Colby. They'd kept the family ranch, no mean feat. Only now . . . Well, it just wasn't enough. Not nearly enough.

By the time she walked back into the bedroom, Dooley had hung up the phone and turned on the lamp on his side of the bed.

"Trouble?" she asked, sliding back under the covers. "What time is it?"

"A little after one," he said. "That was Cal."

Ruth sat straight up, her heart surging, her stomach tightening. "What's wrong?"

"Nothing," he grumbled. "He got his car stuck in the mud off the Springtown Road. I'm gonna pick him up at Ellie Young's and then we'll go pull the car out."

"At Ellie's? At this time of night? Well, what was he doing

. . . ?" Ruth answered her own question. "He's with that TV woman from New York again. What do you want to bet?"

"Good for him." Dooley stood and snagged his jeans from the arm of the chair. "Where's my damned shirt?"

She pointed to the spot on the floor where he'd flung it only a few hours before.

"Why can't it wait till morning?" she asked.

Dooley shrugged into his shirt. "He said there are weapons locked in the trunk he doesn't want anybody fooling with."

"Well, I still don't see . . ."

"Go back to sleep, honey." He came around to her side of the bed and kissed the top of her head. "I'll be back in an hour. Probably less."

Ruth didn't reply, but lay back down and pulled the covers up to her chin, wondering why everything made her angry these days. Why every*one* pissed her off, even by being nice to her. Especially then. And Dooley most of all.

♥

Cal broke the connection and handed the cell phone back to Holly.

"Thanks. My brother-in-law's going to pick me up in a little bit. I'll wait outside so you can get some sleep."

"That's okay. I'm wide awake."

"Yeah," he murmured a little sheepishly.

Who wouldn't be wide awake after spending twenty minutes behind the wheel of a stuck Thunderbird, hitting the gas and shifting gears to no avail, while Cal pushed from behind, further wrenching his bad knee and getting splattered with mud all the while.

They'd finally given up, trudged a quarter mile toward

town before Bobby Brueckner gave them a ride back to Ellie's in the bed of his pickup. Some ride. Some hero.

And not only was Miss Holly Hicks wide awake, but for the past hour or so she'd seemed exceptionally cheerful. Happy as hell, as far as Cal could tell, even while her strawberry blonde hair looked wind-tossed and wild.

"I guess the evening didn't turn out exactly the way we planned, huh?" Holly was perched on the edge of the bed, talking as much to herself as to him while she gingerly eased off her mud-crusted shoes. "But you know what, Cal?"

Cal shook his head. He wasn't sure he wanted to know what. In fact, he was pretty sure he didn't. This was one of those evenings better left to bury without a eulogy.

"I'm glad it turned out the way it did," she said. "I really am."

"Really."

"Uh-huh. I'm sorry about your car, but if it hadn't been for that asshole Tucker and the car getting stuck and all, I think we probably would have made love." She tilted her head, which put her sudden little grin on an adorable slant. "What do you think?"

He shrugged, preferring not to think about it. Where would they have gone, anyway, since they couldn't go to Ruth and Dooley's, or back here? He couldn't see making love to Holly in the back seat of his car or in some sleazy motel. And then there was the whole matter of protection, or in his case, the sad lack of it.

"Anyway," she continued, "I'm glad we didn't. It's just that . . . oh, I don't know. I'm just grateful for the reprieve."

"Reprieve," he echoed mournfully. He'd admired her openness and honesty from the very first moment he met her, but sometimes he almost wished she'd lie a little bit. "Sounds like something you get when you're on death row."

"I don't think you truly appreciate the situation," she said, sounding miffed and misunderstood all of a sudden, her green eyes wide and her oh-so-kissable mouth not grinning anymore, but starting to look unpleasantly prim and self-righteous. "We aren't just any old couple, you know. We're not just any two people who can hit the sack without blinking an eye or thinking twice. This is different. There are certain ethical questions involved here."

"Such as?"

"Well, I'm the producer of your biography, which means I'm the person who needs to be level-headed and clear-sighted and totally unbiased about you. And that's just for starters." She lofted her gaze toward the ceiling. "What was I thinking?"

"Maybe that you found me irresistible," he offered along with a little grin of his own, "in a semi-heroic way."

"That's just the thing." She shook her head and sighed softly. "I do. I find you *completely* irresistible in a semi-heroic way."

"You do?"

Cal wasn't so mentally deficient or sexually stunted that he didn't know when it was time to move closer to the object of his desire. He strode forward, kicked her muddy shoes aside, and pulled Holly up into his arms. But he didn't kiss her. As much as he wanted to, he refrained. This was too important. All of a sudden, it was incredibly important. *She* was important. Crucial. He wanted to get this right. He had to get it right.

"Holly, darlin'," he whispered at her ear. "This is going to happen, you know. With us. Sooner or later. Sooner, if it's up to me. I promise you. We just need the right place, the right time. Do you hear what I'm saying?"

She nodded her head against his shoulder. Her arms lifted to circle his waist. She held him tight.

"That would be nice," she whispered. "Oh, God. That would be heaven."

"Yeah. Close as I'll ever get to it," he said. Cal widened his stance, drawing Holly's hips closer, pressing into her warmth. As far as his body knew, there was no more right time or place than now. He couldn't remember ever wanting a woman so much. He couldn't remember ever wanting a woman at all and not taking her on the spot.

Maybe they'd removed some crucial portion of his brain when they'd repaired his skull. Maybe they'd crossed some wires. Or maybe what he was feeling for this strawberry blonde was so much more than mere physical desire that his baser instincts had given way to a higher purpose. Like love?

Or maybe he was just afraid.

"Holly, Holly," he sighed, pressing his forehead against hers. "I wish . . . aw, hell. When do you have to go back to New York?"

"Wednesday."

"Wednesday!" No. That was too damn soon. It was already Sunday night. He needed more time. "This Wednesday?" His desperation probably sounded in his voice.

"Uh-huh. I have an early flight from Houston Thursday morning." She leaned back and looked up at him, her eyes a deep green and her pretty face all fretted with worry. "I'll be back over the Fourth of July. You'll be here then, won't you?"

"I'm not going anywhere," he said, his voice barely more than a whisper.

She pressed against him once more, curling her arms more tightly around his waist. "Maybe then . . . when the filming's done . . . maybe then we . . ."

Cal smoothed back her hair, let his lips drift over its warm, wild strands. "Yeah. Then. Definitely then."

They stood there for a moment like two people saying goodbye forever instead of agreeing to say hello in a month's time. It made him so damn sad that Cal was almost grateful when he heard Dooley's truck rattle into Ellie's driveway out front.

He tipped Holly's face up and kissed her a kiss that felt so much like good-bye he couldn't even say good night.

♥

After Cal left, Holly lay in bed wide awake, staring at the moonlit flowers on the wall, wishing for the sound of footsteps on the rickety fire escape, waiting—praying actually—for Cal to come back.

They should have made love tonight. No. They shouldn't. They'd done the right thing by postponing it. Hadn't they?

Holly flopped on her side and rammed a fist into the pillow, determined to stop aching for what she really didn't want. Not now, anyway. The right time, Cal had said. When was that? When the biography package was in the can? When his divorce was final? When Holly finally allowed herself to be distracted from her dream?

The perfect place, he'd said. Where was that? Not Texas, that was for sure. Not here. Her perfect place was New York, and she couldn't wait to get back to its narrow skies and gritty streets, its sidewalks with steaming grates, sharp elbows in subways, blissful anonymity, unidentifiable smells and inappropriate shrieks, its thrills and chills, its leers and fears and cheers.

Home.

All of a sudden Holly was miserable. She wanted to go

home, back to New York where her life moved in a straight line along a narrow path called ambition, where she never had to choose between her clear-cut plans and a man, where she was happy all on her own.

She squeezed her eyes closed and called on Rufus to take her there. To whisk her home if only in her imagination.

Tonight her ever-reliable cameraman seemed taller than usual, and she noticed he was wearing hand-tooled boots instead of his normal chewed-looking sneakers. His hair was longer, too, falling in two grizzled braids beneath the bandanna around his head, and he needed a shave. Jeez. Rufus had morphed into Willie Nelson all of a sudden—a clear sign that she'd already been in Texas far too long.

Still, on the sidewalks of New York where anything goes, he didn't look amiss. With his mini-cam high on his shoulder, Rufus widened his stance, rather like a Colossus, in the middle of the sidewalk. Oncoming pedestrians just naturally flowed around him, like a river around a rock, without a backward glance. In slow motion, his lens panned down 42nd Street toward the bright, elegant heights of the Chrysler Building. In the foreground, out of focus, yellow taxis blurred while their horns mingled like clarinets and oboes.

For her part, Holly stood there, imaginary mike in hand, mute. What could she possibly say about the place that hadn't been said before, and better?

It was Gershwin. It was Gotham. It was garlic, lox and bagels, *Breakfast at Tiffany's*, good wines, great newspapers. It was the *new* in news, and where she had to be to get what she wanted.

It wasn't Texas.

She told herself she didn't want Cal Griffin. She didn't. Honest to God. All she wanted was to go home and get on with her life.

♥

Cal unhooked the chain from the tow bar on his brother-in-law's pickup and tossed it into the truck's open bed. "I owe you one, Dooley," he said.

"Glad I could help." Dooley rubbed the axle grease from his hands, then pulled a Marlboro Red from his shirt pocket, flicked a match with his thumbnail, and blew a thin stream of smoke into the still night air. He hardly ever indulged anymore now that Ruth had declared the house off limits.

"I'll follow you home," Cal told him, then only half in jest added, "Guess I'd better put on my flak jacket just in case Ruthie's still up."

"I figured you'd be going back to Ellie's for the night."

"Yeah?" Cal's laugh had a brittle edge, a bitter twist. "Then you must figure I'm at least half the man I used to be, bro. Or that I'm willing to have my sister riding my ass from dawn to dusk for the next couple of weeks."

Dooley took a deep drag from his smoke and gave Cal a long, hard look as he exhaled. "You worry too much about what your sister thinks," he said quietly. "You're better, Cal. Especially in the last few days. I can see that. Can't you?"

The question took him completely by surprise, so much so that Cal found himself taking a few steps back to lean his hip against the front fender of the T-bird. Better? Was he? He crossed his arms, looked up at the starlit sky a moment, then fixed his gaze on the tall, lanky man he'd known so long.

What was Dooley trying to tell him? Just like names and parking-lot colors, Cal feared the subtleties of language still eluded him. "What are you trying to say, Dooley?" he asked.

"Hell, Cal, what I'm saying is you don't need Ruthie and me the way you did when you first came home. You were in pretty bad shape then, and not thinking all that clearly. After that, you started drowning your troubles in booze the same way your old man did. Can't say as I blame you much, either. You were scaring the bejesus out of your sister, I can tell you that. But you've come around. You're better. More like your old self. At least that's how I see it."

"Maybe you're right, Dooley. I don't know. The thing is . . ." Cal's throat constricted. He had to force his words past his closed throat, past his ingrained reluctance to discuss such things, especially with another man. "The thing is I'll probably never be the same as I was."

"Yeah, well . . ." After a last pull on the filter, Dooley dropped the cigarette and ground it under his boot heel. "There are probably some benefits along with the drawbacks of not being your former self. It's not like you didn't make any mistakes, Cal. I'm talking about your personal life now. About Diana."

"Diana." The name sounded more like a curse when Cal said it.

"Well, anyway," Dooley squinted at his watch. "It's getting late. I told Ruthie I'd be home in an hour. You do what you want. For better or worse, you gotta start trusting your own judgment again."

"Dooley," Cal said as his brother-in-law angled into the pickup's driver's seat. "Thanks. For the tow. For everything."

"You bet." His sandy mustache curved up in a grin. "G'night."

♥

Starting up the fire escape, balancing two cold, wet bottles of Perrier from Ramon's and with a pocket full of condoms, Cal's confidence suffered a brief but not fatal setback. He wasn't so sure about his judgment anymore. But after Dooley had driven away, he'd thought long and hard about everything his brother-in-law had said, and had decided that maybe he was right. He *was* better.

He'd spent so long feeling sorry for himself that he'd completely overlooked the fact that he'd improved spectacularly in the past nine months. He'd spent so much time mourning his losses that he forgot to focus on what he'd accomplished since being shot. The worst part hadn't been the physical pain, or even the shame of finding himself abandoned by his wife. It had been the loss of control. In the blink of an eye, with the speed of a bullet, he'd gone from a man in total control of people and events to one who couldn't control anything, including his bowels.

He remembered wanting to die those first few weeks, but not even having enough control to accomplish that. The best he could manage was to pull out IVs, and then they'd restrained him and he couldn't even do that.

But he *was* better, dammit. Dooley had said so, and Dooley Reese wouldn't bullshit him about something so important.

Still, he wasn't perfect. Well, he never had been, except maybe the split second he lunged in front of the president. But he was *better.* A lot better than he was even a month ago. And, by God, tomorrow he'd be better than today. Next week he'd be better than that. Come September, when his medical leave was up, maybe he'd even be back one hundred percent. Well, perfection was probably a stretch. He'd settle for ninety percent.

In the meantime, there was Miss Holly Hicks, whose reprieve was over.

Starting now.

When had he ever run away from a woman he wanted? When had he ever wanted a woman more?

At the top of the fire escape, blissfully free of dizziness, almost free of doubt, he tapped a bottle softly against the door.

♥

Holly had leapt out of bed at the first footfall on the fire escape. For want of a .357 Magnum or a machete, she'd grabbed the heaviest thing she could find—Mel's laptop—and positioned herself just behind the little unlocked door. When she recognized Cal's voice, she didn't know whether to be relieved or furious.

"Cal? What the fuck are you doing out there? You scared me to death."

"Sorry. Can I come in?"

"No," she snapped.

"Holly . . ."

"Oh, just a minute. I'll come out."

She set the laptop down, slipped into the panties she'd slipped out of earlier, gave her oversized tee a tug to make sure it covered everything essential, and opened the door. When Cal edged forward, she planted a firm hand on his chest.

"I'll come out," she said again.

"Chicken."

"You got that right," she muttered, easing one leg and then the other over the threshold of the door. "What are you doing out here?" she asked, settling next to him on the fire escape's landing.

"I brought you a Perrier," he said, twisting the cap off a bottle, then handing it to her.

"Just what I wanted at three in the morning." Actually the cold water tasted wonderful when she took a swig. It was still hot as hell outside, and the iron grating of the fire escape felt as if she were perched on a barbeque.

She reached down to pull her tee discreetly over her knees. Cal, she noticed, was still in his gray suit, only he'd lost his jacket somewhere along the way, the top two buttons of his shirt were undone, and his tie hung loosely around his neck. His trousers were spattered with dried mud from the spinning wheels of the T-bird. His shoes were a mess, their shine long gone.

As for his face, there was a little shaving nick she hadn't noticed earlier. The creases around his eyes seemed to have deepened in the past few hours, and the way the moonlight slanted, she could actually see the small depression in his skull, just at the hairline. Her hero. He looked so tattered, so vulnerable that she wanted to wrap her arms around him and never let go, to keep him warm and safe, which seemed a strange reaction considering that Cal was the one in the protection business.

"I'm glad you came back," she said, tilting her head against his shoulder.

"Are you?" His voice was soft. As soft as the touch of his fingers threading through her hair.

"Yes."

"This is the right time, Holly. The right place. For us," he said. "Here. Now."

"Yes." She closed her eyes and sighed. "I should probably warn you, though. I'm not very good at this, Cal. I . . ."

"Ssh," he whispered, tilting her face up for his kiss. "I am."

Chapter Fourteen

Slower," Cal cautioned himself, as much as he was capable of thinking just then with Holly's hot and supple body beneath his. "Slower, God dammit."

He wanted this moment—this rocket ride, these fireworks—to go on forever. Not just for her sake, so he could take her over the edge, but for his own sake. It had never been like this before. Never this hot, this sweet, this feeling of being turned inside out and upside down and the boundaries between his body and hers obliterated as if they'd melted and reformed as a single being.

Ah, God.

She shuddered beneath him, cried out, clenching him with her calves across the small of his back and his buttocks, urging him deeper inside her until his whole body surged and he exploded from the soles of his feet to the top of his head.

His heart nearly stopped, and for a second he nearly thought he was dead. Jesus. What a way to go! He smiled in the damp crook of Holly's neck.

"My God." Her voice was half sigh, wholly sated. "I have never in my life . . . Well . . . my God."

That pretty much summed it up for Cal, too. He rolled

onto his side, pulling her against him, smoothing his hand
over her hair, her arm, her sleek flank. It occurred to him,
through the post-coital haze in his brain, a haze much more
pleasant than his usual post-operative haze, that he ought to
say something special, something poetic maybe. His Holly
was a writer, after all. She'd expect him to say something
more than just good night. But she spoke before he could
think of anything halfway intelligent.

"You were right," Holly whispered sleepily, drawing his
arms more closely around her and snugging her warm little
butt into his groin.

"About what?"

"You are good, Calvin Griffin. You are very, very good."

Thank God, he thought. It had been so long and he'd been
clumsy getting out of his shorts. Then he'd been too fast, a
little too rough before he'd found her pace, her particular
pleasures. Then there was the awkward pause for protection.
But after that, he'd improved considerably.

"Good enough for government work," he murmured, his
lips exploring the soft flesh of her shoulder. "And, Holly,
darlin' Holly, you're no slouch yourself."

♥

It was well after nine when Holly awoke the next morning. Out of habit, she looked at the clock first before she
turned to the other side of the bed only to find it empty. She
had a dim recollection of a deep kiss, a slow caress, and the
words *workout* and *track*. Cal was gone, and she wasn't sure
whether she was relieved or disappointed. After last night,
she didn't know what she was sure about anymore. Well,
except for being sure that she ached almost deliciously in
places she didn't know it was possible to ache. Her buns

even ached. How was that possible? She felt as if she'd run a marathon yesterday, or more specifically last night. Twice!

She stretched, feeling the aftereffects of lovemaking in every tendon and muscle, taking almost sinful pleasure in the rumpled, untucked covers and the flung-around pillows. She flopped on her stomach, burying her nose deep in the pillowcase, breathing in Cal's distinctive scent, wanting him again, wanton and unethical as it was.

There had never been a morning when she'd lingered in bed, revisiting every moment, every whisper and shiver and touch of the night before. Sex, in her hardly vast experience, tended to be more about hooking up than getting hooked. It had been pretty much a take it or leave it deal. More leave it than take it, actually. Nice sometimes, yet unmemorable. But this . . . !

Holly turned and gazed from bloom to bloom on the wall, studying the pattern's repeat, how the petals and leaves and thorns all fit together again and again, wondering how Cal Griffin fit into her life. He was . . . what?

Unprecedented!

It was the best and the safest description she could come up with at the moment. Anything else would be way too scary to contemplate.

♥

After a long, hot shower, and fortified with a second mug of strong coffee, Holly sat on Ellie's patio where the shade of the big sycamore was already a necessity. God, it was hot. She wished she'd packed a few pairs of shorts or a loose cotton skirt instead of an entire wardrobe of jeans.

Across from her, her hostess was wearing about sixteen yards of pink seersucker that zipped up the front. Her long gray hair was done in a single braid this morning. Ellie lifted it off her shoulder and heaved it over her back.

"Gonna be another scorcher," she said, gazing up through the sycamore's big leathery leaves.

"Ha. What else is new?"

Holly hadn't meant to snort or to sound quite so sour. The weather wasn't Ellie's fault, after all. Hell, Manhattan could be just as miserable as Texas in July and August. Who was she kidding, though? It wasn't the weather that was bothering her. And right now Ellie Young was eying her as if she were about to offer an opinion—a blunt one—about Holly's apparent discontent.

"How're things with you and Cal?" the big woman asked.

"Fine," Holly shot back, vowing that if the next words out of Ellie's mouth were *I know it's none of my business, but* . . . she was going to deck the woman, to wrestle her down to the flagstones despite the difference in their weights.

But Ellie didn't reply, other than to let her lips curve in a rather omniscient and thoroughly irritating fashion. What was she anyway? The Oracle of Honeycomb? The great seer of the Lone Star State? Just what did she think was going on between her and Cal? And—oh, God—just how much noise had they made last night?

"I've got a lot of work to do in the next few days," Holly said, forcing herself to get back on track. "Anybody else you think I ought to interview? What about one of Cal's teachers? Maybe there's a minister who knew him or his family fairly well?"

Ellie's all-knowing grin turned into a laugh. "No Griffin ever darkened a church doorway to my recollection except to get married or buried."

"What about a teacher?"

"That would be Verbena Glover. She taught history and

social studies before she retired a couple of years ago. I put her on that list I gave you, didn't I?"

Holly shook her head. "I don't think so. That's not a name I'd easily forget. Do you think she'd agree to see me? Does she live within walking distance?"

"Not hardly, but I don't have any plans for the rest of the day. I'll take you wherever. Shoot. I owe Miz Glover a visit anyway. It's been a while."

Ellie drained her coffee mug, then stood. "You just let me know when you're ready, Holly honey. We'll make a day of it."

"Thanks. I'd appreciate that." She'd already made quite a night of it. Why not a day, too?

As it turned out, the day was as productive as it was pleasant. Ellie traded her sixteen yards of pink seersucker for half an acre of denim, shoehorned herself behind the wheel of her World War II vintage jeep, and proceeded to tear around the streets of Honeycomb where she managed to slam on her brakes, yell howdy, and introduce Holly to every person who'd ever crossed paths with Cal Griffin or any member of his family.

There was Dave Wexler at the body shop, a former classmate of Cal's who had fond memories of a '71 Datsun that Calvin Griffin, Sr. once put through the rear wall of a car wash. "Cal never cracked up a car, though," Dave told her. "He was always careful, if he wasn't just plain lucky. 'Course, not so much anymore, I guess."

There was Coach Jimmy Joe Holt, now retired to his front porch, who was apparently still smarting after all these years for not convincing Cal to play halfback for the Yellow Jackets. "He favored track and field," the coach said, "prob'ly so's he didn't have to depend on the abilities of others. Cal was like that. Independent. Unto himself, so to speak. That's always been my theory, anyway."

Ethel Johnson had warm memories of Cal's mother's pineapple upside down cake. Mavis Moore still had the mint green bridesmaid's dress she'd worn in Ruth and Dooley's wedding. Edna Gore, who used to work in the high-school cafeteria, remembered that Cal had what she called a powerful affection for tapioca.

Holly met just about everybody in town she didn't know before. The men all swiped off their Stetsons and offered callused hands. The women usually wound up hugging her and inviting her for Sunday dinner. By four o'clock that afternoon, Holly's face ached from smiling, her head was swimming, her notebook was nearly full, and she'd used her last cassette, but she wasn't one bit closer to pinning down her hero.

Worst of all, every time Ellie gunned the jeep down Main Street, Holly couldn't help but catch a glimpse of Cal's T-bird by the track at the high school. He was there longer than usual today, it seemed, but no matter how hard she craned her neck or squinted, she never saw him or his faithful sidekick, Bee. Worried about him—okay, more longing to see him than actually worried—she was just about to ask Ellie to swing by the high school when her denim-clad chauffeur announced, "Now we'll head on out to Happy Acres to see Verbena."

"Happy Acres?" Holly echoed.

"Hell of a name for a rest home, isn't it?" Ellie snorted and pressed her boot on the gas pedal. "We best be quick. They eat supper out there around five."

"Ellie, wait."

The big woman hit the brakes and turned toward her passenger. "What?"

"Well . . ." Holly was ashamed to admit that right this minute she was far more interested in seeing her hero in the flesh than in gathering more data about his past. "You know, I've got so much new information already I hardly know how to organize it. Maybe we could just put Verbena on the back burner for a while, at least until I know just what I want to ask her. Would you mind, Ellie?"

She raised her big denim shoulders in a shrug. "It's your show, honey. You know what you need. I might just zip on out to Happy Acres by myself to pay the old gal a visit."

"Sure." Holly recognized a perfect exit when she saw one. She grabbed up her handbag and reached for the door handle. "Hey, I'll just wander around town a little while and scout some shooting locations. I've been meaning to do that anyway. Scout. You know. Locations. For my story."

"Uh-huh." As she nodded her head, Ellie's gaze seemed to drift in the direction of the high school and her mouth slowly took on that inscrutable curve Holly had witnessed earlier. "You go *scout*, honey. I'll see you later."

"Right." Holly jumped out of the jeep and slammed the door. "Thanks, Ellie."

"You're welcome," she said. Then from half a block away, she waved and called back, "Tell Cal I said howdy, will you?"

Was she that transparent? Holly wondered. Did she have *Crazy for Cal* etched on her forehead? Had she lost all sense of herself as a professional? Apparently so, she decided, when she caught sight of her hero in the distance and her heart immediately vaulted up into her throat.

Holly started for the high school, telling herself it wasn't so unprofessional to want to know the subject of her assignment as well as she possibly could, to explore all the subtle nuances of his personality—forget about his body—any one of which might possibly be the key to his character, the perfect hook on which to hang her story.

She cut through the vacant lot next to the bank, eyes locked on her prize, trying to formulate the single question that would evoke the quintessential response, illuminating the essential Calvin Griffin, Jr. The Who and the Why of him.

She wished she were wearing her navy pinstripe suit with the eggshell silk blouse and the navy pumps that had cost her half a month's salary. She wished she looked like a journalist, like a producer with only one thing on her mind—her story—instead of some jean-clad groupie in battered sneakers whose thoughts kept straying from the Who and the Why of Cal Griffin to the What of him. The whiskery roughness of his jaw. The slickness of his hot skin beneath that gray sweatshirt. The way the supple flesh cushioned the hard muscles of his back and his abdomen. The soft sprinkling of hair there and how it flourished at his beltline and then arrowed down . . .

Jesus. Holly dragged in a breath. She was too young to be having a hot flash, wasn't she?

Halting in the middle of the vacant lot, she pulled a wad of tissues from her handbag and proceeded to mop her neck, then fan herself. This probably wasn't a good time to try to explore either the psyche or the physique of her hero, she thought. She ought to head back to Ellie's and take an ice-cold shower. Cal wouldn't want to be interrupted during his workout, anyway.

Just then she saw him stumble and go spilling forward. Bee, who'd been loping along beside him, scrambled out of his way just before Cal went down, sprawling face-first on the hard surface of the track. Holly gasped and started running toward him, but all of a sudden she stopped, battling her natural instinct to "get the story" as well as fighting the need to rush to help Cal if he were injured. Something told her this was none of her business. Something cautioned her that Cal's privacy right now far outweighed any need she had to know or any assistance she could provide him.

So she stayed where she was and watched, relieved when she finally saw him sit up and sling his legs out in front of him, rubbing his left knee. Nothing appeared to be broken. Thank God he seemed okay. Scraped a little maybe, judging from the way he wiped his hands on his pants, but not seriously scathed.

Bee, too, appeared relieved that his running companion was unhurt. He wagged his tail and nudged his wet nose into Cal's neck. Then, as Holly watched, Cal leaned forward, draped both his arms around the dog, pulled him close, and buried his face in Bee's black fur. From the way Cal's shoulders shook, she thought he might be crying.

Oh, God. Was he? Crying?

Holly's heart held still as her own eyes filmed with tears.

She remembered what Dooley Reese had said to her the other day. She could almost hear him now. *You talk to enough people around town and you'll find out soon enough that the only person who thinks Cal's still got a future in the Secret Service is Cal himself.*

Oh, God. That wasn't true. Cal did know. Better than anyone, Cal knew. And right now his discouragement was almost palpable. Holly could hardly breathe for wanting to put her arms around him and make everything okay.

She watched him struggle to his knees and then, with Bee as a brace, to stand, to shift his shoulders and hips for a minute as if seeking a position free of pain, and then to start forward again, slowly, oh so slowly, his hobble eventually giving way to an awkward jog, then finally stretching into a determined, if graceless, run.

And suddenly, quite unexpectedly, Holly had her hook. It all but slapped her in the face.

Cal Griffin's story wasn't about other people's perceptions of him. It wasn't about whether people in his hometown thought the man was meant to be a hero from the get-go or if they figured he'd never amount to that proverbial hill of beans. His story—his true heroism—was less about doing his job than it was about his monumental effort to return to that job. His heroism had nothing to do with his training or the alertness of his senses or the reflexes of his body that allowed him to take a bullet for another man once, but had everything to do with his courage and willingness to do it again.

The story wasn't so much about what Cal had done in the past, but what he was doing now. Right now. Her piece would open with the scene that was unfolding before her on the hard track, under a relentless sun, in the punishing Texas heat.

A hero in gray sweats, going the distance, refusing to give up.

Chapter Fifteen

What time's your flight?" Cal asked.

"I told you," Holly answered sleepily, almost reflexively.

He sighed into her hair, nudging his knees more deeply into the backs of hers. "Tell me again." He thought she'd said nine-thirty, which would mean they'd have to leave for Houston at five, but he wasn't sure. No surprise there.

"Nine-thirty," she said with a sigh of her own. "Too soon. I don't even want to think about it."

No. Neither did he, but he had to since he couldn't write it down. There was better, and then there was better.

He wished he could stop time. He wished that the doors and windows of this botanical nightmare of a room were hermetically sealed for the next fifty or sixty years, even longer, centuries maybe, and that archeologists would find their bones—his and Holly's—just like this, all wrapped up together, in the year 2500.

He'd never been so happy or so sad all at the same time. He'd never felt so good or so lousy. It was like straddling a fucking barbed-wire fence. Tomorrow at this time Holly would be gone. She struck him as far too happy about getting back to New York.

"Tell me again when you're coming back," he said, hoping he hadn't asked more than half a dozen times in the past few days.

"Next month. Over the Fourth of July. I'm not quite sure which exact day."

"Well, let me know. I'll pick you up at the airport."

"You won't have to. I'll be coming back with my crew, so we'll just rent a van or an RV or something, and drive on down."

"A crew," he muttered. "I keep forgetting about this TV deal. This hero crap."

She jutted her backside into him. "Don't say that. It's going to be really good, Cal. Just wait and see. I've got some terrific ideas."

"I've got a terrific idea," he said, sliding a hand up her flank, over her ribcage, and finding the warm weight of her breast.

"Mmm." A little murmur of pleasure sounded deep in her throat. "That's nice."

"Yeah?" With the flat of his palm, he teased her nipple to attention. "And this?"

"That's even nicer." She moaned. "Oh, God. I don't want to go." She turned within the circle of his arms. There was just enough light to see the sheen in her eyes as they met his. "Love me again," she whispered. "Like the last time."

He smiled, pleased that he had pleased her, made her come, *felt* her come not once but twice. Any awkwardness between them had long since disappeared. He'd learned her body by heart in the past few days as she had learned his. And if he wasn't quite the athlete, sexual or otherwise, that he'd been a year ago, it didn't seem to matter. Along with a good dose of humility these past nine months, he seemed to have learned a patience that served him well in bed.

"Like this?" His lips trailed a stream of kisses from her collarbone to her breasts, from her navel to the nest of soft strawberry blonde hair between her legs, to the soft warm lushness there. "Here?"

"Mmm."

"Or *here*?"

"Oh, God. Yes."

♥

Holly drove the first leg to Houston early the next morning. There was hardly any traffic on the highway for which she was hugely grateful, since she hadn't been behind the wheel of a car since moving to Manhattan three years ago. It was true what they said, though. It was like riding a bike. After only a minute or two she and the T-bird were one, whizzing down the road at sixty-five miles an hour while Cal took what he sheepishly referred to as a "power nap" in the passenger seat.

Poor baby. He hadn't gotten a lot of sleep in the last four nights, had he? Well, she hadn't either, but she was so jazzed by their lovemaking that she barely needed to eat, let alone sleep. Just breathing in Cal's wonderful and exotically masculine scent every night in bed seemed enough to sustain her.

She'd spent her final days in Honeycomb traipsing around town, taking photographs, gathering facts, interviewing new people and re-interviewing old ones, hanging out in the ratty little park while she watched the temperature climb to triple digits on the bank's sign and waited for Cal to end his relentless, nearly religious workouts so their night could begin.

Up the rickety fire escape, in the big walnut bed in the rose-papered room, they weren't even in Texas anymore. It was as if they created their own separate country while making sweet, incredible, explosive love. It was as if they created their own universe.

Holy moly. Talk about your Big Bang theory.

She wouldn't have predicted this, not in a million years. She'd tried to tell herself that her obsession with this man was merely fallout from her job, that as the producer of his biography it was only natural that she eat, sleep, and breathe Calvin Griffin—literally! Whenever she started imagining it might be more, she changed the course of her thoughts and turned them back to her job and the dreams that had sustained her for so many years.

That was precisely what she did just then, even as she held the speeding T-bird to the right of the centerline of the ruler-straight highway. Holly changed the course of her thoughts, turned them east where they belonged, where *she* belonged.

♥

They held hands walking through the airport, only letting go long enough for Holly to wend her way through security. Cal was waiting for her on the other side. He took her hand again as they made their way to the gate.

"Seems like I just got here," she said a bit wistfully.

"Not to me."

Glum. God, he sounded as if the world were about to end, and for a second Holly felt that way, too. Only she made herself feel otherwise. The world didn't end in Texas. Texas was where you left in order for the world to begin.

"I'll be back in four weeks," she said. "They'll go fast. You'll see."

"Not fast enough."

They announced her flight over the public address system

and Cal looped the strap of the laptop over her shoulder while Holly reached into her handbag for her boarding pass.

"Oh, damn," she muttered. "Nuts."

"What?"

"I forgot to pay Ellie for my final day." She pulled out her wallet, riffled through the bill compartment where there were just two singles, a fifty, and her last crisp hundred-dollar bill which she was going to need for the taxi from Newark to midtown. She slid the fifty out and said, "Would you give this to her, Cal? I owe her more, but tell her I'll make up the difference in July."

"Sure." He stuffed the bill in his pocket, then drew her into his arms. "Holly, Holly," he whispered.

Don't say anything more, she thought. *I couldn't bear it.*
"I'll miss you, Cal."

"I'll miss you, too, baby. Holly, I . . ."

Let me go. Let me go. Let me go.

She pulled back just as the gate attendant touched her shoulder and said, "We're ready to close the door, Miss."

"I'll call you," she said, and then ran without looking back.

Inside the crowded plane, she found her seat and fell into it with a muted curse. Her seatmate, a man in his thirties in a pinstripe suit, rimless glasses, and slicked-back hair leaned toward her.

"How's it goin'?" he asked in pure, unadulterated Brooklynese.

"Oh. Fine," Holly said. "Just peachy."

He leaned a little closer, angled his head toward the window and said, "Fuckin' Texas, huh?"

All Holly could do was weep.

♥

Cal stopped by Ellie's before he went over to the track, and he sat in the shade of the big oaks and sycamores along her driveway for a good while, just thinking, as if he hadn't had plenty of time to think on the way back from Houston.

Okay. So he'd parked on Green at the airport and hadn't even had to write it down in order to find the car again. His head was working well enough that he'd remembered to bring the fifty bucks to Ellie without tying a string around his finger. He was definitely better, but being better wasn't much consolation at the moment. And why was he so goddamned surprised and disappointed that his Holly had practically sprinted down the jetway for the plane to New York?

She hated Texas. She'd told him often enough. She'd had a miserable childhood, being taunted if not directly punished for her dreams and ambitions by classmates as well as her own parents. She'd left the state behind her with no regrets, and she'd only returned—reluctantly, it seemed—because of the opportunity to produce his story. Holly loved New York with a passion she probably didn't feel for anyplace else. Or any*one* else.

Well, hell. He didn't blame her. He wasn't all that crazy about his native state, either. If he hadn't been shot, he wouldn't even be here right now himself. She could've asked him to go to New York with her, couldn't she? What did he have but time on his hands these days. It wasn't as if he was working or anything for the next four weeks. But she hadn't asked him, had she? Not that he needed a fucking engraved invitation . . .

"Are you gonna sit out here all day?" Ellie called to him as she stomped down her front steps. "I've been watching you from the front window, thinking you'd be coming up the steps and knocking on the door any minute. Are you all right, Cal? Is anything wrong?"

"No, nothing's wrong, Ellie. Nothing at all. I'm fine. In fact, I'm doing great." *Yeah, right.*

Cal wrenched open his door and got out of the car. "I just stopped by because Holly forgot to give you this." He reached into his pocket for the fifty. "She said to tell you she'd square up when she comes back next month."

"Oh, that sweet thing." Ellie gave a dismissive wave of her hand. "I'm not worried about it."

"Here you go." Cal glanced at the bill just as it passed from his hand to Ellie's. Wait. What the hell? "Wait a minute, Ellie. Let me take a look at that, will you?"

"Sure." She gave it back. "Something the matter with it?"

He squinted in the bright noon sunshine. Damned if old Ulysses didn't look just a tad off kilter on the torn and washed-out bill. Hadn't somebody asked him to check out a fifty just like this sometime this past week? Who was that? Where the hell was it? Not the Longhorn, he was sure. Not El Mariachi. No. Who was it? Where else had he been? And then he remembered. It was Ramon. He wondered how the same limp bill had progressed from the tavern's cash drawer to Holly Hicks' purse. Not that it was impossible, but still . . .

"Listen, Ellie." Cal pried his wallet out of the back pocket of his jeans. "If you don't mind, I'm going to replace that with these." He pulled out two twenties and a ten, then handed them to her.

"No, I don't mind one little bit." She laughed, looked at the money, then back at Cal. "You don't think Holly's trying to pass funny money, do you?"

"Nah. I just thought I'd take this old thing out of circulation." He held the fifty up to the light before he stuck it in his wallet. "It's just part of the job. I do it all the time."

"Oh," she said, sounding surprised. "Well, isn't that interesting? I didn't realize you Secret Service folk did things like that, Cal. Live and learn, I guess."

"Live and learn, Ellie." He leaned forward and kissed the top of her gray head before he slid back into the driver's seat.

"You take care now. And don't be a stranger now that Holly's gone. You remember about that yearbook party coming up Sunday."

"I remember," he said even though he didn't have the slightest intention of attending that gabfest without Holly by his side. "See you later, Ellie."

He was headed for Ramon's. Before he twisted the key in the ignition, Cal looked at his watch. It was a little before one, which meant it was almost two in New York. His Holly was probably somewhere between Newark and her office in Manhattan, smiling no doubt, thrilled to be back home in the Big Apple, tickled to death to be anywhere but here.

♥

It was overcast when she landed in Newark, but by the time Holly's taxi pulled up in front of the Media Arts Building, a light rain had begun to fall. Holly checked the meter up in front, computed a handsome tip, and handed her hundred-dollar bill over the seatback to the cabbie.

"Give me thirty-five back, please, Sol." She'd read the man's name on the posted permit. Sol Majerowicz. Ordinarily she never addressed a cabbie by his first name, but today she felt friendly. More than friendly, she felt magnanimous, so much so that she hadn't even complained about the nasty, soggy cigar he kept in one corner of his mouth and re-lit every five minutes. She merely wrote it off to getting reacquainted with the fragrance of New York.

Sol snatched the hundred, swore out of the unoccupied corner of his mouth, then shoved a key into the glove box and pulled out a beat-up accordion file. "What's with the C notes? My last two fares gave me big bills," he said, peering into the file. "All I can give you is a twenty, lady, and, uh, one, two, three singles."

What? Sol was trying to gouge out a bigger tip by claiming he couldn't make change? Did he think she just fell off a turnip truck at the Newark airport? Well . . . Holly looked down at her jeans and the T-shirt she'd bought as a silly souvenir of the Longhorn Café. She rolled her eyes.

"Maybe you should check the cigar box stashed under your seat," she suggested.

Sol shrugged. "You can take this twenty-three bucks, lady," he said, waving them over his shoulder, "or I can put you back on the meter and take you someplace to get change. What'll it be?"

What'll it be? What'll it *be*? Oh, God. All she could do was laugh as she grabbed the bills and shoved them in her handbag. She couldn't have fashioned a more appropriate welcome to the big city than this.

While she struggled out of the taxi with her handbag and laptop, Sol plopped her suitcase and carry-on at the curb, then beat it back into his vehicle before she could ask him to take the bags to the door. "Schmuck," she muttered under her breath.

Holly stood there in the rain a minute, debating whether or not to leave her heavy suitcase at the curb while she carried everything else inside the lobby. If this were Honeycomb, she could leave her suitcase on the sidewalk all day and nobody would think a thing of it. Here, if it wasn't stolen by the time she got back to it, somebody would have called the cops to report a nuclear device.

She picked up the carry-on and nudged the big suitcase forward with her knee, a few inches at a time.

"Watch it, lady."

"Jesus H. Christ."

"Some people! Sheesh!"

Six men entered the Media Arts building while she was negotiating her way across the sidewalk, one of them just a foot ahead of her.

"That's okay," Holly muttered under her breath, grabbing the door as it was closing. "No. Don't hold the door. I can manage."

Inside the lobby, she cast a baleful glance at the brass elevator doors, then she sat on her suitcase, took out her cell phone, and called Mel upstairs.

"Hey, kid, welcome back. You *are* back, right?" he asked.

"Sort of," Holly said, leaning to her left to avoid losing an eye to a passing umbrella.

"Where are you?" Mel shouted. "This is a lousy connection."

"I'm down in the lobby. Could you send Sammy or somebody down to help with my luggage?"

"Who?"

"Sammy. Anybody."

"Sammy quit yesterday. The ungrateful jerk. What do you want with Sammy, anyway?"

"Never mind, Mel. I'll be up in a minute." Holly sighed, dropped her cell phone back in her purse, and stood up.

Yee-hah.

♥

Ramon's didn't just look dark this afternoon. The place looked downright dank and sleazy to Cal as he settled on a stool at the bar. Funny how a steady diet of Dr. Heineken could alter a person's perceptions, he thought.

Young Rick with his ponytail and pierced ears was on duty today, and Cal stopped him as the young bartender automatically reached for a green bottle.

"Give me a club soda, will you, kid?"

"'Scuse me?"

"I said let me have a club soda. Lots of ice."

The boy actually blinked, which didn't do a whole hell of a lot for Cal's self esteem. "You want a club soda? Seltzer, you mean?"

"Yeah. That's what I mean."

"Oh. Okay. Sure. With a shot of Johnnie Walker or what?"

Cal sighed. "Just the soda."

After Rick poured it and set the glass in front of him, Cal asked, "You know anything about a suspicious fifty-dollar bill that Ramon had last week?"

"Sure. That's practically all he talked about."

"Did he take it over to the bank?"

Rick shook his head. "I don't think so." He punched open the cash drawer. "Seems to me it's still in here. Yeah. Right here under the tray."

Cal held out his hand. "Let me take a look at it, will you?"

"Sure. You think it's a phoney?"

"Nah. I just want to see it again. You don't see too many bills in that condition. Like it's been through the wringer and back."

The kid slid it across the bar and Cal picked it up. Through the wringer. Hell. This sucker looked like it had gone down on the *Titanic*. He turned it over, studying Grant's face. The old guy didn't look all that bright-eyed this afternoon. He'd been hoping that the bill Holly had given him was the same one Ramon had shown him, that there was just a single funny fifty floating around town, in which case he would have just put it away until he got back to Washington this fall.

But now there were two, dammit. He couldn't ignore a pair of bogus bills.

"So, Ramon doesn't remember how he got this?" he asked Rick.

The kid shook his head.

Cal put Holly's fifty next to Ramon's on the bartop and stared at them while he finished off his drink. Twins. Identical twins. The serial numbers were even the same. Shit.

He'd been hoping for something to make him forget about Holly twenty-four hours a day, but this wasn't exactly what he meant in the way of a distraction.

"Tell Ramon I'm borrowing this," he said, putting both bills in his wallet. Standard operating procedure called for bagging them, but it was a little late in the game for prints and he wasn't even sure what his status was as an investigator while he was on medical leave.

"Borrowing it? Hey, I dunno, man. He's not going to like that," Rick said.

"Yeah, well, I'm not crazy about it myself, kid."

♥

Mel was going to be tied up in a production meeting until four o'clock, so Holly settled in at her desk where she found a good-sized stack of pink while-you-were-out messages in addition to a week's worth of mail and eighty-seven email messages on her computer. She felt as if she'd been gone a month rather than just a week. And somebody—probably that jerk Sammy—had left a half-filled coffee cup on top of her calendar and spilled Sweet 'n Low all over her keyboard.

Not quite ready to dive back into work, Holly took the rank coffee cup to the ladies' room, where she flushed the moldering dregs and then washed the cup with hot water. While she was rinsing it, Maria Bianchi from research came in to freshen her makeup.

"Hey, Holly. When did you get back?"

"Just a few minutes ago," Holly said.

"You were where?" Maria leaned toward the mirror over the sink and studied her bronzed eyelids. "Arizona? Oklahoma?"

"Texas."

"Ha. Same difference," the researcher said as she reached into her handbag and came up with a tube of mascara. "So, how was it?"

"Oh, fine. Nice, actually." There wasn't a shred of sarcasm in her tone, but Maria seemed to hear otherwise.

"Yeah. I'll bet." While she stroked more black gloss on her lashes, her gaze strayed to Holly in the mirror. "What's that say? On your shirt. The Lohengrin Café?"

"Longhorn. The Longhorn Café."

"Gawd," Maria moaned. "You must really be glad to be back."

Not as glad as I thought I'd be, Holly almost said. She gave the coffee cup a final swipe with a paper towel. "Well, I better get back to my desk. There's a week's work waiting for me."

"I noticed. I put a copy of that pool tape you wanted, the one of the assassination attempt, right by your phone. Did you see it?"

"No. I'll go take a look. Thanks, Maria."

"Sure." She managed to talk at the same time she was dragging lipstick across her lower lip. "I'm still trying to come up with some more footage for you. There was a guy there with a video cam but he's jerking everybody around over the price. If CNN comes up with it in the next week or two, maybe I can get you a sneak peek. I'll let you know."

"Great. Thanks."

When Holly got back to her desk, she saw the tape right where Maria said it was, next to her phone. Other than the film from the private citizen's video cam, this pool tape was the only visual record of that day in Baltimore. A cameraman from CBS had been on duty then for what was supposed to be an uneventful afternoon. Then Thomas Earl Starks and his M-16 had changed all that.

Holly sat down and just stared at the black rectangular box. She'd seen the footage dozens, maybe even hundreds of time. It was practically all any station showed for a couple weeks last September in the media's typical overkill of a big story. She'd watched it almost clinically, wishing the cameraman had been just a little closer, that he'd remained standing throughout the incident instead of hitting the pavement like everybody else in the line of fire.

Except for Cal, of course.

Oh, God. All of a sudden she could hardly breathe. How was she going to be able to watch the man she loved get shot again and again? It would kill her. It would be like taking a bullet herself. It would . . .

Whoa, Nellie. Where did that come from? The man she loved? Had those words actually passed through her brain?

The man she loved. Holly tried out the thought once more. It made her stomach flip and her mouth kind of slide into a grin she couldn't control and her heart almost tickle inside her ribs. She glanced at her watch, wondering where he was right now, deciding he was at the track with Bee while the sun beat down on him and bounced off the chrome of the T-bird parked nearby. She pictured the stupid roses in her room at Ellie's and the big bed, empty now, maybe freshly made up for another guest.

She wanted to cry, but that was the last thing she should do, so instead she reached for the stack of pink messages. None of them struck her as earth-shattering or in need of immediate replies. Several of them intrigued her.

There were five—no, six!—messages from a Diana Koslov. One of them was written with three names. Diana Koslov Griffin. All of them were marked *Urgent*. That had to be Cal's ex-wife, but why in the world, Holly wondered, would the woman be calling her? And what the hell was so damned urgent? Then, just as she was sitting there, literally scratching her head, the phone on her desk chirped. She answered it with her usual greeting.

"This is Holly Hicks."

"Oh, thank God you're back," a husky voice exclaimed.

Holly didn't recognize it. "May I help you?"

"I hope so, Ms. Hicks. This is Diana Koslov. Well, actually Diana Griffin. I want to talk to you about this biography you're putting together on my husband."

Husband. The word sort of ricocheted inside Holly's head. *Husband.* "Your husband?"

"Yes. That's right. My husband. Cal. Calvin Griffin. I don't suppose you're aware of it. Well, actually hardly anybody knows. Not that it's a great secret or anything."

A husky, sexy, supremely self-confident laugh filtered through the phone. It struck Holly as the way a lioness would laugh. Well, if lionesses laughed.

And then the woman stopped laughing and said quite clearly, "Cal and I are back together."

Chapter Sixteen

It's nice having you back at the dinner table, Cal," Ruth said, setting a final serving bowl on the table before she sat down herself. "I mean that. I really do. Maybe we should open a bottle of wine."

With Holly gone, Cal didn't feel much like celebrating, but then neither did he want to announce his newfound sobriety only to be reminded—at length—of his father's major sins and shortcomings. He gestured toward the tall glass beside his plate. "Iced tea's fine with me, Ruthie."

"Yeah, honey," Dooley said. "I just poured myself this great big glass of milk."

"Oh, all right." Not bothering to hide her disappointment, she helped herself to some rice, and passed the bowl to Cal. "Those are fresh peas in the risotto. From the MacCauleys' garden. Bev brought them over this morning. And here, Cal. Take some broccoli now. There's just butter and lemon juice on it. Nothing fancy or scary."

Actually he liked broccoli, but his sister seemed to have more fun if she thought she was force feeding him veggies, so Cal winced and fidgeted and grimaced a bit as he let a few bright green florets tumble onto his plate, then passed the bowl to Dooley at the other end of the table.

He could almost hear Holly's voice asking him what kind of vegetable he'd want to be. God, he missed her. He didn't even have her phone number, but one call to Washington after dinner would soon remedy that.

Ruth's chicken, with its stuffing of sharp cheese and ham and fresh herbs, practically melted in his mouth. Having lived in Washington so long, and having circled the globe with the president, Cal was no stranger to fine cuisine, and Ruth's cooking ranked among the best he'd ever had. She really should have her own restaurant, he thought, but refrained from saying it out loud for fear of setting her off.

"How is Bev MacCauley?" he asked, not that he cared about their neighbor so much as he felt obliged to add a bit of good conversation to Ruthie's good meal.

"She's fine. Still talks up a storm," Ruth said. "In fact, she told me something pretty interesting this morning. Seems like that Bingham fella—you know, the real estate guy—is snooping around her place, too. He's even been out wandering around Charlie Cutler's place, if you can believe that."

"Well, he can't be too interested in ranching then," Dooley said between bites of chicken. "Ol' Charlie hasn't cleared any brush in the past fifteen or twenty years. It's a damned paradise for javelinas and wild turkeys over there."

Although Cal had been largely focused on Holly's pretty face the day they'd encountered the real estate agent, he suddenly recalled something Bingham's client had mentioned. "They're not looking for ranch land," he said now. "I think they're trying to put together some acreage for a hunting preserve."

"He told you that?" Ruth asked.

"Uh-huh."

"Doesn't surprise me all that much," Dooley said. "They've done that with a couple places over in Kleberg County and down in Kenedy County. Pretty successfully, too. They're importing all kinds of livestock from Africa. Springboks. Nilgai. Hell, even wildebeests, I hear."

"Wildebeests." Ruth snorted.

"Well, honey, people are willing to pay a lot of money to hunt exotic critters, I guess."

A little glimmer of an idea flickered to life in Cal's brain. It was probably stupid and pretty misguided, considering the source, but he decided to mention it anyway. What could it hurt?

"You know, you might want to think about consolidating with the MacCauleys and Charlie Cutler and some others. Why let all those easterners have all the fun and reap all the profits? You could put together your own ten or twelve thousand–acre hunting preserve and still keep enough fenced pasture for Dooley's bulls and the MacCauleys' long-horns."

"You know how I feel about hunting," Ruth said dismissively, putting an effective damper on the discussion.

But at the other end of the table, Cal noticed that Dooley looked a little more contemplative than usual. Maybe he wasn't a complete lame brain. Maybe his idea wasn't such a bad one after all.

♥

It was after nine when Holly finally got home to her apartment. She and Mel had stayed late at the office to go over her ideas for her script and to finalize the shooting locations. In addition to returning to Honeycomb in July, Holly was going to have to visit the site of the assassination

attempt in Baltimore, the Secret Service's headquarters in
Washington and their training facility in Glynco, Georgia.
They decided that would give them plenty of background
footage.

When Mel dropped her off in front of her building on
59th, he had playfully punched her arm and said, "No rest for
the wicked, kid." Holly had searched his face intently then,
wondering if her boss was implying something in "wicked"
above and beyond the usual cliché. Did he mean she was just
going to have to work hard, or could he tell somehow that
she'd broken a cardinal rule of journalism by going to bed
with the subject of her piece? Had the logo on her Longhorn
shirt suddenly transformed itself to proclaim, "I slept with
Cal Griffin and all I got was this lousy T-shirt"?

Cal and I are back together.

She couldn't get that sentence out of her head.

Once inside her apartment, the first thing she did was turn
on the television, not simply to get a much-needed news fix
but to supply herself with some background noise to drown
out Diana Griffin's haunting words.

Cal and I are back together.

And Holly couldn't for the life of her recall how she'd
responded when those words were spoken on the phone. She
was fairly sure she responded vocally, other than just sitting
at her desk feeling gut punched and out of breath and dizzy.

Cal and I are back together.

Surely she'd said something. A startled little "oh" no
doubt, if not an audible gasp. She did remember saying
brusquely to Diana, "I'll have to get back to you" before
slapping the phone back in its cradle.

She turned the TV up another notch before she went to the
refrigerator, where, if the gods had been sympathetic, she'd
have found a Sara Lee coffee cake awaiting her. Instead,

there were three yogurts, two of which had expired, and what was left of the split of champagne she'd bought last week to celebrate her promotion.

Jesus. Was it just a week? It felt more like a month. Shaking her head, Holly reached for the chilled little bottle, plucked out its plastic stopper, and drank the last flat ounce—gack—just before the phone rang.

It was probably Mel, who typically remembered something he'd meant to tell her when he was in the middle of the New Jersey Turnpike. Thank heavens for speed dial. Tonight he was probably calling to clarify exactly what he'd meant by wicked.

"What?" she asked when she picked up the receiver.

"Hey."

Oh, God. It wasn't Mel.

"Hey," she responded. The word sprang from her lips automatically even though Cal was the last person on earth she wanted to talk to right now. She wasn't prepared to be cool and unconcerned, to converse with him as if she'd never even kissed him much less gone to bed with him, to come across as if she weren't angry and hurt, sounding not like *Sleepless in Seattle* but *Wretched in Manhattan, Devastated in New York*.

"How did you get my number?" She asked the very first question that popped into her head. It seemed neutral enough. At least it was better than hanging up.

"Ve haf our vays, liebchen."

Cal was laughing. Laughing! God. How could he laugh? How *could* he when all Holly wanted to do was cry? She was hardly able to breathe, much less talk.

"Just a minute," she told him. "I've got something on the stove."

As if there really were a pot about to boil over, Holly put

the phone down on the bed and walked briskly into the small galley kitchen, where she stood for a moment, motionless, her head a blank and her heart as heavy as a stone. *Don't just stand here. Do something,* she told herself. So she reached down, opened the door of the oven, then let it slam closed. She opened the refrigerator, stood in its cool wash of light a second, then slammed that door closed, as well. She went to the sink, turned on the cold water, and bent forward to slurp from the tap.

None of the frenetic activity helped her know what to say to Cal, though. It wasn't like her to avoid a confrontation. It wasn't her habit to skirt an issue. To skulk. To pussyfoot. Hollis Mae Hicks was not a pussyfooter, by God. She was used to saying exactly what she felt, and she told herself she ought to pick up the phone and do just that.

Cal and I are back together. What do you have to say about that, bub? Care to comment, asshole?

Oh, but just now, just this minute, she couldn't bear to hear one of those knee-jerk male responses. A *What are you talking about?* or an *It's not my fault,* or a *Give me a fucking break, will you?*

Holly stalked back to the bedroom and picked up the phone from the bed, hoping against hope that her caller had grown bored while she was gone and had hung up. She didn't hear a dial tone, but at least he wasn't laughing anymore.

"Still there?" she asked in a tone neither sweet nor sour.

"Still here," he said. "I miss you."

The stone in Holly's heart increased to the size of a boulder, pressing against her lungs, hampering her ability to inhale or exhale properly. *I miss you, too. Oh, God. I'll be missing you the rest of my life.*

"That thing in the kitchen . . ." she said. "I . . . uh . . . I need to get back to it."

He didn't say anything then. To Holly it seemed less an absence of sound than a dark, profound silence—almost palpable across two thousand miles.

"Cal?"

"Yeah, well, listen . . ." Now his voice was brusque and all business. "I don't want to keep you. I just called to ask you a quick question anyway. About that fifty-dollar bill you gave me at the airport. The one for Ellie."

"What about it?" *So you don't really miss me, then? You called to ask about some stupid money?*

"Do you remember where you got it, or maybe remember who gave it to you?"

"No," she answered, hardly bothering to hide her irritation.

"Did you get it at Ramon's?"

"I don't know," she snapped.

"Think. This is important."

Think? Here's what I think, buster! Why did you even bother to say you miss me when it's obvious you don't? And when did you get back with your wife? You should have told me. Damn you, Cal. That was important. Not some fucking fifty-dollar bill.

"Think, Holly," he said again. "Please."

"Oh, all right."

Holly really didn't have to think. She clearly recalled the moment when she got the fifty yesterday in change from Hec Garcia at his print shop after she'd used his Xerox machine to copy Cal's yearbook. She'd handed Hec a crisp hundred and he'd given her the tattered fifty along with a few smaller bills and forty-two cents in change.

"Hec Garcia gave it to me yesterday," she said.

"At his print shop?" Cal asked.

"Yes. I did some copying there. What's the big deal?"

"No big deal."

There was that bottom-of-the-ocean, sunken *Titanic* silence again on the other end of the line, and Holly wondered if he was preparing a confession or framing an apology or working up to an offhand remark about his reconciliation with his wife. If that was the case, she was fairly sure the top of her head was going to explode with anger and the phone was going to melt in her fist.

But all he said was "Well, I'll let you get back to whatever it is you need to get back to."

And then he hung up.

Just like that.

♥

Cal didn't know how long he sat on the pulled-out sofabed with the dead phone in his hand. Long enough for the sun to set and for darkness to creep into each corner of his room. He had no idea what time it was. What difference did it make? All he knew was that he felt like the biggest fool on the planet.

Yeah. Sure. He'd anticipated that Holly would get sucked back into the rat race once she was back in New York. He just hadn't expected it would happen quite so fast. One minute he was kissing her good-bye; the next minute she was kissing him off.

Just like that.

If he hadn't been such a coward, he'd have asked her whose voice he heard in the background and what the hell was so important in her kitchen that made her sound so damned distant and distracted on the phone.

He'd called to tell her how much he missed her, how much he wanted her, to tell her he didn't want to wait four interminable weeks for her return to Honeycomb, to say he was thinking about flying to New York, thinking about her, thinking about the two of them, together again, maybe always.

She hadn't given him a chance to say much of anything before she raced away from the phone, and by the time she came back Cal was already feeling like a fool. The funny fifty was the last thing he wanted to ask her about, but as a defense, he put on his Secret Service hat and pretended the money was the only reason for his call.

Hec Garcia. He'd think about that tomorrow and decide how to proceed. In the meantime, he was tempted to drive into town, and reclaim his seat at Ramon's while renewing his old acquaintance with Dr. Heineken and Mr. Johnnie Walker.

"Cal?" Ruth knocked softly on his door. "I was just going to make some popcorn for Dooley and myself. Do you . . . ?"

A wedge of bright light from the hallway appeared as she opened the door.

"What are you doing, sitting here in the dark?" she asked, her tongue making a soft, admonishing cluck.

"Just sitting."

"Are you all right, Cal?" After flipping the switch for the overhead fixture, she stood peering at him in the sudden wash of light. Worry furrowed her brow and dragged down her mouth. "Are you feeling okay? You look a little pale to me."

"Fine." Actually now that he thought about it, a headache was flaring in his right temple.

He must've winced or something, because his sister sighed as she settled beside him and lifted her hand to test his forehead for fever. He had a split-second impression of his mother doing that same thing, and it occurred to him that only his mother and his sister and perhaps a nurse or two had ever done that. It struck him as pretty sad. But just then probably anything would've struck him as pretty sad.

"You're nice and cool," Ruth said, removing her hand. "Were you on the phone?"

Cal looked down at the portable handset. He'd forgotten it was still in his hand.

"No," he said. "I was going to make a call, but I changed my mind. It wasn't important."

"Want some popcorn? I make it the way Mama used to. Remember? On top of the stove in that heavy black kettle?"

"Yeah. I remember. Maybe later."

"Aw, Cal." Ruthie reached up and smoothed her hand across his back. "I wish I could snap my fingers and have things go back to the way they were a year ago. Before Baltimore. Well, maybe two years ago. Before Diana."

"That'd be a nifty trick," he said, almost wishing it were possible, even as he realized that if it hadn't been for Baltimore, he never would have met Miss Holly Hicks. For all that was worth now.

She sighed as she leaned her head against his shoulder. "Seems like we're pulling in two separate directions over the ranch, doesn't it? About selling it, I mean. This restaurant thing. It's so important to me, Cal. But so are you, sweetie. I just worry—"

"Too much," he said, cutting her off. "Don't worry about me. Go ahead and sell the place, Ruthie. I'll be going back to Washington in September, and after that I probably won't get back here more than once every two or three years."

"You think you're that much better? Dooley says he's noticed it, but . . ." Her voice drifted off, as if she didn't truly

want to confront him over the subject of his health or lack of
it.

"I'm just about back," he lied. "And by September I'll be
a hundred percent. You want me to call that real estate agent
and tell him that was all bullshit last week? Just say the word
and I'll do it."

"Maybe," she said. "Let me think about it. I better go
make that popcorn for Dooley. You sure you don't want
some?"

"No, thanks, sis. Hey, flip off the light on your way out,
will you? I think I'm going to try to get a little sleep."

♥

Half an hour later Ruth and Dooley had made a good-
sized dent in the huge bowl of buttered popcorn that sat
between them on the couch.

"This is good, honey," Dooley said, reaching for another
handful. "Think we should save some for Cal?"

"He went to bed a while ago."

"This early? Is he feeling okay?"

"Hard telling," she replied, drawing her feet up beneath
the folds of her robe. "Dooley, you didn't say anything to
him about Diana calling, did you?"

He shook his head. "Nope. Not a word. Why?"

"I just wondered. He seemed kinda down tonight. I
thought maybe you told him she was trying to get in touch
with him."

"Nope."

"The bitch," Ruth muttered. "I wonder what she wants
with him now."

"Probably just looking for more money in the divorce set-
tlement. That'd be my guess."

"She's got something up her silken sleeve. I'd bet the damned ranch on that."

Dooley chuckled. "Don't do that, honey. We can't afford it."

She reached for a perfectly popped, butter-drenched kernel, chewed it thoughtfully, and then said, "Cal said he'll be going back to Washington in September."

"Well, I wouldn't bet the ranch on that, either."

"I want my restaurant, Dooley."

"I know." He patted her knee. "We'll figure out something, honey."

Chapter Seventeen

Over the course of the next four weeks, Holly became increasingly convinced that Murphy's Law had been misnamed. It should have been named Hicks' Law because everything that could possibly go wrong with her Hero Week project did. With a vengeance.

It started with a cold, the one she caught almost as soon as she got back to New York, a whopping, Texas-sized and Texas-bred infection she no doubt picked up on her flight home from Houston, or maybe it was a parting gift from Cal, in which case she hoped he had one, too, and worse. At any rate, it was a monster cold that had her crawling home from work on Friday, then hardly getting out of bed until she absolutely had to on Monday morning.

"You look like shit, kid," Mel said upon seeing her, and then promptly put her in a cab and told her to stay home till Wednesday.

The next week her health was substantially better, but her luck certainly hadn't improved. She drove through a torrential rain to Baltimore with Chris Keifer, her favorite cameraman, to get some footage of the site where the shooting had happened the year before. Just as they reached the hotel, the rain stopped, the sun broke through the clouds and things seemed to be looking up for Holly. But only for a moment. It turned out that so many ghoulishly curious sightseers and assassination buffs had caused so much disruption in the vicinity that the hotel management had recently bricked up that exit and torn up the adjacent sidewalk, or what was left of it after people kept chiseling out chunks of pavement where Thomas Earl Starks' bullets had ricocheted and the President's protector had been gunned down.

After that, still in hopes of some decent B roll, she and Chris made a visit to the emergency room eight blocks away where Cal had been rushed that day. But Hicks' Law prevailed once more when they discovered the place locked down tight with signs posted that it was temporarily closed while undergoing renovation.

"Good thing it wasn't closed last September, huh?" Chris said. "Your hero would probably be a goner."

Holly pretended she didn't even hear that. She wished she *hadn't* heard it because her emotions were so conflicted where Cal was concerned that in a tiny, cobwebby, cruel corner of her heart she almost wished he were dead or at the very least that she hadn't met him.

In the end, all the trip to Baltimore had yielded was a halfway decent crab dinner at the company's expense, and that forlorn moment of thinking about Cal before she once more banished him from her head.

Her trip to Washington a few days later didn't go much better. She had set up an interview at the Treasury Department with the Secret Service's public liaison guy, Special Agent Timothy Tull, who turned out to be about as forthcoming as a tree stump. What Holly basically needed to know was what extra qualifications, both physical and mental, were required for an agent to be selected for duty on the

President's protective detail. What it was that Cal had that few other men did. What it was he'd lost and was struggling so hard to regain. And she'd been hoping for an anecdote or two to enliven her production. Something along the lines of *And then there was the time that Cal . . .* or *Wait'll you hear about the time when he . . .*

But Secret Agent Tull seemed to take the Secret part of his title a bit too seriously, and he spent the better part of the interview politely but firmly refusing to divulge the simplest of details, all the while regarding Holly as someone who was trying to weasel highly classified information out of him, or as if she were the front woman for Murder, Incorporated.

When she finally closed her still-blank notebook, shook his hand and said with obvious sarcasm, "Thank you, Agent Tull. You've been *so* helpful," the guy didn't even crack a smile. It only made her appreciate Cal's wonderful sense of humor all the more.

For a few moments every day, usually when she was about to drift off to sleep, Holly would allow herself to think about him—not as the storybook, stoic hero whose biography she was producing, but as the very real and vulnerable man she'd fallen for during her brief stay in Honeycomb. She'd picture him at a distance, dressed in his gray sweats, doggedly circling the track with his faithful companion, Bee. She'd picture him up close, allowing herself to drift in the blue depths of his eyes, to shiver beneath the touch of his palm, to wrap herself in the subtle Lone Star cadence of his voice.

It was a voice she hadn't heard since her first night home because Cal hadn't called her back. On the other hand, Mrs. Calvin Griffin had called her at least half a dozen times, inquiring about the shooting schedule, offering suggestions about wardrobe and lighting and location. Always the location.

"Why film in that awful little town?" the woman kept asking. "It means nothing to my husband, after all. It's simply where he's from, you know. Just an accident of birth. Why bother with Honeyville when there are such lovely settings in Washington? Our condo has a divine balcony and I've just redecorated."

"Honeycomb," Holly had corrected in the first few calls.

"Excuse me?"

"Honeycomb. The town's called Honeycomb."

"Oh, that's right," Diana always said before getting it wrong again.

Holly stopped correcting her. Diana obviously wasn't interested in facts.

Each call from Mrs. Griffin concluded in a similar fashion. Holly, weary of gritting her teeth and nursing a headache, would abruptly inform her that she had another call, after which Diana would say, as if she hadn't said it numerous times before, "Oh, and I told you I have the tapes of my appearances on *Good Morning America* and *Larry King*, didn't I? There are a couple rather nice sound bites if I do say so myself. Whenever you'd like to look at them, just let me know. You've got my number, right?"

Holly had her number, all right. The woman craved the spotlight and seemed thrilled to bask in its reflected glow whenever her husband was in it. That explained the lovely Diana. But what Holly couldn't even begin to comprehend was not just why Cal had married her in the first place, but why he'd chosen to reconcile with the bitch.

Against her will, against her better judgment, she kept thinking about all those boxes stacked against the wall in Cal's room. Diana had just crammed her husband's life into cartons and shipped them off to Texas, including their wedding picture and that sad, sawed-off gold band that signified their union.

She'd be damned, Holly vowed, if she'd give this selfish, egocentric, blood-sucking chick anything more than a passing mention in her production. If she mentioned her at all.

♥

Cal deliberated two long weeks over what to do about the bogus bills. He shouldn't have taken so long in his capacity as an officer of the law, whether his status was active or not, but he was reluctant to simply turn the money over to agents in a field office and then be told to go home to his rocking chair. Fuck that. He needed a little action, something more than just lifting weights and hobbling around the track, otherwise he'd go nuts thinking about Holly, who was back in New York and presumably happy as a clam in a bowl of Manhattan chowder.

During those two weeks, he stopped in Ye Olde Print Shoppe a couple times, ostensibly to copy some documents for Ruth and Dooley. Hec Garcia had seemed happy enough to see him, but there was a wariness in the guy that Cal couldn't overlook. There was an edginess that had nothing to do with the fact that the two of them had been adversaries in high school. As far as Cal could tell, Hec looked guilty as hell.

He finally decided to take the bills to the field office in Houston where they created an instant buzz.

"Have a seat, Griffin," Mike Squire, the Special Agent in Charge of the office said, pointing to the chair across from his desk.

The man's military bearing was straight out of the Marine

Corps, vintage Viet Nam. He was probably only a year or two from retirement, Cal guessed. His credenza was loaded down with framed portraits of kids and hunting dogs, and his desktop was stacked a foot high with manila files.

"Good job with the President last year," Squire said almost gruffly.

"Thanks."

"Now give me the quick skinny on how you got these bills."

All the while Cal spoke, Agent Squire nodded as if he already knew the details. And when Cal stopped, the man opened a drawer and tossed a rubber-banded stack of currency on top of his littered desk. Cal only had to glance to know that they were identical to his two.

"I'll be damned," he said. "What's up?"

Squire stared at him hard. "What's your status, Griffin? I haven't had time to call personnel yet, and I'd rather not waste time with those paper pushers if I don't have to."

"I don't blame you," Cal said, striving for the perfect tone—a bit of healthy *Semper fi* mixed with confidence and enthusiasm. "I'm just using up the last two months of my mandatory medical leave, then I'll be going back to Washington on active duty." *Maybe. I hope.*

Squire bought it, thank God, because the next words out of his iron-clad mouth were, "Okay. Sounds good to me. We could use an extra hand with this operation."

That operation, as the Special Agent in Charge detailed it, was a pretty big one, even though it wasn't centralized. Because he'd been on leave, Cal hadn't been privy to the investigation of a counterfeiting ring that had set up fairly recently in the border states of Texas, New Mexico, Arizona, and California. The key players had managed to distribute some fairly decent threaded paper to willing print shops in the southwest, usually places about the size of Hec Garcia's shop. The printers got a buck or two for every fifty they produced, and the bills were collected and then distributed at or near border crossings, where the recipients, fresh from Mexico, weren't all that familiar with U.S. currency.

According to Agent Squire, the counterfeiters had crossed the million-dollar mark in April, and were well on their way to their second million. A million here, a million there, and pretty soon they'd be talking about some real money.

The Secret Service had been reluctant to move in on the operation until they had pinned down a substantial number of print shops. But now that they had identified at least eight in each of the four states, they were ready to make their move, as well as make a big splash in the news.

"Seems we haven't had much good press since you took that bullet for Jennings," Squire said. "Washington wants this operation to make the front page so it's going down on the Fourth of July. Kind of our own little fireworks display. I'll make sure Garcia's place is on the list. We'll keep you posted."

"Great," Cal had said, trying not to sound too eager, or like a man desperately in need of some real fireworks as opposed to the female variety. "I'll be looking forward to it."

♥

On Holly's last half day at the office, before she was due to fly back to Texas late that afternoon, she wondered what else could possibly go wrong because it seemed as if everything already had.

The Al Haynes bio for Hero Week was excellent and nearly in the can. The Neil Armstrong segment, on the other hand, was a complete and unqualified mess with so little original content that a high school sophomore could have put it together with some paste, a pair of blunt scissors and a modicum of research on the Net. Mel would have fired the producer, Harriet Hyde, but the woman had outfoxed him by tendering her resignation along with her skimpy script and ninety-seven minutes of file footage for the forty-eight-minute piece.

If things kept going like this, Mel wasn't going to have any hair left for that stupid comb-over of his.

"Can you fix this?" he asked that final morning when he slapped Harriet's script on her desk.

"Got a match?" Holly asked.

Mel didn't laugh, but Holly did. God, if she didn't laugh, she'd cry.

She fiddled with the script for a couple hours and then, just as she was straightening up her desk prior to leaving for the airport, another grenade got lobbed into her office when she got a call from Wesley Cope's agent, informing her that the Country and Western star had received a last-minute invitation to headline the Independence Day celebration on the Mall in Washington, and thus wouldn't be available for filming in Honeycomb until the first week of August.

When Holly passed that tidbit along to Mel his face turned so purple she thought he was going into cardiac arrest. One of her boss's claims to fame was being able to say "fuck" in twenty-three languages, and he covered at least nineteen before he growled, "We'll sue him to Nashville and back. We'll sue his country ass off."

That sounded good to Holly, but it didn't do much to solve her problem of what the hell she was going to do in the meantime without her narrator.

"Maybe I'll just cancel my flight," she suggested, trying not to sound half as hopeful as she felt.

The longer she could put off seeing Cal again, the happier she'd be. Well, not happy exactly. Just less miserable.

"Not much we can do in Honeycomb without Wesley Cope and it's probably too late to bring anybody else on board," she said. "I'll just stay here, re-tool the Griffin script, get rid of all the Fourth of July stuff and . . ."

"You're going," Mel said, adding another expletive in a twentieth language. "You've just been promoted to narrator."

"Mel! I can't . . ."

He swore again. "Don't give me any of that I can't crap, Holly. Let's not forget I've seen all those tapes you sent to CBS and ABC and every media outlet east of the Mississippi, the ones where you do the writing, the video, and the narration all by your little Lone Star lonesome self."

"Well . . ." She wasn't going to deny that she was pretty good, but still . . .

"And now that I think about it, if we're gonna be cutting back on this Fourth of July segment for the piece, you might as well do the video, too. No need to take Chris Keifer with you." He almost grinned. "Wait'll I tell Arnold and Maida we're saving them about ten thousand bucks. We'll probably both get bonuses this year, kid."

"Oh, good," Holly moaned. "That's great. That's just wonderful. I can use my bonus to change my name after this low-budget bio—written, directed, filmed, narrated, produced and all the popcorn you can eat provided by Holly Hicks—gets laughed at all over the industry."

"I've got confidence in you, kid." Mel looked at his watch. "You better get going now or you'll miss your plane."

♥

If Hicks' Law had been consistent, Holly's plane would have crashed somewhere between Newark and Houston. The worst thing that happened, though, was when she spilled some coffee on Mel's laptop. Its screen fluttered and blipped for a few seconds. Holly's heart stopped. But then both the screen and her heart resumed their normal rhythms.

She'd been using the computer in an attempt to watch the footage of the assassination attempt. The tape had sat on her desk for four weeks, during which she'd merely stared at its black plastic casing, telling herself she'd view it tomorrow. Or tomorrow. Today, however, she'd run out of tomorrows. She had to watch the tape in order to figure out how to fit it into her piece—whether to use it as prologue or to feature it chronologically in Cal's life story.

One of the guys in Technical had transferred it to a CD-ROM for her this morning and she was determined to use part of her two-hour flight to watch it. When she'd spilled the coffee, she was already on her fourth attempt.

Each time it was the same. She'd watch the gaggle of press and onlookers gathered outside the hotel door, then the door would open and out would come those stern-faced men in gray suits with their little yellow Secret Service pins on their lapels and their earpieces planted firmly in their ears. First came two, and then came Cal. Each time she saw him come through that door just ahead of the President, her heart would start beating harder, a lump would lodge in her throat, and a feeling of dread would settle in her chest like a lead weight. Each time he came through the hotel door, Holly would hit the computer's pause button, freezing Cal's image on the screen.

He looked so competent, so totally in control, so hard and

impervious to harm. He looked . . . God! He looked as if
bullets would bounce right off him. But because Holly knew
what was coming in a matter of mere seconds, because she
knew that Thomas Earl Starks was lurking in the parking
garage just outside the camera's view, Cal looked vulnerable, too. She could almost discern the color of his eyes,
almost feel his body, all that hard muscle and hot blood and
the myriad textures of his skin. Focusing on him so closely,
she almost couldn't breathe.

And each time she reached that precise, heart-stopping
moment in the film, she'd go back to the beginning because
she couldn't bear to see what happened next. It wouldn't
have surprised her if she'd somehow spilled the coffee on
the computer on purpose, hoping to short out the CD-ROM
drive to prevent any further viewing of the film.

She finally closed the laptop and put it back in its case,
telling herself she'd better stop thinking about Cal last September, and start thinking about herself this July. What with
losing her narrator and her cameraman, her maiden voyage
as a producer was beginning to look a lot more like the
Titanic than the *QE2*.

Walking from the jetway into the gate area, Holly couldn't
help but glance at the concrete post where she'd first seen
Cal. Not that she expected him to be there this time, of
course. Not that she even wanted him to be there. Still a
little tic of disappointment pulled at her lips and she had to
remind herself all over again just how angry she was at him
for making her believe he cared about her when he was still
obviously in love with his wife.

As she slogged to the car rental counter with her luggage,
Holly kept waiting for the *I Hate Texas, Anywhere But Here*
blues to hit her. But strangely enough, she didn't recoil a bit
from the sight of Stetsons and string ties and Tony Lama

boots. There was even something sweetly familiar and vaguely comforting about the *y'alls* and the *yeps* and *nopes* she picked up from passing conversations.

Much to her amazement, she didn't even want to slug the cowboy at the car rental counter when he smiled and said, "What can I do for you, little lady?"

Traffic was blessedly light and the closer she got to Honeycomb, the wider and more beautiful the sky became with long slashes of orange and brilliant pinks. She turned onto Main Street just in time to see the neon lights blink on at Ramon's and the numbers on the bank's thermometer dip from triple to double digits.

It was eerily like coming home.

And when Ellie Young came down her front porch steps and threw her big soft arms around her, Holly almost cried for joy. She'd never had a sister, but this was how she imagined it would be, coming home to one.

"Welcome, Holly. Welcome back. Lord, it's good to see you."

"It's good to be here," Holly said, realizing how sincerely she meant it as she tightened her embrace around the big woman. "It really *is* good to be back."

"Lemme help you with these bags," Ellie said, opening the back door of the car and hauling out a suitcase.

"I can't wait to see my old room," Holly said.

"Oh. Well, now . . ." Ellie set the suitcase down on the driveway. Her welcoming smile turned sour and upside down. "We've got a couple little problems here."

"Problems?"

"Uh . . . yeah. Seems I've got another guest, and she insisted on the Rose Room. Just wouldn't take no for an answer."

"Oh." Holly tried not to let her disappointment show. It

was just a room, for heaven's sake. A room with memories she ought not to revisit. It was probably for the best, not seeing it again or sleeping in the bed where she'd slept with Cal. "That's okay, Ellie. Really. I don't mind so much. So who's this other guest?"

"Well, now, that's the other problem," Ellie said.

"Excuse me?"

"It's Diana Griffin. Cal's wife."

Chapter Eighteen

Early on the morning of the Fourth of July, not long after dawn, Cal opened his eyes. When he realized what day it was and how long this day threatened to be, he promptly closed his eyes again and tried to program himself back to sleep. He'd only slept a few hours the night before after driving back from Houston.

Special Agent in Charge Mike Squire was one of those dinosaurs who didn't believe in email, conference calls, or any other forms of twenty-first-century communication when it came to one of his operations. He wanted to be eyeball to eyeball with his men before a job went down, so Cal had had to return to the field office in Houston on the afternoon of the third to go over final instructions for the raid on Hec Garcia's print shop.

It was standard operating procedure to inform if not include local law enforcement, but given the rather parochial nature of Honeycomb's finest and considering the fact that Sheriff Bates was still on vacation in Alaska, it was decided to bypass the customary nod to the local authorities and to inform Deputy Jimmy Lee Terrell only after the operation had succeeded.

Which it would, Cal thought sleepily. Tonight at nine or so, right after the fireworks started at the high school, he and Agents Reed and McGovern would kick in the door of Ye Olde Print Shoppe, locate the stash of threaded paper plus any counterfeit bills that might be there, and then proceed to locate and arrest Hec. If it went according to plan—and Cal could see no reason why it shouldn't—the whole operation would be over before the final blast of fireworks blazed across the sky above the high-school football field.

He drew his forearm across his eyes to block out the rays of the rising sun coming through the parted curtains. His only concern about the upcoming operation was his own performance in it. He could actually feel a butterfly or two in his stomach, a sensation so alien to him that he wondered if maybe he wasn't coming down with a virus or food poisoning or something.

What the hell was he worried about? During his career in the Secret Service, he'd been in situations a hundred times more complicated and dangerous than what was going down tonight, and he'd never blinked so much as an eyelash beforehand.

When he'd worked undercover in Miami and it came time to make the bust on the heavily armed compound where the Colombians were cranking out credit cards as a little side business to the drugs, he hadn't thought twice about being the first guy over the fence and through the front door. Same for the bust on the Mob in Jersey in '99. He could list dozens of special ops that hadn't cost him the loss of a good night's sleep or a minute of anxiety.

Even when he was a kid, he never thought twice, much less once, about jumping into a fight or taking any sort of physical risk.

That was it, of course. He was thinking now, and not just

twice, but over and over again, worrying himself sick. What if he forgot something or got confused tonight? What if his knee froze at a critical moment? What if he fucked up? What if he lost control of the situation, something he'd never ever done?

Get your mind on something else, Cal told himself. Think about sex. That was always a guaranteed distraction. Only now, in the past month, any thoughts he had of sex were no longer faceless or generic. They were of Holly. Her wild hair and her warm skin, the fragrance and taste of her, the way her supple little body conformed to his, and how their separate bodies had learned so quickly to give and take and blend into one single scorched and blissful being.

He couldn't think about sex without thinking about Holly. Maybe he'd never be able to separate the two. She had worked her way into his head as thoroughly as she'd worked her way into his heart. Damn her.

No way he could get back to sleep now. He levered up and swore out loud.

Holly was probably back in town now. He thought that Ellie said she expected her on the third. He'd be glad when all this fucking hero stuff was in his past.

"Cal?" his sister called from the other side of the door. "Are you awake? Can I come in?"

Ruthie barged through the door before he even had a chance to answer. She looked ticked, which seemed to be the way she greeted every day lately, but this morning she looked a bit more ticked than usual. She looked downright pissed.

"That woman's in town," she said, crossing her arms as she stood at the foot of the open sofabed. "She had the nerve to come here, looking for you, but I wouldn't let her set one foot inside. I think she meant to stay here. Can you imagine that? Dooley drove her back to Ellie's place."

Cal rubbed his eyes, then ran his fingers through his hair. "Okay. I'll take care of it. She's my problem, Ruthie, not yours."

"I'll be so glad when you're done with her, Cal."

"Yeah, well, it shouldn't take long. How much can they film in Honeycomb? A day or two and all this hero business will be over."

"I figured that's why she was here. The bitch. Standing all sweetness and light at my front door, acting like she's family and trying to talk herself inside."

"I'll take care of it," he said again, surprised at the hostility Holly had evoked in his sister. It hadn't been a love match, but they'd seemed to get along well enough last month if he remembered correctly. Of course, remembering wasn't exactly his strong suit these days. "I thought you liked Holly," he said.

"Holly who?" Ruth snapped.

For a second Cal wasn't certain they were engaged in the same conversation. Jesus. He half suspected that Ruthie was trying to gaslight him. Or maybe it was the lack of sleep that was scrambling his head so badly this morning. All of a sudden he couldn't even think of Holly's last name.

"Holly," he said. "You know. The producer from New York. I thought you liked her."

"I do," Ruth said, shrugging. "Well enough, I guess. Why would you even ask?"

"Oh, I don't know. Calling her a bitch was a pretty good clue that . . ."

"I wasn't talking about Holly." Ruth rolled her eyes heavenward while she clucked her tongue in supreme annoyance. "Judas Priest, Cal. I was talking about Diana."

"Diana?" He sounded even more baffled than he felt, if that was possible. "My Diana?"

Ruth snorted. "Yeah. *Your* Diana. But not for long, I hope."

♥

Holly woke up early. Hells Bells, she'd hardly slept the night before what with listening for sounds coming from Diana Griffin's room. The fact that she didn't hear anything didn't mean there wasn't anything going on in there, though. She knew only too well how that big soft mattress on the antique walnut bed could muffle sounds of passion.

Oh, God. At least she hoped so, although it didn't make much difference now, she supposed. Ellie would have been the only one who'd heard them, and Holly doubted very much that her hostess was going to pass that juicy bit of gossip along to the woman who now resided in the Rose Room across the hall.

Holly remembered this room from her earlier stay, and she clearly remembered why she'd chosen the rose-papered suite over this one, with striped wallpaper throughout the room. The dark green stripes on the cream background would take a sickening pitch every few panels. It was particularly bad on the south wall, the one at which Holly was forced to stare as she lay sleepless in bed.

Even good old reliable Rufus had let her down last night. She couldn't summon up her cameraman no matter how hard she tried. Maybe he was on strike, she thought. Maybe he didn't want any part of this low-budget production for Hero Week. Hell, neither did she anymore.

♥

Cal laid rubber pulling out of the driveway at Rancho Allegro and had the T-bird up to ninety in a matter of seconds, but the closer he got to town, the more he came off the accelerator. It had occurred to him that he should probably be heading in the other direction. Not toward Honeycomb, but away.

His suspicion was confirmed for him when he pulled into Ellie Young's driveway and saw her coming down the front steps with a look on her face that seemed to say "Well, you damned fool. Just what are you planning to do with these two females?"

He didn't have a clue.

"Morning, Cal," Ellie called. "You're up early. Happy Independence Day!"

"Same to you," he answered, getting out of the car and slamming the door.

Ellie wrapped her meaty arms around him, then stepped back, grinning up at him like a Cheshire cat who'd just swallowed Tweety Bird. "You're a mighty brave man, Calvin Griffin," she said. "Which one did you come to see?"

He dragged in a breath. "My . . ."

Before the word wife was out of his mouth, his actual wife shot out of Ellie's front door. "Cal! Oh, God. Cal! Look at you! Just look at you!"

He probably did look different to her, he thought. The last time Diana had seen him he was in the hospital, horizontal and semi-conscious. She, on the other hand, looked pretty much the same—thin as a rib of celery, with her mane of honey blond hair and her makeup already in place at seven-thirty in the morning. But why he'd ever considered her beautiful was beyond him now.

When she hugged him, Cal was nearly overcome by fumes of Fendi. Her signature fragrance always smelled more like insecticide to him than expensive perfume.

"Sweetheart," she cooed against his ear. "Oh, God, you look wonderful. Sexier than ever, I must say. And what a darling car. It's a Thunderbird, right? Is it yours? I just adore it."

Christ. Had she always spoken this way? Like a human Gatling gun? Cal didn't know how to respond or what to respond to, so he just ignored everything she'd said and asked, "Have you had breakfast yet?"

"No," she exclaimed. "That would be lovely. Do I need to change?"

He stepped back a foot or so to take her in, from the tips of her lizard boots, past the designer concha belt circling her waist, to the massive chunks of turquoise strung around her wrists and neck.

"No need to change. You look very . . . um . . . western."

"Oh, good. That was the look I was going for. Where shall we go for breakfast?"

Ellie, who had been viewing this spectacle from the other side of the T-bird, piped up. "Take her to the Longhorn, Cal. She'll like that. It's real . . . um . . . western."

"The Longhorn," Diana chirped. "Oh, I love that. You know Honeyville isn't at all what I expected. Well, how do we get to this Longhorn place? Do we walk? Drive? What?"

"Let's walk," Cal said.

"All right. Let's do. Oh, but wait, sweetheart. Why don't we invite your producer to come along with us? I'm just dying to meet her. We've spoken on the phone, of course. I gave her some terrific ideas. Let's invite her, shall we?"

While Cal stood there dumb as a post, Ellie picked up the conversational slack. "I don't think Holly's up yet," she said.

"Yes, she is. I heard her in the shower before I came

downstairs. I'll just run back up and ask her about breakfast."

Diana disappeared as quickly as she'd appeared, leaving Cal and Ellie staring at each other across the hood of the car.

"You could leave right now," she said, doing her best to suppress a pretty nasty grin. "I surely wouldn't blame you."

"Well, I would leave, Ellie," he drawled, "but then they'd have to put me on Coward Week, wouldn't they?"

"Good luck," she said, then shook her head and added, "You know, I can't for the life of me picture you married to that woman."

"Neither can I, Ellie." He sighed. "Neither can I."

♥

How did she get here? Holly wondered bleakly as she sat across from Cal in a back booth at the Longhorn Café. How could this be happening?

That woman. Diana the Huntress. Diana the Harpy. The Devil Woman. She was part bulldozer, part pit bull, and all Harper's Bazaar with her Size 2 designer jeans, a half ton of gorgeous turquoise jewelry, and her obscenely long, blood red acrylic talons. She had barged into Holly's room without knocking, introduced herself as Mrs. Calvin Griffin and then intoned, "You must join us for breakfast. I absolutely insist." She was so insistent that Holly finally agreed to meet them at the Longhorn just to get rid of her.

So here she was in a rear booth at the Longhorn, across from Cal, alone with him because as soon as she'd arrived, Diana had looked at her turquoise beaded watch, realized it was nine o'clock in Washington, and had rushed outside in order to make a "crucial" call to somebody on her cell phone.

Holly picked up the knife from the place setting in front of her, pondered its blade a moment and her own reflection there, then put the utensil down with a sigh.

"What's the matter, Miss Manhattan? Thinking about using that knife to slit your wrists now that you're back in Texas?"

Her gaze lifted, meeting his. It was the first time they'd actually made and maintained eye contact this morning. Oh, God. Oh, damn. How could she have forgotten the pure, unadulterated blue of his eyes?

"No," she said. "As a matter of fact, I was thinking about plunging it into your lying, cheating heart."

His gaze didn't waver and those blue eyes didn't even blink when he answered, "I never lied to you, Holly."

"Well, maybe not in so many words, Cal." She forced a note of breezy who-gives-a-shit into her voice. "I'm a big girl, after all. Nobody put a gun to my head. I mean, I knew the risk I was taking by getting involved with a married man."

"What risk? What the hell are you talking about?"

Holly cocked her head toward the window, outside of which Diana was striding back and forth, her cell phone at her ear. "You and your wife. You're back together. Kudos, Cal. Congrats. Bon Appétit. May you live happily ever after and all that crap."

"Diana told you that." It wasn't a question, but rather a blunt accusation.

"Right after I got back to New York last month." She smiled with a kind of sweet venom. "Imagine my surprise."

He swore and picked up his own knife, curling his fingers around it until his knuckles were white. "Why the hell didn't you just ask me?"

"You never called me back!"

"I never called you back, god dammit, because you were so fucking busy with whoever it was who was with you that night."

She remembered brusquely telling him she had something on the stove, slyly implying that she wasn't alone. "My feelings were hurt," she said.

"Jesus, baby, so were mine!"

Holly just stared at him then, at the tension in his jaw, the hard, determined set of his mouth, and most of all the sheen of moisture in his eyes. She'd been lied to a lot in her thirty-one years. But if ever there was a look of truth, an expression of bone-deep honesty, this was it. Oh, God. It was, wasn't it?

"So you're not back together?" she asked, hating the little quaver in her voice.

He shook his head.

"Then why did she . . . ?"

"Are you kidding me?" He gestured with the knife in the direction of the window. "Look at her. She's a goddamn drama queen. She wants in on this TV thing, that's all. It doesn't have anything to do with me."

"But you *are* still married to her." She cocked her head. "Why *did* you marry her, Cal?"

"Damned if I know."

"That's not an acceptable answer," she said bluntly.

"Okay." He sighed, closed his eyes a second and then said, "I married her because I was thirty-eight years old and didn't have a family to call my own. Because I was sick and tired of sleeping in hotels. Sleeping around, if you really want the brutal, unvarnished facts."

"Well, you can use a little varnish," Holly cut in, figuring ignorance was bliss where Cal's sexual past was concerned.

"I don't know, Holly. Hell, I was just ready to settle

down. The time seemed right. Diana was there. She said yes. It just seemed to happen somehow. It's a lousy reason, but I don't know how else to explain it to you or even to myself. Just believe me when I tell you it's over. The divorce papers went back to her attorney last month, all signed, sealed, and delivered. I mailed them the morning after we made love the first time, as a matter of fact."

"Really?"

"Really."

"You didn't love her?"

"I didn't even know what love was." He reached across the table to grasp her hand. "Holly, not until I . . ."

A pungent blast of Fendi signaled Diana's return, and Holly pulled her hand away.

"Well, my dears, all hell is breaking loose in Washington. Let me tell you," Diana moaned, sliding into the booth next to Cal. "Senator Ferriss' daughter was arrested last night after a car chase through Georgetown at ninety miles an hour. Can you believe that? In Georgetown. It's lucky she didn't take out a pedestrian or two. She's out on bail, but Jack Ferriss' people, idiots, all of them, don't have a clue about spinning this thing. I've got to get back there. Right now."

"Oh, that's too bad," Holly said.

Cal didn't say a word. Actually, he looked as if he were holding his breath. Either that or he was trying hard not to yell whoopee.

Diana looked at Holly. "I know that puts a terrible crimp in your production schedule, Holly," she said, "but there's really nothing I can do."

"Oh, that's okay."

"I'll get back to you from Washington as soon as I possibly can. Naturally, we still have the option of filming there."

"We'll work it out," Holly said sympathetically, without

the slightest intention of working anything out where this babe was concerned except celebrating her exit.

Just then, Coral—who'd been up to her blond beehive in taking orders and refilling coffee cups—sidled up to their booth. "Mornin', folks. What can I bring y'all?"

Diana glanced up, appeared to look right through the waitress, then frowned and picked up her menu.

"Coffee, Coral," said Cal. "You got any of those great Danishes today?"

"Sure do, Cal." She looked at Holly. "How 'bout you, hon?"

"Same for me," Holly replied.

"And you, missy?"

Diana looked back up at Coral. "I'll have eggs Benedict, a croissant, unsalted butter, and a large pineapple juice with shaved ice. And tea, please. Earl Grey, if you have it. With lemon."

Coral's pen kind of hovered over her order book for a moment, and then she looked at Cal. "She's kidding, right?"

"I don't think so," Cal said.

"Ooo-kay." She made a quick notation in her book. "That'll be three coffees and three Danish. Be right back."

♥

Two hours later Holly was walking—sauntering, actually —around Ellie's yard, getting a feel for the expensive video cam she signed out of the production department at the VIP Channel. It was light years beyond her own, which she'd picked up cheap from the station where she worked in West Virginia.

Ellie, who'd been gone since breakfast, clomped down her back stairs. "Hey, what's goin' on? I just went up to check on Diana's room and her stuff's all gone. I didn't miss any early fireworks, did I?"

Holly laughed, sighting Ellie in her lens. Her hostess' big denim dress just about filled the frame. "No, you didn't miss any fireworks. Diana and her PR firm had a crisis with a Senator's kid in D.C., and being on the evening news in every major market trumped the VIP Channel's comparatively meager viewership."

"So, she's gone?"

"Yep. Cal drove her to Kingsville to catch the bus to Dallas."

She laughed again, this time to herself. Even before they'd left the booth at the Longhorn, Diana had started with her arm twisting, wanting somebody to drive her all the way "to someplace civilized. Dallas. Houston. I really don't give a flying fuck."

When Cal said he didn't have time to make the trip today, she still wasn't going to take no for an answer and she continued to press until Holly, suddenly inspired, told her, "The Thunderbird's only licensed in this county. He can't drive you any farther than the bus station in Kingsville."

Diana looked more appalled than shocked or disappointed. "I've never heard of that." She turned to Cal. "You can't drive your car out of the county?"

"That's right," he said. "It's a special registration because of the steel plate in my head. A damned nuisance, too."

"Well, that's absurd."

"No," Holly said with a shrug. "It's just Texas."

"You expect me to . . . to take a . . . a bus?" The woman could hardly get the word out.

"Yep." Holly and Cal had replied in unison, trading glances, both of them almost cracking up.

Ellie's laughter boomed across the backyard now. "I'm

trying to picture that City Slicker on the bus from Kingsville to Dallas."

"Not a pretty picture, is it?"

"No, indeedy. Well, one good thing about it, though."

"What's that?" Holly asked.

"You can move back into the Rose Room, honey. I'll just go and strip the bed."

"I'll help," Holly said, already envisioning Cal coming up the fire escape when he returned from Kingsville this afternoon.

Yee-hah.

Chapter Nineteen

In this part of south central Texas, the Fourth of July was just about always crystal clear and hellishly hot, and today was no exception. Cal would've loved to have put the top down on the way to Kingsville, but Diana—with her high-maintenance hair and foot-long false eyelashes—wasn't exactly a top-down kind of woman, so he hadn't even suggested it.

Breezing along with the needle dancing around the speed limit, he found himself wondering again why he'd ever married Diana Koslov. Granted, he had felt a profound urge to settle down last year, an urge that had been building with every succeeding birthday in his thirties. But why Diana? Other than the fact that he was her lover at the time, Cal couldn't come up with a single reason.

If he made a list of the qualities he prized in a wife, Diana's sexual enthusiasm might have made it in the top dozen or so, but that was about it. She didn't have a sense of humor to speak of. That was important to him. A sense of humor like Holly's. Diana's intelligence wasn't stellar. Her curiosity was limited to the people and events in her own small coterie of socialites, politicians, and hangers-on, the people who paid her handsomely to get their names in or out of the paper, depending on the story.

It suddenly occurred to Cal that a better question than why he'd married *her* was why the hell she'd ever married *him*. After all, he was just as wrong for her as she was for him. He figured this was a good time to ask as they were only a few miles from Kingsville now, and after he put her on a bus he'd probably never see her again—he hoped—no matter how long he lived. He drummed his fingers on the steering wheel, waiting until she broke the connection on the phone that had been attached to her ear for most of the trip.

"I've got a question for you, Diana. No big deal. Just something I've been wondering."

"What's that?" she asked, then added, "Oh, would you roll your window up a bit more, Cal? This wind is absolutely ruining my hair."

While he cranked up the window all the way and turned the AC down a notch, he cast about for a way to phrase his question so it wasn't insulting to her. Why he cared about that, he wasn't sure. In all honesty, though, Diana probably wouldn't recognize an insult if it bit her on her bony ass. "When I asked you to marry me last year, Diana, why the hell did you ever say yes?"

"What?" She sounded surprised, even slightly amused, and far from insulted.

"I said when I asked you to marry me last year . . ."

"I heard what you said, Cal." She laughed as she pulled down the sun visor, adjusted its mirror, and fiddled with an eyelash. "Darling, don't you remember? You didn't ask *me*. I asked *you*."

He shook his head in disbelief, keeping his eyes on the two-lane road, doing his best not to blink in complete befuddlement or to look half as lame brained as he felt. She'd proposed to him? "No," he said. "I don't remember that."

"Well, I do. I asked you. It was a year ago today, come to think of it. The Fourth of July. Funny, isn't it?"

Oh, yeah. A real riot, he thought. "You proposed to me? Why?"

"Why? I told you, Silly. As a matter of fact, I confessed to you right before you left for Baltimore last September. We had that terrible argument and . . ." She snapped up the mirrored visor and stared at him. "God, Cal, you really don't remember, do you? The little wager I had with Penny Price? Well, not so little actually. She's still bitching on a daily basis about having to pay up the inches she owes me in her column."

Jesus H. Christ. He did remember now. It was as if Diana's words had jarred something loose in his brain, probably something lodged right beneath the metal plate. Penny Price and Diana were pals in a back-biting, cat-fighting sort of way. Penny wrote a gossip column—Penelope Tells All—in one of Washington's glossy chi-chi magazines, a column in which Diana, Queen of Public Relations, coveted coverage for her clientele.

Suddenly he remembered something else Penny had once written in her column about him as the most eligible as well as most elusive bachelor in the White House. He'd taken more than a little ribbing about that in the West Wing. Now a tiny light bulb went on somewhere in the dim recesses of his skull.

"You had it all planned?" he asked, already knowing the answer. "Right from the start? Beginning with that red eye flight from L.A.?"

Diana didn't even have to answer. Her feline smile, somewhere between a cougar and an alley cat, was far more eloquent than any words she might have spoken.

"You married me on a fucking bet," he muttered, slapping the steering wheel with the flat of his hand.

"Well, we had some great moments, darling. Oh, come on, Cal. You've got to admit that. And if you're worried that someone might find out, don't. Trust me, no one knows a thing but Penny and me. I'm certainly not telling, and I've got enough dirt on Penny to guarantee that she won't ever say or print a word of it. Not to worry, love. And I meant what I said, you know. You really do look sexier than ever."

After that remark, it hadn't really surprised him when Diana had suggested a farewell tryst in the rest room at the bus station. Cal had politely declined. Actually what he'd told her was that by the time his Viagra kicked in, she'd already be halfway to Dallas. Her look of pity and disgust was exactly what he'd expected, and he figured that would preclude any further invitations for Olympic-class sex from his soon-to-be ex.

After he put her on the bus for Dallas, Cal thought about what she'd said while he was driving back to Honeycomb. He wasn't sure whether he was relieved to know that the marriage hadn't been his idea, or ashamed to discover that he'd been so thoroughly duped, beginning in an airplane lavatory at 35,000 feet above the earth.

He almost laughed out loud, recalling the look on Diana's face when he'd mentioned the Viagra. He'd have to remember to tell that Viagra thing to Holly. It was almost as good as the Creeks and Greeks and the goats, if he did say so himself. God, how he loved to hear her laugh. Well, on second thought, maybe it wasn't such a good idea. Holly, despite her vibrant sense of humor, probably wouldn't think it was so damned funny, his being hit on by another woman. Particularly Diana.

Or maybe Holly wouldn't really give a shit. Maybe she was one of those women who just loved the one she was with. Him in Texas. Somebody else when she got back to New York.

After what he'd just learned about his marriage, who was he to judge a woman's wiles or whims or motives? He'd made a mess of that even before he'd gotten shot.

The little round clock on the dashboard told him he had eight hours before the Hec Garcia bust went down this evening. One good thing. His problems with the women in his life had certainly made him forget all about the butterflies in his stomach.

♥

There was no mistaking Cal's tread on the fire escape or the accompanying acceleration of Holly's pulse. She'd spent the past few hours, while waiting for him to return, filming B roll of the annual parade on Main Street, where it had begun to feel less like the Fourth of July than Old Home Week, only far better than her actual old home.

Nita Mendes called out and waved to her from the back seat of a red Caddy convertible that was draped with blue and white crepe paper. Bobby Brueckner from the bank leaned down from his two-story-high palomino in order to present Holly with a little plastic flag. Coral, stationed in front of the Longhorn, handed her a doughnut with red, white, and blue sprinkles and wouldn't even consider letting Holly pay.

"Pardon my asking, hon," Coral asked with a telling roll of her eyes, "but where's that too-sexy-for-her-clothes ex-wife of Cal's who was with y'all at breakfast?"

"Gone," Holly said, licking patriotic sprinkles from her fingers. "Long gone. He drove her to Kingsville to catch a bus."

"Good riddance," Coral said. "Though I'd rather you said he'd put her in a gunny sack and taken her down to the creek and pitched her in."

Holly laughed, then asked the waitress to move out into the sunlight so she could get a better picture of her.

Coral patted her blond beehive and scooted her chair out of the shade. "You gonna put me in your movie, hon?"

"Sure," Holly said, even as she realized that she was doing most of this filming for purely personal reasons. It wasn't extra footage for Cal's story. It was for herself. For her own private archives. She wanted to remember everything about this day in Honeycomb. Everything and everyone.

Especially the one who was coming up her fire escape right now. She opened the door before he had to knock.

Cal stepped over the threshold, gazed around the rose-papered room, then drew Holly into his arms and whispered, "I hate to admit it, but I'm starting to develop a fondness for this damned wallpaper."

Holly laughed, loving the feel of his arms around her, the hard warmth of him against her, the way his lips drifted over her hair. "We're probably the only couple in the world who doesn't have 'Our Song.' We have 'Our Wallpaper' instead."

She began to pull away, but Cal drew her even closer against him.

"Holly. Listen to me, baby. I'm sorry I hurt your feelings."

She shook her head against his chest. "It's my fault," she said. "I should've known better than to believe anything Diana said. I'm a journalist, for God's sake. I should've checked my facts."

"Next time, just ask me, okay? I'll never lie to you."

She angled her head up, grinning even as she grimaced in mock horror. "There's going to be a next time?"

"Not if I can help it."

As long as her face was properly tilted and just a few convenient inches from his face, Holly lifted on tiptoe and pressed her lips to Cal's. "Mmm. I've been wanting to do that ever since breakfast," she said. "I've been wanting to do that ever since I left here last month, actually. I missed you. Oh, God, I missed you, Cal, even when I was mad as hell at you."

Cal took her face in both his hands and looked deeply into her eyes. "I missed you, too, babe. I had myself convinced that you, well . . ." He lifted an eyebrow. "So there's nobody in New York I need to beat to a pulp or put out a hit on?"

"Nobody," she said, planting little kisses from one edge of his smile to the other. "Well, except maybe the people in charge at work. The ones who keep cutting back on my budget for the piece about you on Hero Week. I'm half tempted to beat them to a pulp myself."

"Holly, this hero business . . ." His expression turned from sexily sweet to almost grim. He swore harshly, then reached for her hand, led her to the big walnut bed, and sat her down. "As long as we're being so honest, there are some things you really ought to know."

"Wait!" she exclaimed, feigning a look of horror. "Oh, God. Oh, no! You're not about to tell me you don't have a Superman costume on under your clothes, are you?"

"I'm serious here."

"So am I," she said, unable to stop laughing even as he glared at her.

When he sat on the bed beside her, Holly reached for the top button of his shirt. "Well, I guess I'll have to look for myself. Just think of me as Lois Lane, checking out her facts."

He caught her hand in his, pressed her palm flat against his chest where Holly could feel the strong and solid beat of his heart. "Be serious for a minute and listen to me, will you?" he said. "This is important."

"All right."

Holly sucked in a breath. It wasn't easy, sobering up her expression. She was just so damned happy to be with Cal that it was all she could do not to skip around the room, stripping off her clothes, piece by piece, while whistling "Happy Days Are Here Again."

"There." She exhaled slowly. "Okay. What is it that's so important?"

Cal brought her hand to his lips, kissing her fingertips. "It's about this hero business. I haven't lied to you, exactly, but . . . Well, I haven't given you the whole truth, either."

"Which is . . . ?" Holly knew a lot of things about Cal that he hadn't told her himself, but she didn't have a clue what he was about to confess, and his serious demeanor was starting to make her nervous. Very nervous.

"I've probably given you the impression that, once my medical leave is over in September, I'll be resuming my duties with the President right where I left off last year." He paused to clear his throat. "That . . . uh . . . that might not be the case."

Now that she knew exactly what he was going to say, Holly didn't want to hear it. She'd heard it before from just about everyone in town, most notably Cal's brother-in-law, Dooley Reese.

About the only one who thinks he's got a chance to get back is Cal himself.

"Holly, listen . . ."

She touched a finger to his lips. "No, you listen to me. I don't think I've ever told you about my daddy, did I?"

He shook his head, blinking, as if to say *What the hell does your daddy have to do with any of this?*

Holly scooted back on the bed and patted the place beside her. "Come here. Just stretch out and close your eyes and listen to me."

"All right." There was a note of skepticism in his voice, but he settled beside her, taking her hand in his. "I'm listening."

"My daddy lost a foot in Viet Nam. His platoon wandered right into an ambush one afternoon. Their point man, Harris—he was a Private first class and only with the unit a few days—was hit first, a terrible wound I guess because he lay there screaming while the others dived for cover wherever they could find it."

Holly paused for a moment to gather her thoughts. She hadn't revisited her father's war story in such a long time. He'd never told it to her himself. Not one word. She'd spent years uncovering the story herself, combing through the papers her mother had saved, tracking down and interviewing the men who'd been in Corporal Bobby Ray Hicks' outfit.

"As I understand it, they were caught in a crossfire with the bullets coming so fast and furiously that nobody could even raise up on an elbow to fire back. This went on for two or three hours, and all the while Private Harris was screaming."

"Jesus," Cal breathed.

"Their lieutenant radioed for a helicopter, and told everybody to hold their positions until it came, which was probably a wise call since he didn't want to lose any more men. Well, to make a long story short, when the chopper landed a few hundred yards south of them, everybody started running for it. Except my daddy, who started running north to where Harris was."

Holly sighed. "The reports from the men who made it to the helicopter were all identical to the last detail. Daddy came crashing out of the underbrush with Private Harris slung over his shoulder. He took three steps, and then a land mine exploded and blew off his foot right there."

Cal muttered a quiet curse and held her hand more tightly.

"If he'd been six inches either side of it, everything would've been different, and I don't think he ever got over that," Holly said. "He survived, of course. Harris survived, and apparently tried half a dozen times to express his gratitude but my father wouldn't listen. Daddy got a Purple Heart and a Bronze Star and a bitterness in his heart that ruined his life more than the loss of his foot."

"So, that's why his daughter doesn't believe in heroes."

"He didn't believe in them. He thought of himself as a fool. A loser. Not that he ever said so. At least not to me. But when he came home to Sandy Springs, he ripped down the bunting hung to greet him, he threw his medals in the trash, and pretty much quit living. Loving, too, for that matter."

Holly turned toward Cal, levered up on her elbow. "And the point of that long digression is what I'm focusing on in my piece about you. It's not about the heroic deed itself. It's not about what somebody does in the blink of an eye. It's about what he does with his life afterwards."

Cal reached up to twist one of her curls around his finger. "How'd a self-pitying bastard like that ever have such a smart and thoughtful little girl?"

Ignoring his question, Holly continued. "The point isn't whether or not you take up at the White House right where you left off in September. The point is that you're fighting so hard to do it. If there is such a thing as heroism, then that's the essence of it."

"Maybe," he said. "I don't know."

"Well, I know. I've seen you out there on the track when you didn't know anyone was watching. I've seen you fall and get back up. Again and again. That's what it's all about."

"Yeah, well, I'll tell you a little secret, Miss Holly Hicks." Cal levered up on his elbow now so their faces were nearly touching. "All that work I've been doing . . . making it back to the level where I used to function doesn't seem as crucial to me as it did a month or two ago. Back then I didn't have anything else in my life but the job."

"And now?" she whispered, thinking she knew what he was going to say. *Hoping* she knew what he was going to say.

"And now there's you." The fingers just toying with her curls slid more deeply into her hair and he brought her face even closer to his. "Holly, I'm half in love with you."

Oh. Her heart felt as if it were opening like a rose within her chest. An entire bouquet of roses. A million blossoms crowding out the air in her lungs. For a moment she couldn't even speak, but only gaze at her own reflection in Cal's bluer-than-blue eyes . . .

. . . which suddenly began to look worried.

"Did you hear me?" he asked, sounding as worried and uncertain as he looked. "I said I'm half in love with you, Miss Holly Hicks."

God. She was so happy, so ridiculously joyous, so incredibly over the moon that all she could do was burst out laughing and ask, "Which half?"

♥

Cal would've been content to spend the next twenty-four hours in the big bed on Ellie's second floor. Hell, he wouldn't have minded spending the next twenty-four years there as long as Holly was with him. They'd missed lunch and dinner, and Cal found himself wishing they could dial up room service so they didn't have to leave the bed, or get dressed, or even loosen their embrace.

"Are you awake?" he whispered, sliding his hand along Holly's smooth, warm flank.

"Mmm. I'm basking in the throes of afterglow here."

He raised his wrist to check his watch. "The fireworks are going to start in about ninety minutes."

She moaned into her pillow melodramatically. "Oh, God. More fireworks?"

Cal smiled, wondering what could be better than loving a smart woman who held back nothing in bed, a beautiful woman who was as greedy for his body as she was generous with her own. They had set off their own fireworks, no doubt about that. Sparklers and Roman candles and climaxes that were almost blinding in their intensity. They'd nearly scorched the roses on the wall.

He wished she could have known him when he was at his best. He wished he could *be* at his best again. Then he realized he was thinking too much—his new curse!—because the butterflies made their presence known in his gut.

It was time to get his body out of bed and his head in a place where he was ready to focus on work. Agents Reed and McGovern would be arriving soon to meet him about half a mile east of town. After that, if all went well, he and his Holly ought to be back here, neck deep in roses, before the Fourth of July turned into the Fifth.

Chapter Twenty

By eight-thirty that evening the grandstand at Honeycomb High School was so crowded that people sat shoulder to shoulder, hip to hip. Holly wouldn't have minded so much if it had been Cal's muscular shoulder and lean hip on her right, but it was Ellie's soft shoulder and ample denim-covered hip. On Holly's left was the far slimmer Ruth Reese in a pretty summer dress, who looked happier and more at ease tonight than Holly had ever seen her.

Gazing around her through the lens of her camcorder, she almost had to laugh because the crowd looked more like one gathered for a rodeo than for Independence Day fireworks. There were more Stetsons and plaid western cut shirts and string ties than she'd seen in any one place in the past decade. There was enough hair spray on the women to shellac every building in town. Funny thing was though, that instead of being repelled by the Texas couture and coiffures as she had been a month ago, Holly found it all almost comforting now in its predictability and reassuring somehow in its down-to-earth casualness.

It amazed her, too, how many faces she recognized as she panned the crowd. There was Coral sitting next to a good-looking guy in a white shirt and bolo tie, probably Mr. Coral. Not far away, there was Bobby from the bank. Holly smiled, wondering if the fireworks would reflect off his bald head. There was Ramon, who must've left Rick in charge at the bar. There was Nita Mendes, and Cal's classmates Jen and Carol whom she'd met at Ellie's. Good grief. There was gun-toting Kin Presley and his run-around wife, smooching in the top row of the stands.

It suddenly occurred to Holly that she knew more people in Honeycomb after a few days than she did in New York after three years. There, outside of work, she hardly knew anyone. She didn't even know who lived across the hall from her in 12-B.

She never thought she'd use the words Texas and happy in the same sentence, but that was exactly what she was thinking right now. She was happy being back in Texas. Who knew? Maybe she'd have been happy in Sandy Springs all those years ago if she hadn't spent all her time trying to get out of it.

Her piece for Hero Week, she sensed, was going to be kinder and gentler than originally planned now that Texas no longer felt like a giant pool of quicksand.

She wanted to tell Cal, but not long after they'd all sat down, he had disappeared, claiming he needed to move his car so that no errant fireworks made the convertible top catch fire.

Still, even in his absence, Holly was having a grand time. A good ol' time. For a brief moment, she and Ruth and Ellie had huddled like the witches in Macbeth, raking Diana over a bed of hot coals. The impromptu roasting of Cal's ex surprised Holly, especially considering the company—the mature and rather matronly Ellie, and the heretofore cool-natured Ruth. But the three of them had sat cackling and hooting and rubbing their hands with glee until Dooley, sitting beside Ruth, had finally leaned over and shushed them with a stern, "All right, ladies. That's enough."

"How's your restaurant planning coming along?" Holly asked Ruth. "Are you still trying to sell the ranch?"

Cal's sister looked surprised. In truth, Holly had been prepared for a scathing reprimand over the titanium incident, but Ruth's voice was quite pleasant when she asked, "Didn't Cal tell you?"

"Uh, no." Holly thought it prudent not to tell her that she and Cal had mostly confined their recent conversations— their intercourse, actually!—to *Yes, Yes, Oh God, More* and quite a few *Mmms* and *Ahs*. And then there was Cal's "half in love" confession which Holly had laughed off because it was just too scary to even think about at the time.

"We're not selling the place," Ruth said. "We're going in with some of our neighbors and starting up a hunting preserve. A pretty fancy one, actually. It was Cal's idea."

"Really."

"Yep. Next week we're meeting with an architect about building a first-rate lodge where we can accommodate about two dozen guests at a time."

Dooley leaned into the conversation, grinning beneath his droopy mustache. "Where Ruthie can cook up a first-rate storm for about two dozen guests at a time."

"That's terrific," Holly said. "It all worked out perfectly for you, didn't it?"

"Sure did," Dooley said, draping an arm around his wife and pulling her against him.

"I guess it did at that," Ruth said, turning to smile at her husband.

Holly sighed. Well, at least one of the little dramas she'd been following in Honeycomb had come to a happy ending.

That was nice. As a journalist, Holly liked closure. It remained to be seen how her own little drama would conclude.

She turned off her camcorder and returned it to its case. It was getting too dark to film now, anyway. The fireworks ought to be starting soon. Where in the world was Cal?

♥

Agents Reed and McGovern were late, so late that Cal looked again at the little spiral notebook in which he'd written their names and the time and location of their meeting. The fact that he was parked east of town in the right place at the proper time wasn't much consolation. Where the hell were the agents from Houston? The fireworks would be starting at the high school in a matter of minutes, and all that noise and hoopla was supposed to serve as the distraction when they—Griffin, Reed, and McGovern—broke into the print shop.

He pulled his cell phone from the glove box and punched in the number of the office in Houston only to get a recording that informed him that no one was currently in the office and that if this was an emergency, he ought to call his local 911 number.

Oh, sure. Now there was a good idea. That would put him through to Deputy Jimmy Lee Terrell, who was currently prowling around town in his big cruiser, looking to bust kids with firecrackers and cherry bombs.

The only good thing at the moment, Cal decided, was that the butterflies in his stomach had packed up their fluttery little wings and flown elsewhere. He held out his hand, just to reassure himself of the steadiness there. Good deal. Steady

as a rock. Cool as the proverbial cucumber. Special Agent
Calvin Griffin was back . . .

. . . and wondered what the hell he ought to do. This hit
on Hec Garcia's shop had to take place tonight at the desig-
nated time when all the other sites in the Southwest were
being hit, or else the opportunity for a clean sweep by the
Secret Service would be lost. No way was Cal going to be
responsible for that, especially when his current status with
the service was questionable at best, if not downright shaky.

At the moment, without further word from Houston, he
didn't see that he had much choice but to proceed with the
operation as planned.

He got out of the T-bird, opened the trunk, and put on the
Kevlar vest he hadn't worn in nearly a year. He slipped his
pistol into the waistband of his jeans. Then he slid back
behind the wheel and headed toward town, where the first of
the fireworks—a patriotic red, white, and blue dazzler—was
lighting up the sky.

♥

Holly sat *oohing* and *aahing* right along with the rest of
Honeycomb's population when the sky overhead burst into
an amazing display of red, white, and blue. But even as she
oohed and aahed, she kept wondering why Cal wasn't back.
How far away did he think he had to move his car to keep it
safe from sparks, for heaven's sake? The next county?

She reached down to give a reassuring pat to poor old
Bee, who'd been slinking around the grandstand all evening
and then had finally worked his way under Ellie's long denim
skirt, as if he'd been through this before, knew just what was
coming, and wanted to be somewhere dark and safe when the
heavens above exploded. The old dog gave a quiet little *woof*

when Holly touched his head, as if to say he was doing as well as could be expected under the circumstances and thanks for your concern.

The sky had barely cleared of the red, white, and blue when another firework shot up and flared out in a pulsing shower of brilliant white. Holly almost laughed because the burst of intense light suddenly reminded her of an orgasm. A fairly recent one, in fact. God. She must really have it bad, she thought, if she was seeing orgasms exploding in the sky over Honeycomb, Texas.

That train of thought led directly back to Cal for obvious reasons, and Holly looked to her left, past Ruth and Dooley, toward town, to see if she could see him anywhere. Hard as she tried, she couldn't discern his now oh-so-familiar form. But over on Main Street something caught her attention. She was certain that she saw the reflection of blinking lights on a police car or a fire engine or some sort of emergency vehicle.

Everybody else was looking skyward, so she was apparently the only one to notice that something was going on in town.

Holly reached for her camera.

"I'll be right back," she told her companions.

♥

It had been a piece of cake getting into the print shop. One of the major benefits to a small town like Honeycomb was that nobody felt obliged to use dead bolts, so Cal had simply slipped the lock with a credit card. Once inside, though, he realized his first mistake, hoping it would be his only one. He didn't have a flashlight. Not only did that make it impossible to find Hec's stash of threaded paper in the

cluttered shop, but it dramatically increased the odds that
he'd stumble over something in the dark and break his
fucking neck.

He felt along the wall adjacent to the front door, and
touched a plastic wall plate with four switches. Bypassing the
first, which he figured would be the main switch to light the
entire shop, he flipped the third switch, which brought on the
fluorescent bulb above the copy machine. That was good.
There was just enough illumination to do a thorough search
while hopefully not arousing too much suspicion.

He started with the locked cabinet behind Hec's cash register, silently congratulating himself for keeping a universal
pick on his keyring all these months, thinking maybe his
skills weren't quite as rusty as he'd feared. Hell, if he didn't
pass the physical for the Service, he could always make a living by breaking and entering.

He had just squatted down and started opening boxes and
riffling through the papers inside when Deputy Jimmy Lee
Terrell clicked on his fucking bullhorn.

"You there in the print shop. This is the police. Come out
with your hands over your head. Now."

Cal stayed where he was, low, behind the counter on the
theory that Jimmy Lee would be only too happy to shoot first
and ask questions later.

"It's Cal Griffin, Jimmy Lee," he called. "I'm in here on
federal business."

"Cal? What do you mean? Federal business? Nobody told
me. Does Hec Garcia know about this?" the deputy's voice
boomed.

Jesus. Cal groaned and rolled his eyes. He probably
knows about it now. "No," he said, and then added, "You
want to turn that amplifier down, Jimmy Lee? I can hear
you fine."

"You got a warrant, Cal?"

"There's one on the way from Houston."

"You need a warrant."

"It's coming, Jimmy Lee."

"I don't know about this."

♥

Holly was cutting through the dark vacant lot adjacent to the bank, heading in the direction of the police cruiser with its deck of flashing lights, when she heard the deputy's voice blasting over the bullhorn. He was talking to Cal! Hard as she tried, though, she couldn't hear Cal's replies. What was he doing in the print shop at this time of night? What was Jimmy Lee saying? Something about a warrant?

What the hell was going on? Her ambulance-chasing instincts kicked into high gear and her nose for news began to twitch like crazy when she suddenly remembered that Cal had inquired about a fifty-dollar bill she'd gotten from Hec Garcia.

Glad that she hadn't left her camera behind in the stands, Holly paused just long enough to pull it from the case.

♥

"I'm afraid I can't allow you to proceed, Cal. No warrant. No search. Now that's the law."

Okay. So maybe his other mistake had been not bringing Jimmy Lee into the bust, Cal grudgingly admitted to himself. But maybe there was still a way to bring Deputy Dawg into the operation.

"I could use your help, Deputy," Cal called out to him.

"Turn out those damned lights and come in here so I can give you the deets. All right?"

"Not without a warrant, I'm not. You come out and we'll wait for the proper paperwork. Do you hear me, Cal?"

Christ. They probably heard him in Houston. "Okay. Give me a couple minutes, will you?" He started whipping off the tops on boxes under the counter, examining the papers they contained.

"Cal?"

"What?"

"Are you armed? Because if you are, I need to ask you to hand over your weapon."

Continuing to scrutinize ream after ream of paper, Cal called back, "I'm a federal agent, Jimmy Lee."

"I know that," he squawked. "But it's my jurisdiction, dammit, Cal. Now come on."

"Yeah. Yeah. Okay. Give me just a minute."

♥

Holly hovered in the shadows of the bank door, still trying to figure out what was going on. A block to the south, the fireworks seemed to be building to some sort of deafening crescendo. Each successive boom nearly had Holly jumping out of her skin. She was debating edging forward toward the squad car and questioning the deputy about this weird stand-off, when all of a sudden she spied Hec Garcia approaching the print shop from the north.

Whatever Cal was doing inside, Hec's appearance didn't seem to be good news. He was carrying a rifle, too, which was definitely bad news. If she only knew the phone number of the shop, she could use her cell phone to warn Cal. But since she didn't have the number, she figured the next best thing would be to sneak around back of the place and try to warn him from there.

The journalist in her suffered a brief and rather painful attack of ethics at the mere thought of inserting herself into a situation, but the half of her that was half in love with Cal Griffin quickly overcame her qualms.

She slipped out of the bank doorway and crept around the corner.

♥

"Okay, Cal. That's it. Come on out. Toss your weapon out first."

"Yeah. Yeah."

Cal shoved aside a plastic file box under the counter, and lo and behold, just behind it was a flat gray metal box with a cheesy little padlock dangling from its hasp. He took his keys from his pocket, inserted his handy dandy pick, and plucked the open lock from the gray box. "Well, hello, Dolly," he murmured pulling out a piece of pale green paper whose fine threads nearly jumped out and bit him.

"Cal!"

The hair on the back of his neck stood up when he heard Holly's voice, and turned to see her standing in the doorway of the shop's back room.

"Get down," he snapped.

She dropped to the floor immediately, then whispered urgently, "Hec Garcia's outside. He's got a rifle."

Cal swore as he motioned Holly closer to him behind the counter. "What the hell are you doing here?" he asked her once she was beside him.

"What the hell are *you* doing here?"

"Working," he said gruffly while he undid the Velcro fastenings of his vest then shrugged out of it. "Here. Put this on. Hurry."

"A bulletproof vest?"

"Put it the fuck on."

She stared at him stubbornly. "Well, what are you going to do . . . ?"

Before she finished her sentence, the glass in the shop's front window shattered. Cal shoved Holly's arms through the vest and snugged the fittings tight.

"Just stay down, Holly. I mean it." To emphasize his point, he pressed his hand into her back to flatten her against the tile floor, then he jerked the gray metal box from underneath the counter. "If anything happens to me," he said, "make sure Jimmy Lee gets this, okay?"

"What is it?"

"Ssh," he hissed.

Jimmy Lee's bullhorn squawked again. "Did you shoot that window out, Cal? Dammit. I'm serious now. You're under arrest for destroying private property."

Another shot hit the fluorescent light over the counter, showering Cal and Holly with glass and plunging the shop into darkness.

"Are you okay, baby?" Cal asked her.

"Sort of."

"Just stay there. Don't move." He swiveled to call out the front window. "Jimmy Lee, Hec Garcia's the one who's shooting. You need to take cover. You hear me?"

"I don't care who's shooting, Cal. It's you who's under arrest, god dammit, and . . ."

Another shot cracked, and judging from the squeal of the bullhorn, it hit the deputy and his amplifier as well.

Time to stop playing sitting duck, Cal told himself.

♥

In the dark, Holly lay face down, afraid to move so much as a micron, not only because of the flying bullets but because there was glass all over her, even in her hair. She was vaguely aware of Cal slowly edging away from her. "Where are you going?" God, her mouth was so dry she could hardly speak.

"Just stay here." He touched her cheek. How could his hand be so cool and steady? How could his voice be so calm? "Stay down and don't move, Holly. I'll be right back. It'll be all right."

"I don't think I can move," she said. "My whole body feels like jello."

When he didn't answer, Holly realized he was already several yards away, his shoes crunching on broken glass as he headed toward the back door. She would've gotten up and followed if she'd been able to move.

And then she didn't hear anything except the reverberations of the fireworks over at the high school. Boom! Ka-Boom! Boom, boom, boom! The grand finale. One final explosion that she could feel in her chest where it was squashed against the floor. Or maybe it was her own heart that was exploding again and again.

While cheers and applause rose up in the distance, closer—somewhere near the front door of the print shop— she heard heavy footsteps. Slow and heavy footsteps.

She squeezed her eyes closed and hoped like hell that the bulletproof vest Cal had thrust on her was muffling the sound of her thudding heart.

Another footstep. Then the harsh metallic click of a rifle cocking. Another footstep, crunching glass, coming her way.

Holly curled her fingers around the box that Cal had placed beside her. She stopped breathing for a second, tried to focus inward, to find an iota of strength, and then, suddenly, her fear seemed to evaporate like a red mist around her. What took its place was an anger that poured through her veins and a voice hammering at the back of her brain.

After a Bronze Medal burst of heroism, her father had just lain down and quit in the face of adversity, but she wasn't Bobby Ray Hicks. She was Hollis Mae Hicks, who didn't know the meaning of the word quit. And she just plain refused to die in the dark on a dirty linoleum floor in fucking Texas!

And, by God, there was no way in hell she was going out without getting the story first.

She tightened her fingers on the metal box, drew in a lungful of air, and got ready to get up. She'd throw the box at her attacker, and if that wasn't enough, then she'd throw herself. With all the glass in her hair, she could probably do considerable damage.

♥

Cal was coming up behind Hec when he saw two shadows shift inside the print shop.

But which was Holly's?

Unable to fire for fear of hitting her, he did the next best thing.

"Hec," he yelled, stepping out into the streetlight, holding up his hands with his pistol high over his head, and praying—Jesus!—that his reflexes were still intact, still there, even at ninety percent, eighty percent, seventy-five.

One shadow moved. Turned. And as it turned, light glinted off the rifle's barrel.

Cal brought down his weapon, locked his arms, and squeezed off one, two, three, four shots. All to the head before it hit the floor.

Chapter Twenty-One

If Holly had had a mike in her hand and a live feed, she would have looked directly, even gamely, into the camera and said, "All hell broke loose in Honeycomb this evening after the fatal shooting of alleged counterfeiter, Hector Garcia." But she didn't have a mike and her camcorder had disappeared. All she had were Cal's arms wrapped tightly around her, which was pretty much all she wanted in the world at the moment.

The reports from his four pistol shots had emptied the grandstand at the high school and brought everybody, including Bee, running to Ye Olde Print Shoppe on Main. There, without his bullhorn and suffering a minor flesh wound to his cheek, Deputy Jimmy Lee Terrell was hard pressed to control the milling throng.

Cal let go of Holly only long enough to hug his sister, who looked at first as if she'd rather slug him before she threw her arms around him and held him tight, muttering, "I swear, Calvin Griffin, you're gonna be the death of me yet."

Dooley shook Cal's hand and slapped him on the back. So did Ellie and bald Bobby from the bank and Ramon and even Tucker Bascom, who ground out an apology of sorts along with his congratulations. Coral kissed him, right on the lips.

And while all this was going on, a black SUV turned onto Main Street and pulled up right behind the deputy's cruiser. Agents Reed and McGovern jumped from the vehicle and, their faces grim, took Cal aside.

Ellie grasped Holly's arm. "Honey, let's you and I go back to my place and see if we can't get some of that glass out of your hair," she said. "I wouldn't mind pouring a little snort of whiskey, too, while we're at it."

After half a bottle of shampoo and nearly a whole bottle of conditioner, Holly's hands were bleeding from tiny cuts, but she was reasonably sure that every last shard of glass was gone. She put on her robe and joined Ellie on the front porch, where the two of them shared a nightcap.

"Some night," Ellie said. "I don't think we've had this much excitement in town since my great-great-grandfather, Augustus, shot the mayor and two councilmen for refusing to put in a proper sidewalk. 'Course, he only winged 'em."

Holly squinted in the direction of Main Street. "I hope Cal's all right. I thought he'd be back by now."

"Oh, I suspect there's a lot of red tape to be hassled with after something like this." Ellie took a sip of her whiskey, and laughed. "Speaking of tape, Jimmy Lee had the print shop wrapped up like a birthday present in yellow tape, didn't he?"

Holly could barely mount a smile. "Cal could've been killed. He gave me his bulletproof vest, and then he stepped out into the streetlight, practically asking Hec to shoot him."

"I'm sure he knew what he was doing."

"Even so . . ." Holly shivered.

"You're pretty fond of him, I gather. I mean, more than just business associates."

"Pretty fond," Holly said, then, "Very fond." She almost said half in love.

"Yeah. I can tell. With Cal, too. You've been good for him."

"Think so?"

"I know so," Ellie said. "And let me give you a little piece of advice even if you're not asking for any. Don't let Ruth scare you off. You hear?"

"It isn't *that* serious, Ellie."

Even as she spoke the words, Holly was wondering if she meant them. How serious was *that* serious? Was it being so frightened for Cal that she'd been willing to risk her own life to protect him? God. Tonight when he'd stood in the street light, calling Hec to distract him away from her, all Holly could think was that she ought to do the same thing—yell out to Hec to turn him and his rifle away from Cal. She had just opened her mouth to scream "Here I am" when the four shots rang out.

Just what that said about her feelings for Cal, Holly wasn't sure. Maybe it was simple instinct. Maybe she would've done the same for anyone. For Ellie. For Ruth or Dooley. Hell. Even for poor ol' Bee.

But she did know that if Hec had fired into the light, if Cal had died . . .

"If he died . . ." she said out loud, her voice cracking all of a sudden.

"But he didn't," Ellie answered. "No use wasting time with might-have-beens or should-haves. Maybe the Man upstairs figured he owed him one for what happened last year."

"Maybe."

They finished their nightcaps in silence, each staring through the darkness toward Main Street where they could see lights going out one by one, until the only illumination remaining was in the vicinity of the print shop.

After Ellie went to bed, Holly carried a second glass of whiskey upstairs, then sat at the top of the fire escape waiting for Cal. When he appeared suddenly, as if out of nowhere, she had just enough ninety-proof fuel in her system to call down to him, "Romeo, Romeo, wherefore art thou?"

He stood there a moment, his hand pressed to his heart, grinning up at her. It was so ridiculously romantic that Holly thought her heart might break, just crack right down the middle. Suddenly everything seemed to catch up with her—life, death, love or whatever it was she was feeling—and tears began streaming down her cheeks.

"Hey, don't cry." Cal took the rusty steps two at a time until he was beside her.

"I'm not crying." She swiped at her face with the back of her hand. "My eyes are just leaking."

"Uh-huh. Bourbon, no doubt."

He took the glass from her hand and finished it off in one gulp, then sighed with a weariness that sounded bone deep. "God, I needed that."

"Ellie's got more downstairs. Shall I . . . ?"

"No," he said in a voice roughened by the liquor, and more. "Now all I need is you."

♥

They made love as if they were alone in the Lone Star State, as if they were the last two people on the planet, as if it might never happen again because death seemed very real and all too close, merely a block away, a few hours back.

They made love as if they were celebrating life and the

Fourth of July and New Year's Eve and Valentine's Day all wrapped into one.

They made love as if they were delirious just to be alive, together, in a big walnut bed in a room full of roses.

They made love as if they were wholly—not half—in love with each other.

And they slept, finally, deeply, wrapped in each other's arms like two lovers clinging tightly to life.

♥

The bleep of her cell phone tugged Holly out of her warm blanket of sleep. She eased out of Cal's arms, trying not to wake him, then reached for the phone on the table beside the bed.

"Hello?" Her voice sounded like sandpaper.

"Kid?"

"Hi, Mel."

"I've got good news and bad news. Which do you want first?"

"Neither," Holly said.

"Are you sitting down?"

"Sort of." She stretched out her foot a languid few inches across the mattress, encountering Cal's warm calf. "Okay." She sighed. "What's the bad news?"

"They cancelled Hero Week."

"What?" Holly sat up so fast that she pulled all the covers off her bedmate, whose reflexes, even asleep, kicked in and had him sitting up nearly as fast as she did. Both of them were blinking.

"What's the matter?" Cal asked.

Holly shushed him, and yelled into the phone, "They *what*?"

"They cancelled it. Pulled the plug. Killed it. Fucking Arnold and Maida put their screwball heads together yesterday and decided that heroes are a cliché. Overdone. Last year's news. They want to do Great Chefs Week instead."

"They can't do that," she howled.

"They already did."

"What's wrong?" Cal asked before she shushed him once again.

"Well, great," she said. "Peachy. This is just dandy. Now that my career is swirling down the toilet, I guess you better tell me what the good news is."

"Are you sitting down?" Mel asked again.

"Hey, I'm flat on the fucking floor, Mel."

"Well, you better get up, then, because CBS called. They like your tapes, kid. A lot. They want to talk to you about a new program they're putting together called *60 Minutes More*."

Holly stopped breathing. The roses on the wall began to blend into one another and pulsate from the crown molding all the way to the floorboards. She wondered if a person who was already sitting down could faint.

Then she managed to drag just enough air in her lungs to say, "Mel, I can't breathe."

"That's okay, kid. Air's bad for you anyway. Now get your Texas ass back to New York. Pronto."

♥

It was a dream come true.

It was a nightmare.

Holly cried and laughed all the way to Houston.

Cal felt like crying and laughing, himself. Laughing because Hero Week had gone belly up, and he was off the hook. Crying because he was about to put his Manhattan Chili Pepper on a plane when all he wanted to do was keep her close beside him. For days. Weeks. Years. For fucking ever.

He wasn't good at good-byes. No. That wasn't true. He was great at good-byes. In thirty-nine years he'd probably said more than his fair share of them and then turned his back with a smile of relief on his face.

Now, standing at the gate just minutes before his Holly was going to fly out of his life, he was at a loss for words. Even good-bye.

He shrugged the strap of her laptop case off his shoulder. "Go get 'em, Tiger," he said, looping the strap over her arm.

She gazed up at him, her eyes glistening with tears. "I wish we had more time. Oh, God, I wish . . ."

Cal looked at his watch, mostly because it was too painful to look at her face. Christ. He'd rather take a bullet for her than watch her cry. "I should probably get going," he said. "I told them I'd be at the field office by three for the debriefing about the shooting last night."

"What if I didn't go?" she asked, reaching out to grab his sleeve.

"What the hell are you talking about?"

"What if I didn't go? What if I stayed here?"

I'd be happy, he thought. *I'd be so goddammed happy.*

"You'd regret it all your life," he said.

She nodded. "I know. I know it. Only . . ."

The gate attendant gave the final call for her flight to Newark.

He took her pretty face in both his hands, cupping her chin with his thumbs. "I'll be back in Washington in two months. I'll spend all my days off in New York."

"Half your days off," she said, trying her best to laugh.

"What?"

"Half your days off because you're only half in love with me."

He kissed those just-about-to-pout lips, then turned her toward the jetway. "Go. I'll call you tonight. I'll see you in two months. Maybe sooner."

Holly turned back. "How much sooner?"

"Until I can't half stand being apart from you. Now go."

♥

Five hours later, trying to negotiate the distance from the curb to the front door of the Media Arts Building with her suitcase, her carry-on, her handbag and Mel's laptop, attempting to maneuver east to west when half the population of midtown Manhattan was moving north to south, Holly raised her fist and screamed, "I'm walking here!"

Not that anybody cared. Not that anybody even heard her. Certainly nobody paused on their way to wherever it was they were going in such an all-fired hurry.

"All-fired," she muttered to herself, shoving her suitcase forward another foot. "Now if that just don't beat all. Here I am, Holly Hicks, about to be a producer at CBS, and I'm talking like I've got cow shit on my Ferragamos."

She was still muttering under her breath when she finally reached her office.

"Welcome back, kid," Mel boomed.

Holly dropped into the chair across from his desk. "Mel, I'm conflicted."

He rolled his eyes toward the ceiling. "Tell me about it," he groaned.

Now, as Holly well knew, in Texas when somebody said

"Tell me about it" they meant quite sincerely "Tell me about it. What's wrong, hon?"

But she wasn't in Texas. She was in New York, where "Tell me about it" meant "Listen to this."

So she sighed and listened to Mel as he began to rant. "You're not going to believe what Arnold and Maida, those two loose screws, want to do now."

♥

"I miss you," Cal said on the phone that night. To Holly he sounded a million miles away as much as he sounded right there in the same room.

"Do you miss me completely or just half?" she asked.

"I miss you completely."

Holly smiled. "That's good because I'm half out of my mind with missing you."

She could almost feel his smile, almost feel the blue warmth in his eyes, the tenderness of his touch when he answered, "Well, that's not half bad, I guess."

They talked for an hour, maybe more. The debriefing about Hec's death had gone fine, as Cal had anticipated, and his actions were deemed appropriate under the circumstances. The sheriff had come back from his vacation and had demoted Jimmy Lee from deputy to patrolman. Tomorrow Cal planned to get back out on the track with Bee, and then he was going to help Ruth and Dooley come up with a preliminary plan prior to their meeting with the architect about their hunting lodge. Ellie sent her love.

"Everything's just about the same in Honeycomb," he told her. "Except you're not here."

"I wish I were," Holly replied, shocking herself because

she truly meant it. She wished she were in Texas. And then she laughed. "I can't believe I said that."

Later that night, lying in bed with Manhattan noise and neon coming through her window, she called on Rufus to take her back to Honeycomb.

It may not look like much, this small and tattered town on a wide spot on a dusty road in Texas, but if you take the time to look closely, Honeycomb is a veritable hive of activity.

Rufus pans slowly past Ramon's, the Longhorn Café where Coral's standing by a table at the window taking an order for biscuits and gravy, the print shop with its shattered front window and yards of yellow tape flapping in the hot breeze. His camera swings south to the track where Cal and Bee are making their second circuit.

Whether you believe in heroes or not, Honeycomb isn't a half bad place to go looking for one.

Chapter Twenty-Two

In spite of all the time he'd spent over the years in the White House, Cal had never been inside the Oval Office. But now, in early September, on the one-year anniversary of the assassination attempt, he was standing just outside the door to that famed room, waiting for his appointment with President Jennings.

"Congratulations, Griffin," Special Agent Terry Young-blood said to him from his post by the ante-room door. "I heard you passed the physical at Glynco with flying colors."

"Thanks," Cal said without elaboration. The fact was that, even though he'd passed the rigorous tests last week, his flying colors hadn't flown quite high enough to earn him a resumption of his duties on protective detail. He'd been bitterly disappointed for about a minute, partly out of pride and partly on principle, and then he realized that such rigorous, all-consuming, living-out-of-a-suitcase duty wasn't what he wanted at this point in his life.

Even if his performance scores had—by some extraordinary fluke of nature—landed him once more in the top echelon of Secret Service personnel, Cal would've declined the assignment. He just didn't want it anymore. He didn't need it, that feeling of mental and physical control, that macho mastery and mystique.

He wanted Holly Hicks. He needed her.

With each passing day from July to September, missing her more and more, he realized that he needed her to feel happy and whole. He needed her smarts and her sass, her coolness under fire, her hot little body beneath his.

For him, excitement used to be preceding the President off of Air Force One, or walking mere inches away from the Democrat Jennings when the man plunged open-handed into a crowd of hostile Republicans. Excitement used to mean knowing he stood as the last physical barrier between the President and harm.

But now his notion of a heart-stopping moment was witnessing Holly Hicks smile in her sleep, or watching her hair dry after she showered and seeing how each curl seemed to have a mind of its own and a God-given direction that would not be denied. Excitement would be knowing he was going to wake up beside her every morning for the rest of his life. Putting kids to bed on Christmas Eve. Teaching a son to ride a two-wheeler. Braiding a little girl's curly, unruly hair.

All of which was exactly what Cal intended to tell Holly this afternoon after his meeting with the President. How long could it take for Jennings to tell him again how grateful he was for his sacrifice last year? He was going to pick up his divorce decree and an engagement ring—not necessarily in that order—and then take the shuttle to New York. That city had never been his idea of a place to live happily ever after, but if his Holly was there, and if she were his, then he'd be happy enough. And, hell, Ruthie could visit once or twice a year and get her fill of New York restaurants.

The door to the Oval Office opened and Janet Adcock stepped out, brandishing a clipboard and looking like she needed a quick nicotine fix. Cal had forgotten what a long drink of water the Press Secretary was. Her eyes were level with his when she greeted him.

"Cal! Welcome back."

"Janet. You're looking good."

Her gaze warmed appreciably, even a bit flirtatiously if Cal was still a judge of such things. "You're not so bad yourself, Agent Griffin. Hey, I'm sorry that hero program didn't work out. I was really looking forward to watching it."

He muttered a quiet, restrained oath. "What's this all about, Janet? Why does Jennings want to see me?"

She gave him one of her famous I-know-but-I'm-not-telling looks, then said, "He's waiting for you." She gestured through the door. "Go on in."

"Is that Cal Griffin I hear out there?" the President called.

"Yes, sir."

"Well, come on in, son. Janet, move aside and let him through."

♥

After the CBS people called with their decision, Holly put the phone back in its cradle and just stared at it for a while. Her hands must've been sweating because there was a little spot of moisture on the back of the black handset that took a minute or two to disappear.

She was vaguely aware of Mel walking past her open office door, then heard him swearing as he stepped back and stood there gazing at her.

His normally gruff voice went soft with concern when he asked, "What's up, kid?"

"CBS just called," she answered rather tonelessly.

"Aw, damn. Aw, fuck." He stepped inside and closed the door behind him. "Hey, I'm really sorry, Holly."

She simply stared at her boss then, blankly, as if he were an inanimate object, a coatrack or a floor lamp, one with a bald glass dome. Shouldn't she feel upset right now? Holly wondered. Shouldn't her stomach be roiling or, at the very least, shouldn't her temples be beginning to throb with the first pangs of a headache? What was the expression on her face that was making Mel go all soft and gooey?

"Oh, that's okay," she finally said, still amazed by her own sense of calm.

Mel sagged in the chair across from her desk. He looked more like a basset hound now than his usual Rottweiler self. "Don't worry about it. You're good, kid. Better than good. You've got real talent. One of these day those idiots at CBS will be kicking themselves that they didn't snatch you up when they had the chance. You'll see. They'll be eating their hearts out—you mark my words, kid—that they didn't offer you this job."

Holly smiled wanly. God. She felt as if she were having an out-of-body experience, as if she were watching herself talk to her boss, as if she hardly recognized her own voice. "That's the odd thing, Mel," she said. "They did."

"Pardon me?"

"They offered me the job. A producer's spot on the new show. I told them no."

"You told them no," he echoed. "You said no to CBS?"

Holly nodded.

He came out of his chair as if the seat had just caught fire. Leaning over her desk, his hands planted on her blotter, he growled, "You said no to fucking CBS?"

She nodded again.

"Holly," Mel breathed. "Jesus, kid. Why?"

"Well, they wanted me to produce pieces out of London and Paris for the next two years."

"Yeah. So? That's not exactly like asking you to transfer to Reykjavik or Kabul, you know, or even fucking Texas. Shit. London and Paris. I know at least fifty guys who'd sell their own grandmothers for a chance like that."

He raised his hands and gestured toward the ceiling, then bellowed, "Hell, Holly, are you completely nuts?"

God. Maybe she was. Maybe she really was crazy, Holly thought, because a grin was working its way across her lips and there was nothing she could do to stop it.

"No," she said. "I'm completely in love."

♥

She was still sitting at her desk an hour later, trying to clamp down on the shit-eating grin on her face—at least that's how Mel had described it—when they buzzed her from Reception.

"There's a guy out here to see you," Rhonda said in a voice that didn't quite carry her characteristic Brooklyn, Bay Ridge, been-there, done-that, seen-it, yeah, yeah tone. She sounded a bit breathless, in fact.

"Who is it?" Holly asked.

"I dunno. He won't give me his name. Just says he needs to see you." Rhonda's voice dropped to a whisper. "Actually, um, Holly, he's wearing shades and a gray suit and he looks like a narc. I think he's here to arrest you."

Even as her heart somersaulted, Holly had to bite her lower lip to keep from laughing like an inebriated loon. "Send him back, Rhonda," she said.

"Are you sure?"

"Oh, yeah. I'm very sure."

She put the phone down and went to her door just for the pleasure of watching him approach. But as she stood there, it occurred to Holly that maybe Cal was coming to tell her good-bye. Oh, God. He'd told her he had a meeting with the President this morning. Maybe Jennings had prevailed on him to return to his former detail. Maybe Jennings had pulled strings so that Cal's not-quite-good-enough scores were now good enough to resume protective duty. Maybe . . .

He pushed through the glass double door from the hallway and came striding toward her through bustling secretaries, dropped files, stacks of tapes and other hazards like a man who was so perfectly in control that nothing could deter him.

He was tan. He was fit. Holly almost cried because in the eight weeks since she'd seen him, his stride was more secure and he held his head just a little bit higher. He radiated confidence. He wore it like cologne.

And when he dragged his dark glasses down and pierced her with the laser blue light of his eyes, Holly thought she might never breathe again.

"Don't say a word," he told her, propelling her into her office and closing the door behind them. "Not one word. Just sit and listen to me."

Holly sat.

Cal paced.

"I know how you feel about Texas, and I know how much this CBS thing means to you . . ."

"Well, actually—"

"Just listen to me, dammit."

"All right."

Ah, God. She loved the stern, granite set of his jaw. The tension she detected in his body as he paced from her file cabinet to her window, and back. The little beads of sweat she could see on his brow. This wasn't a good-bye after all.

Holly settled back in her chair to savor it.

"I love you, goddammit," he said, bashing his fist into the top drawer of her file cabinet before he turned toward the window again.

"I love you, too," she said softly, not certain whether he heard her or not.

"And if New York is where you have to be, then I have to be here, too. I can do that. If that's what you want . . ."

"All I want is you," she said just in case he was listening.

"But I've got a proposition for you, and I want you to hear me out before you answer. Okay?"

"Okay."

"I met with President Jennings this morning, and . . ." He stopped pacing and planted a hip on the corner of her desk. "This isn't for publication, Miss Sixty Minutes, by the way. I guess the man still thinks he owes me for last year. I don't know. But he told me he's not going to accept the nomination next week . . ."

"Whoa. Hold the phone. That's big news," Holly exclaimed.

Cal's dark blue glare kept her from springing out of her seat.

"I told you it's confidential," he said. "The reason Jennings told me is that he wanted to offer me the job of heading up security for him after he leaves office in January."

"What? In Washington? As his head Secret Service guy?"

"No. As private security. If I accept, he'll decline the service's protection. Basically, the man's throwing me a bone— a pretty big one—out of gratitude."

"Well, that's good, isn't it?" she asked, wondering why

Cal didn't seem happier about what sounded to her like an honor.

"Not exactly." He sighed. "The hitch is that he won't be staying in Washington. He and the First Lady will be going back to . . ."

"Texas!" The word sprang forth on a burst of laughter that Holly couldn't stifle. "Oh, God. You're going back to Texas."

"This isn't funny," he growled. "I want to be with you, Holly." He wrenched an envelope from the breast pocket of his jacket and tossed it on her desk. "My divorce papers."

While Holly was looking at the envelope, Cal tossed something else on top of it. A small square box.

"There's a ring in there," he said.

"So I gathered."

He ripped his fingers through his hair, and Holly's heart melted when she saw the indentation above his right temple, just behind the hairline. She remembered how he'd stood in the streetlight, calling out to Hec to distract him. She remembered how she'd called out at the same moment, ready to take a bullet for Cal.

"Here's the thing," he said. "After the President offered me the job in San Antonio, I told him about you."

"Me?"

"He's going to be building his library there, in San Antonio, with all the exhibits and whatever it is they put in Presidential libraries. I told him you're a first-rate documentary filmmaker, and that you might be interested in putting together his official biography for the library."

"Wow."

Cal obviously mistook her exclamation of awe for sarcasm because he went on, "Okay. It's not CBS. I realize that. But it would be something special, having your name on a production like that, that would be seen by thousands, maybe millions of people, over the next century. It's not CBS, but it's a pretty big deal."

"It's a very big deal," Holly said.

"So . . . so you'll consider it?"

"I'll take it," she said. "What's in the box?"

He levered off her desk. "What do you mean you'll take it? What about CBS?"

"I turned them down."

"You got the job?"

"Yes, I got the job and I turned it down because they wanted me to go to London and Paris, and I didn't want to be half a world away from the man I'm half in love with."

Cal blinked, and for the very first time since Holly had met him, he looked lame brained. Stupid. Completely and gorgeously befuddled.

"What's in the box?" Holly asked again, trying with all her might not to laugh at the man she loved, who was looking absolutely gut punched at the moment.

"Jesus. Holly." He picked up the little jewelry box and came around to her side of the desk. "Sweetheart."

He winced, getting down on one knee, and Holly knew it would be even harder for him to get up. The ring was too big and its beautiful pear-shaped diamond immediately slipped to the underside of her finger, but Holly wasn't even looking.

"You'll marry me?" Cal asked.

"Yes. Oh, yes."

"Even if it means you have to go back to Texas?"

"Yes."

His blue eyes sparkled. "Even if you don't believe in heroes?"

"Doesn't matter," Holly said. "I believe in you."

About the Author

Mary McBride has been writing romance, both historical and contemporary, for ten years. She lives in St. Louis, Missouri, with her husband and two sons.

She loves to hear from readers, so please visit her Web site at MaryMcBride.net or write to her c/o P.O. Box 411202, St. Louis, MO 63141.

THE EDITOR'S DIARY

Dear Reader,

People always say home is where the heart is. But no two people ever resisted home as much as Holly Hicks and Leigh Mitchell in our two Warner Forever titles this June.

Susan Andersen said, "I'm hooked on Mary McBride . . . she's an author headed to the top of the lists with a bullet!" and that statement couldn't be truer in **Mary McBride's MY HERO.** Secret Service Agent Cal Griffin took a bullet for the President and became a media sensation. He's just the person to give a jump-start to TV producer Holly Hicks's career. The only catch: she has to return to Texas where she grew up, and a small town world she so desperately wanted to leave behind. And as soon as she arrives, the battle lines are drawn. The last thing Cal needs is a hounding reporter, but Holly is determined to get her story. And soon these two people that rub each other the wrong way find that there's nothing Cupid loves more than a challenge. . . .

Moving from the heart of Texas to a small town in Indiana, we find **Susan Crandall's BACK ROADS** which Mary Jo Putney calls a "gripping debut novel that shows a keen eye . . . for the nuances of the human heart." Leigh Mitchell has never left home—in fact, she is the town's local sheriff. She has always been sensible and responsible and suddenly, she just can't take it anymore. On the verge of turning thirty, Leigh needs a change. She longs for excitement and romance, so when a sexy and mysterious stranger asks her for a ride on the Ferris wheel one moonlight night, she can't resist. But the longer this stranger is in town, the more upside-down home becomes for Leigh and the more she can't bear it without him.

To find out more about Warner Forever, these June titles, and the authors, visit us at www.warnerforever.com.

With warmest wishes,

Karen Kosztolnyik

Karen Kosztolnyik, Senior Editor

P.S. As the summer heats up, crank up the AC and grab a cool glass of lemonade—you're going to need cooling down when you read these upcoming titles: **Sandra Hill** presents a woman escaping her fiancé only to find trouble in the form of a sexy pilot in **TALL, DARK, AND CAJUN**; and in **DON'T TELL**, author **Karen Rose** pens a spine-tingling romantic suspense debut about a woman who risks everything for the chance at a new life.